A
Dish Best
Served
Cold

A tale of roses, revenge and risotto!

By Tracy Baxter-Syer

New Generation Publishing

Dr Wendy,

Merry Christmas! Enjoy the read.

Love

Tracy

This book is dedicated to my lovely husband and children and parents. Thanks for all your support and unwavering belief. I hope I won't let you down. It's also for my wonderful friends and family who inspired me with their random funny tales and behaviour. You know who you are! It's for Michelle, who planted a seed that just grew and grew. And for Darin Jewell whose encouragement brought me this far. Thank you each and every one, you are all priceless gems. xxx

The Smelly Brown Stuff hits the Van Driver...

At about ten thirty – and fortunately following his last delivery – Ralph burst in through the door of the shop; successfully rattling the door and the connecting shop window in his wake.

He filled the doorway with his massive frame and brought in the most horrendous smell of what seemed to be raw sewerage. I glanced up from my work and screwed up my nose at the vile and violent pong. I then noticed something on Ralph's clothing and stared quizzically at him. He seemed to have curry paste or sauce all over his jacket.

I began to speak, in order to find out the cause of his intrusive outburst when I was stopped dead in my tracks by an obviously irate Ralph. "You and your bright bloody ideas! Look at the bloody state of me, woman! Can you not tone down your floral statements a bit? Either that or you can deliver the bloody things yourself! Look at me, I'm all covered in baby shit!" he ranted.

"Oh my God, Ralph, I'm so sorry!" I pacified, whilst just barely resisting the urge to laugh uncontrollably.

"Yeah? You don't look very bloody sorry! Your mouth might be saying it, but your face, well, that looks as though you are finding it all highly amusing. I'm going home to get changed. I'll be back for the afternoon deliveries if I can get rid of the smell of shit!" he blustered.

Before I could answer him, he swung round and stomped angrily out of the door, almost crashing it off its hinges in his wake. It amused me that the one thing in life that Ralph could not abide was the offerings from a baby's nappy. As the eldest of eight children, in a family where his father spent all of his time at the watering hole and his mother taking in washing, most of Ralph's childhood had been spent wiping noses and bottoms. His most unpleasant and enduring formative memories were of changing nappies and the smell of the nappy bucket in the outside lavatory. Nothing was more certain to make this bear grizzly in every sense of the word. Whoever had given Ralph that particularly faecular tip couldn't have chosen more wisely!

And it was obvious that the 'charms' of my floral offerings were getting ever more flamboyant. 'So, chalk it up, Zoe,' I thought to myself, 'that's another dissatisfied customer!'

I felt that I was really getting to grips with the newest angle of my job. Maybe I would even treat myself to a raise...

Chapter 1

I tapped impatiently on the desk with my Biro and absent-mindedly pushed an unruly strand of my frizzing, mousy hair out of my eyes. I flipped the leaves of the diary back and forth, back and forth, all without managing to really view the contents of the pages (even without the hair getting in the way).

Wickedly I was still sniggering to myself over Ralph's earlier misfortunes – even though I knew I shouldn't – when a movement from outside caught the corner of my eye. I slowly turned my attention to the window and beyond, watching as a middle-aged woman with wiry, fair hair and careworn blue eyes stared blankly at the flowers in the window. It occurred to me that I wasn't the only one looking without seeing. Do any of us ever truly see what is right in front of us?

The woman raised her gaze, looking through the window and briefly caught me eyeing her. She smiled a little wanly and so I returned this. This woman was almost familiar, but I couldn't quite place her. That nagging feeling of thinking that I should know her began niggling away at the back of my head.

All the while, front of house, I was vaguely aware that I was still smiling inanely at the woman in front of the window; but now she was walking away. Maybe I had frightened her with my inane grin and fuzzy appearance? I must resemble Animal from The Muppet Show! No matter, I had a feeling she'd be back.

I went back to flipping the pages of the diary. It was a welcome if pointless diversion. I began working again on my flipping and tapping percussion and toyed briefly with adding in the sound of the tape being ripped from its reel. Surely it would then sound even *more* annoying. Trouble was, I was the only one in the shop to hear the dreadful cacophony so I'd just be annoying myself.

Finally it occurred that this time I ought to actually read the contents of the diary. 'Do some work Zoe' I chided myself. Then I realised that I had to make a decision. Which was the more important, the hand-tied bouquet for the much-admired Ms Black, or the 'revenge' bouquet for Ms Mosslee? Hmmmm... Ms Mosslee was in line for a good one. She had hurt both her best friend and her live-in partner. She had copped off with the former's partner at the latter's birthday party.

The curious thing with customers who came in for revenge was that they were always eager to divulge why. Of course I was always willing to provide a listening ear; little did they know it but later I enjoyed writing the stories down. I thought they might make interesting reading someday for someone. And for the hurt parties it was a bit like therapy without the enormous fee. Given the tale told by the errant Ms Mosslee's partner – and the highly emotional state that both he and Ms Mosslee's best friend were in when they visited the shop – I should try to enjoy making this one extra-special! I had just the right stuff to do it with because I'd been saving it especially for such an occasion!

Well now; whilst revenge bouquets were always more fun to make, the two dozen red roses for Ms Black were the most urgent. They would need to go on the delivery van within the next hour. I looked over at the numberless clock and decided that I would sort out the hand-tied, and then reward myself with a damn good laugh making up a vile concoction for Ms Mosslee.

I brought the roses and exotic fern fronds out of the cold room and set about the hand-tied first. I sung along with Robbie on the radio, and danced to Abba as I worked, and in no time at all it was ready to go. I couldn't help but secretly envy Ms Black her admirer. Just like Ms Black the man was a local accountant of good standing. He was young and handsome in a solid sort of a way, and with an obviously large bank balance judging from the amount of large floral 'I will pursue you till I get you into my bed's' he sent out.

It would be a shame if he ever got around to proposing marriage to Ms Black, because then the shop's profits would plummet! In the floristry game you quickly learn that there aren't many married men who are willing to buy their wives flowers on such a regular basis as Ms Black's admirer bought them for her. And I considered that just like all the rest of his gender, if he ever managed to ensnare her for his wife he would probably stop trying to impress her with his lovely big overblown floral gifts. Still maybe some of that was just my jaded old opinion? He could be the exception to the rule. Someone had to be...

I stood back to better take in my handiwork and smiled softly to myself. It wasn't half-bad. The velvety red of the roses contrasted beautifully with the large, deep green fronds of ferns. I knew I wouldn't turn it down if a deliveryman showed up at my door with it!

It had been a seriously long time since I had received anything from an admirer, secret or otherwise. I couldn't bring myself to canvass for admirers though, not since Nick. His name still made me shudder, even now. I carefully lifted the hand-tied being careful to take the bubble of water it stood in from the underneath. Then gently I set it on the floor to the left of the door, ready for Ralph to pick it up on his next collection if he returned.

Then I turned back to the revenge bouquet. So far it had been a bit of a long and strange sort of a day, and concocting these things always made me feel better. However, as much fun as they were to make up I was certain that, for myself, I most definitely would not like to have a delivery man show up at my door with one of my 'I hate you' confections to offer...

I crouched down behind the counter and began to scrabble among the shelves until I found the dangerously chipped and damaged vase I had been saving for just such work. I had found it at a car boot sale as I did so many of my revenge work findings; it was of thick 70's style earthenware in a shade that could probably best be described as 'vindaloo diarrhoea'. Lovely! Next, I scouted in the 'on its way out' bucket, to see what was suitably dead-dying-mouldy-stinky enough for my needs and, lastly I brought some oasis just big enough to fit the job.

The oasis was actually pointless if you took into account it was there to feed and water the flowers (only if you sensibly kept it moist with water and flower food as my 'care of flowers' card suggested) but it was necessary in order to hold the flowers in position. They might have been on their way out but in order for them to be at their worst – believe it or not – they needed arranging into the least attractive arrangement. The station was now playing 'Beautiful Day' by U2, so I whacked up the radio and began to sing loudly – and, some might say, tunelessly – along as I worked.

Within a matter of minutes it was done. The rotting and brown-tinged double white chrysanthemums echoed the sentiment of the vase perfectly. The crispy, yellow leaves of the (not so) lucky dying bamboo set the whole thing off to perfection. I hoped that Ms Mosslee would appreciate the irony of the work of fart that now graced the counter in front of me, and not attempt to cut short Ralph's life with it. He'd suffered enough for one day! I laughed out loud at my audacious floral sculpture, and then crinkled up my nose at the putrid smell.

Just as I was picking up the vindaloo vase to stand it down with the other afternoon deliveries, Ralph came bounding through the door. I set down the unpleasant container and its contents then returned to the counter, leaned over it to turn down the radio then turned to face him.

"Wow, great timing, Ralph. I've just this second finished," I told him.

"Eugh, what's that horrid smell? Is it me? Do I still pong of baby shit? Or have you been eating sprouts again?" Ralph quipped.

"Very funny! No, it's the retaliation of the chrysanthemums. See, if you don't use them and they accidentally get left somewhere too warm, they go off and smell foul. Speaking of smelling foul, what happened to you this morning?" I questioned.

He glared at the contents of the brownish vase on the floor and whinged "Oh, no, is this another revenge job? Two in one day? The baby shit was due to that creation you sent out this morning. The recipient was carrying a full nappy bag when she answered the door and she was so thrilled with your horrific floral homage that she gave me the contents of the nappy as a tip! Between that and what happened with the last revenge job I think I've had enough punishment." He regarded the fetid offering on the floor. "Shall I need my riot shield this time, do you think?" he asked, only half jokingly.

I looked Ralph up and down. He was six foot four and almost as wide as he was tall. A bear of a man, he didn't appear to be the sort of person you would want to argue with, unless you were on a suicide mission. "No, I don't think you will need it. Not just to fend off another weak and feeble woman."

I grinned and Ralph narrowed his eyes in return. We were clearly remembering a previous delivery of a "revenge bouquet" to a 'lady'. She turned out to be well, not much of a lady at all. In fact according to Ralph's description of her as he recounted his adventure later, she looked like 'a docker in drag and could have played in the England Rugby team and upped their chances of winning tenfold'. Ralph's bruises had only just faded from that job, and thanks to the overzealous use of cologne the smell of the baby faeces had only just faded too.

"Huh, *ladies*! I don't think there are many of those left in this town! You realise I'm going to sue this time if I get assaulted?" he grinned back. Then he bent and began to pick up the floral tributes and load them into the van. He took the revenge bouquet and loaded it last, chuckling as he did so. "This is your worst yet, I think. You never know, the recipient might even want to thank *you* for your handiwork in person!" He winked as he spoke and I grimaced back at him.

"Have you got any big mates that wouldn't mind working as bouncers?" I wondered.

"Hah, you can look after yourself. You're quite a scary lady you know," he said with a knowing look.

"Oh, that's a comfort, I'm sure. How long will those deliveries take? I'll put the kettle on and break out the chocolate Hob-Nobs," I promised.

"Well, provided I don't need to go back via A and E – coz this vase looks like it could do some damage if her aim is any good – I should be a couple of hours,"

Ralph guessed.

"Ok, see you later, then," I smiled.

I watched him leave and then set about clearing away the floral remains from the last works. Wiping my hands on my apron, I leafed slowly once more through the diary to see what would need to go out first in the morning. There was a wreath and a couple of small sprays, a small and simple bouquet, and lastly a cyclamen plant in a pretty pot.

The door slid open quietly as I was mentally planning how I would be best to do the work, and an elderly lady hobbled through it. She carefully watched where she walked and on reaching the counter said, "I have to be careful how I go these days. I once slipped on a slimy bit of leaf in a flower shop and did myself a bit of an injury."

"Oh, I hope it wasn't in this shop. My assistant and I do try to keep the flower debris off the floor, but sometimes the odd leaf or stem still manage to escape the bin! They can be quite cunning, you know, flowers," I explained.

The old lady smiled a soft smile and responded, "Yes, I have a garden full, and just like children they never do quite what you want them to. Maybe that's why they're grown in nurseries? Anyway, could I take one of your ready-made bouquets from the barrow, please?"

"Did you want the pink and whites, or the orange and creams?" I questioned as I moved from behind the counter.

"Mmmm, I think my friend is more the pinks and whites sort of a girl, please," the elderly lady replied.

I selected a full and flouncy bouquet and fetched the pink and white ready-made concoction from the flower barrow just outside the door. Carefully I wrapped it in bright white paper with a star motif. Then, eyeing it for a second, I thoughtfully added a big, lime-green bow to echo the colours of the stars on the paper and enquired, "Would you like a card to pop in with this?"

"That's very kind. Could I have a get well one, please?" replied the elderly lady.

We had one in stock. It was with pink gerberas on a white background so I took one of those and carefully put it into a small envelope with a sachet of flower food and a care card. The lady took several minutes to locate her purse, and just the right amount of cash to pay with her obviously arthritic hands. She shuffled deliberately out of the door that I had now hurriedly darted around the counter and held open.

Next I went into the cold room and brought out some flowers for the wreath I wanted to make. It was for a man, so I collected blue and white flowers and some mixed foliage from the flower buckets. Pulling a small wreath ring down from the shelf, I turned up the radio once more and set about my work, placing the wreath ring into the sink and snicking the stems from the flowers.

An hour and three quarters later there were snicked stems, leaves, thorns and oasis dust all over the counter but the three funeral jobs were ready to roll. I wrote out the cards and discreetly tucked them onto the display prongs whilst saying a silent goodbye to the people they were for. I can't remember how or why I started doing this, only that it seemed to me somehow respectful, so I continued.

Then, to cheer myself up and lift my now somewhat sombre mood, I peeled a good length of bright yellow cello-wrap, and some bright orange tissue for the backing for the bouquet, and set about making something altogether more jolly in the way of a bouquet. I used all my favourite sunrise colours – reds, yellows, oranges, cerise pinks and a little cream – for this. Soon the bouquet was ready. Small, but perfectly formed I thought. I stood all of the work back in the cold room where it would be safe.

Afterwards I went to search amongst the good pots for something in a 'shade of purple' for the cyclamen. It didn't take me long to find a lilac pot with what appeared to be tiny purple plums (at least I hoped that was what they were) bordering the top. At this point I smiled at something one of my friends had told me... if you drew a face on a scrotum, whom would you have a portrait of? Gordon Brown! Didn't quite get to the bottom of how she had found that one out, though.

I placed the cyclamen in the pot, decorated it with a large purple bow, and stuck in the prong with the card. This could stand quite happily out of the way on the floor until the morning.

Then, although I actually wanted to sit down and wait to meet myself coming back, I set about hurriedly sweeping up the flower snippings and shovelling them into the bin. I didn't want any of my customers suing *me* for taking a tumble on escaping flower detritus!

Pretty soon it was all ship – or even shop – shape. Work done!

I turned my waning attention to the back of the shop, put on the kettle and began to make some tea. Whilst waiting for the kettle I noticed that the shelves were a bit dusty and earthy in places here and there. 'Tardy bint' I told myself as I took down a feather duster and began idly and half-heartedly dusting away at the shelves, and in the front at the fake ivy garland along the trellis separating the front from the back of the shop.

As I started to dust the front display, I noticed the careworn woman I had seen earlier, hovering by the door once more. I fixed her with a bright smile – although given what had happened earlier when I did this it was a risky strategy – but this time she didn't turn and move away. She tentatively slipped open the door and glided as though on well oiled casters into the shop. (I thought only nuns could move like that?)

After a few minutes browsing she approached the counter, smiled nervously at me and began "Hi. Me again! I don't know if you'll recognise me, but I was in about five months ago for a dog-food pie. Do you still do them?"

"Of course, although we do prefer it if you call them 'sneak and kid-me' pies. I must admit, I thought I recognised you when I saw you peering through the window earlier," I confessed.

"Yes, I thought long and hard before coming in, because I don't want you to think that I feed my husband your pie as a regular occurrence. It's only in extreme circumstances that I resort to this. Although, I

14

have to say your pies are rather difficult to tell from other shop-bought real pies," the woman giggled nervously and it triggered my memory. I remembered when I had last seen the woman now standing in the shop.

She had last purchased a dog-food pie when her husband had been getting some very explicit text messages from another woman. His wife had found them when she had mistakenly picked up his phone instead of her own (they had the same type of phone).

Instead of confronting him – in truth, she didn't strike me as the confrontational type – she'd decided to secretly send him up and then tell all their friends what she had done. She now gladly told me that the day following his ingestion of the last pie, he'd been given a warning from his boss. He earned this when he'd accidentally sent a sexually explicit reply he'd meant for his mistress to his boss, who was also female. His wife found this out through one of his colleague's wives at a works party. It was a strange side effect of my 'revenge foods' that many people reported ill luck seemed to befall the eater slowly after.

Must have had something to do with the extra 'special' ingredients...

Anyway, the fact that she was back here meant that this woman's husband wasn't any the wiser to her 'game' as yet, but I didn't like to pry for information. I preferred to wait for my customers to volunteer information. Luckily for me, most of them did. Of course, it went without saying that I would never break ranks and tell the opposite party who was hitting them or why they were being hit.

I turned and went into the back of the shop to the small freezer in the corner. Opening the door, I moved my stash of homemade chilli-chocolate ice cream (heavy on the chilli), which went down well with those wishing to gain revenge on the sweet-toothed. There at the back was what I was looking for, the box marked 'sneak and kid-me pies'. Carefully I took out the box and removed one of the hand-made delicacies.

No one would guess from looking at it that it contained only the finest dog food, despairingly mixed with gravy, flavoured with disappointment, garlic and finest herbs. Into the pastry, I was always careful to crumble only best butter and heartache. The overall effect was a pie that tasted wonderfully garlic-y and meaty with a rich pastry crust that melted on the tongue, leaving no taste of the venomous cocktail of emotions with which it had been laced. To be honest I found making them to be a form of therapy for my own pains. I had done since I had made the very first one for my own errant lover two short years ago, after only the seventh time he had let me down. He turned up late for a concert leaving me standing outside the venue waiting for him. If only I was the confrontational type! I smiled softly to myself as I selected a pie and brought it to the front of the shop.

I offered the customer the beautifully formed hand made pie. When she showed her satisfaction with the article I carefully placed it in a brown paper bag. The lady smiled her wan little smile again and told me "He really enjoyed the last one. He keeps asking me to bake another. I hope you won't mind, but I told him it was homemade. It just seemed easier somehow. I can hardly tell him they're only for revenge purposes, so I have to keep telling him I'm just too busy to bake one for him. He'll think that today's his lucky day! If only he knew... I'm not ready to tell him that I'm onto his game with his floosie yet. Not quite enough saved up in my 'rainy-day account' to get a decent place to live on my own. Thanks for this; no doubt thanks to his fun and games I will see you soon." And handing over her money she left without waiting for a receipt.

Repeat business means a satisfied customer!

I again turned into the back of the shop and attempted to put the kettle on to boil for some tea. A quick glance at the clock told me that it was five to four, and very soon Ralph would be back through the door if he'd made it unscathed from his deliveries. I took down two cups from the top of the shelf above the kettle and set them on the counter top. Then I put in two tea bags and went to the cupboard to find the Hob-Nobs.

As I brought the biscuit barrel over to the counter

with the other tea things, it occurred to me that I could experiment with a nice line in dog-chocolate covered biscuits and Florentines for a bit of a revenge Christmas special. I routed out the notepad from the rear pocket of my jeans and noted this idea, adding to it by possibly putting in chilli as an ingredient for the Florentines so as not to forget. Then I removed the chilli from the ingredients list. I was becoming a tad too reliant on it as a weapon. Instead, I replaced it with dog chocolate. Result!

The shop bell rang out as I was doing this, and I finished and looked up to find Ralph reading my notes over my shoulder. "Oh dear! Not another one of your mad ideas for people wanting revenge? Is it food or flower based? Will I need an asbestos suit to deliver it?" Ralph enquired.

"This one is just for a bit of a Christmas special, so we can always hire you an asbestos suit for a short term if needs be. Maybe we can get an attractive red and white furry edged asbestos Santa suit for that seasonal touch?" I replied. He raised his eyebrows, rolled his eyes and wandered into the cool room to check out tomorrow's deliveries against the delivery sheet and line them up in order of time.

I hurriedly put away my notepad and made the tea. Eventually, the two of us sat perched comfortably on stools at the back of the shop, companionably munching on Hob-Nobs and enjoying the inactivity and the peace.

As I crunched into my second biscuit whilst absent-mindedly brushing away the stray crumbs from my apron, I wondered, "How is life in the new house, then Ralph? You have hardly mentioned it since you moved in."

Ralph, now on his fourth biscuit, munched thoughtfully and at last said, "Well, it's ok. The neighbours seem kind enough and there isn't much noise considering it's a terraced, but there's just something about the place that I can't put my finger on. I'm not sure why Kerry fell in love with it, but I can't even get to grips with liking it at the moment. It's got that air of 'it's gonna be really expensive to maintain' about it. Mind you, so does Kerry, but I still ended up loving her, didn't I? I suppose it'll be alright when I get used to it," he chuckled.

"Well it would help if you spent some time in it. Doesn't Kerry get fed up that you work all day, and then go off to snooker, rugby, and football whenever you get the chance?" I probed.

"Nah, she has her own hobbies and friends. The house is always full of bloody women talking about girl stuff. " He pondered for a second, and then added, "At least, I don't think she minds. We don't seem to get much time to talk with our hectic social lives. I have never asked her."

"Wow. You want to watch it, you might end up on the receiving end of a sneak and kid-me pie if you carry on down the rocky road of no conversation and no time together!" I pointed out only half joking.

"Is that the voice of experience?" Ralph questioned. In reply I picked up a nearby tea towel and flicked Ralph with it on his arm. He laughed at my sad attempt of violence and said, "You ladies! All so aggressive these days! If we are resorting to this, I'll take your sage advice and get off home. See if I can't rescue my relationship before it's too late."

I climbed off my stool (it's difficult being only five foot three inches short) and proceeded to cash up and switched off the till and then Ralph and I washed up the tea things. Due to the darkness Ralph insisted that he take the bin to the skip out back of the shop and off he manfully went hauling it over his shoulder to empty it. I thought I'd better get on with 'ladies' things'.

Carefully I dried up the mugs and put everything away onto the now clean and dust-free shelves. Then taking off my apron, I put it in my bag to take home for a good wash as it was looking a bit green and slimy. As Ralph re-entered the shop and set the bin down, I turned off the radio and swung both of our coats down from the pegs behind the back door. Lastly giving the shop one quick glance over to check that there was nothing forgotten, I turned out the lights and turned the sign on the door to closed.

"Bye, Ralph. See you in the morning," I said.

"I'll just wait until you're in your car and safe first, if you don't mind," he returned.

"There really is no need. Like you said before, I'm quite scary when I want to be." I attempted to lighten the conversation, but Ralph was having none of it.

"Yes, but the local louts and hoodies are scarier even than you. And as I've already explained to you, the nights are drawing in and it's dark, so if it's all the same to you I'll wait until I can see you're safe," he told me forcefully.

"Ok, thanks, Uncle Ralph," I grinned.

It was early November and the nights had drawn in it seemed to me much faster than in previous years. It was almost as though someone had turned out the lights at a little after four o'clock, with an immediate effect on the remains of the day.

I skipped hurriedly across the car park and climbed into my little purple metallic Fiesta. As I did so, I caught sight of myself in the window of the shop, and wished that I hadn't!

I was more than a little shocked to see that I actually looked a bit like an escaped mad woman at that moment. My mousy brown hair had mostly come loose from its scrunchie. It was hanging about my face and shoulders in frizzy strands, while my faded jeans and baggy t-shirts looked like they'd been wrestled from a bag lady. Time to radically sort out my appearance! Maybe I was taking this 'wild and free' look a bit far.

Once in the car, I quickly locked the doors – you read about women getting into cars and perverts and criminals getting in behind them or when you have to stop at traffic lights – and turned on the lights. This illuminated Ralph, who I noticed was still watching me intensely. I waved tentatively and he waved back before slowly turning to walk to the van. The van even under the orange street lighting I could see was grimy and in desperate need of a good clean. The dirty days of autumn were taking their toll on the roads as well as on the moods of the public at large. They were no longer spending unnecessarily, but were saving their loot for Christmas. I could tell this from the contents of my till.

I turned on the engine and began the short journey home. Somewhere on the way, I made a snap decision to stop at the shops and get hold of the ingredients to experiment with dog-chocolate biscuits and dog-chocolate Florentines. It would give me something to do, and my ever-hungry Springer Spaniel Flo would be happy to test market the biscuits for me. I have to admit that I was slightly worried about test-marketing the Florentines – because it was bad for dogs to feed them things containing nuts and raisins – but I would cross that rickety bridge when I came to it.

Then I had a thought, but it was so mischievous that it made me snigger! I considered asking my friend Sal to take them for her pig of a lazy husband to test. The thing with Peter – Sal's old man – was that it was guaranteed that they'd barely get over the front door step before he had sniffed them out and snaffled them from me. He'd test marketed the pies when I first made them for the shop on Sal's insistence – they'd had a huge fight when she'd discovered that their joint account was all but empty.

I suppose it would depend on just how disenchanted Sal was with Peter at the moment. Would she be angry enough to send her husband's internal organs on a rollercoaster ride without the fun of the rollercoaster? I knew he was still not putting into the household budget and leaving Sal to pay all the bills from her wages, but would that be enough to tick Sal off? Still, it hadn't been enough to make her leave him so far...

"If you don't ask, you don't get" I reasoned with myself. "Besides which, if I give Sal a call, I could try and set up a bit of a social for us" I told no one in particular. "It's been quite some while since we had a girls' night out, and I could do with something to break up the long, dark evenings."

I couldn't help wondering whether I should take up a new hobby or night class of some kind. The thing is, I'm not sure that I'm ready to meet new people. Some people aren't worth meeting. Some people are like Nick.

I shuddered. Best not go there! I'd better call in at the 7-11 and get the groceries I need. "And then I should try to stop talking to myself!"

Chapter 2

I called in hastily at the supermarket and threw in all the ingredients I thought I would need for my latest innovation in revenge technology, and also found a lovely-looking piece of salmon in their fridge that would do for my tea. Maybe I should buy a 'sad old trout' to match my demeanour, but isn't fish supposed to be brain food? I would definitely buy the salmon then - I wasn't all that keen on trout, sad or not. My brain could always almost certainly do with a bit of a boost these days.

I thought it would be ideal to stick it in my steamer with some baby new potatoes and garden peas. I was pretty sure there was half a small pot of watercress sauce lurking in my freezer too. I had saved it from the last time I had salmon for tea. I remember thinking it would come in handy, and now it would. I could use it up to go along with this juicy, pink Piscean morsel. Yummy!

After a brief in-depth conversation with the grey – and somewhat tired-looking – checkout assistant, on the merits of omega 3 oil and her arthritis, I continued on my journey.

Some young joker in a souped-up Fiat Punto attempted to cut me up at a roundabout. The traffic at this time of day was inevitably murderous for such a small town, and there was always some idiot willing to pull across the entrance or exit to block your way; but this particular idiot was in a class of his own. I could make out his ghostly features behind the wheel and could see that he was openly staring and grinning at me as I sat waiting. His car was deliberately and obtrusively thrown in a blasé fashion across my path. After a minute of irritation and without thinking it through – not knowing if I could or could not be seen due to the darkness – I pointed at the man, then pointed at my baggy pink t-shirted right breast. As I did so, I mouthed the words 'You are a right tit!'

His pale features looked aghast for a second, and then his teeth lit ultraviolet in the darkness showing that he was grinning broadly as he pulled away.

Cheek of him! It wasn't meant to make him smile!

I continued on my way unabashed and allowed myself a small smile of satisfaction for brightening the pillock's day.

Eventually pulling into my driveway the security light illuminating the gravel track, I felt relief that the workday was done. Not that I disliked my work – far from it – but it had been a tiresome and lengthy day. Taking the bags of shopping from the back seat I locked up the car and let myself in to the warm sanctuary of my house. The living room and kitchen lights were on, and there were small muddy paw marks just visible in the dim shadows of the length of the hall. I turned on the hall light and bent to fuss Flo who was now running around my calves like a dog with two tails. Flo deposited her favourite toy, a small fluffy Hedwig owl at my feet and licked at my face as I patted her soft head. It felt good to be home.

This was the only sort of welcome that was welcome in my book. Warm, wet and furry to excess! It had been a good couple of years since I had allowed a man to be the one welcoming me in through my front door. Nick had done a great job of seeing to it that I couldn't bear the thought of having one within a mile range, let alone sharing the same address. Even now thoughts of him made me feel angry and bitter.

Putting these thoughts aside for later, I forged on into the kitchen opened the back door for the dog to go out, and put away the shopping. All of the baking ingredients could be left on the granite surface for later use along with the dog chocolates. The salmon and a handful of potatoes from the fridge with peas from the freezer went quickly into the steamer. Better not get the baking ingredients all mixed up with my lovely dinner. I then set the timer, let in the dog and set out to go upstairs to take off my outdoor things and put on my comfortable, warm slippers. This was almost a metaphor for what my life had become.

On my way through I put on the kettle and checked my answerphone for messages, whilst opening the mail that my dad had placed on the hall table. There was just one message on the answerphone from a desperate-sounding Joy.

I had known Joy for the last seven years since she took up with Duncan. Duncan had been a friend of mine since I took my floristry City and Guilds at the local college, he was there doing A levels. The thing with him is, the longer you knew Duncan, the more confused about the basic mechanics of life he appeared to be. To an outsider, he tended to give the term 'fuckwit' a really bad press with his bizarre habits and hang-ups. Once you knew him well though, you'd realise that Duncan had a complete inability to think in straight lines. He was generous, funny and thoughtful, but not in the usual, obvious ways. At the moment he was having a problem finding work due to his unusual specialism.

It was a pity he couldn't get a job complaining because when I had last seen him, this was rapidly becoming one of his greatest talents. In some ways it was a pity I liked him so much or I could offer him work test-marketing my delicacies.

Anyway, due to his strange problems of the moment, Joy was practically on her knees with exhaustion most of the time. I shook my head sadly, and made a mental note to call Joy back later.

Upstairs I went into my walk-in wardrobe – bit of an extravagance this, but as I'm not planning to share the house with anyone else I can use the precious space within as I see fit, it was only a box room before – and hung up my well-worn coat and took off my boots.

Catching sight of myself in the mirror, I made a mental note that not only was I looking more like a bag lady and less like a businesswoman, but my pasty, fair skin was looking a little pinched and could benefit from a facial. My cheeks, however, were flushed from the warmth of the house, along with my small button-nose, giving me the appearance of a gout sufferer. Nice!

I put away my boots and put on my warm, furry, beige slippers – a fashion article which quite sums me up at the moment – then descended the stairs and went into to the kitchen. Halfway down the stairs, I could hear the kettle clicking off and realised that I was more

24

than ready for another lovely cup of Earl Grey with a big spoonful of honey.

As I made it, I remembered that I'd heard this kind of tea referred to in Ireland as 'Silver Tea', and there and then as I put the teabag into the cup and added the water and honey, I thought the name was apt. It did almost turn to watery liquid silver, in a tarnished sort of a way.

I slid the almost empty biscuit barrel out of the cupboard and selected a digestive from it. Flo sat salivating eagerly at my feet, so I posted the biscuit into Flo's anxious little mouth, telling her, "Last one Flo. We're now officially out of biscuits." Not really understanding, the dog happily wagged her tail and pranced off down the hall with her treat.

As I put away the now empty biscuit barrel, the dog chocolate caught my eye and I made an executive decision to – whilst I had a little time – start preparing the ingredients for the 'Flo-rentines'. This made me laugh out loud as I did it. But laughter wasn't a welcome addition to revenge goodies. So once the stuff was prepared, I reversed my decision and thought I'd better leave the making of them until after I had eaten. No sense in ruining a good meal with thoughts and memories that would put me off my food! This way, I reasoned, it would give me a chance after dinner to get into the 'zone' without wrecking my meal or digestive system.

I retrieved the watercress sauce from the frozen wastes of my freezer and placed it into the microwave to thaw and heat. I watched absent-mindedly as it went round and round on the turntable, absorbing shortwave radiation therapy and in no time at all the microwave stopped. I took out the sauce, almost burning my fingers, and stirred it, then returned it the turntable to finish off heating it up.

Right on cue the steamer timer pinged, so I took down a plate from the cupboard and began to load it with the deliciously fragrant contents. Then the microwave cheerfully announced that the sauce was ready. Perfect timing! So I poured slowly and deliberately over the contents of the plate, licked the drip from my finger, and went into the living room armed with a knife and fork, – fighting irons, my Dad calls them! – and my welcome cup of 'silver' tea. I turned on the flat screen TV (another little extravagance purchased impulsively on a rainy afternoon from a rather attractive but far too old salesman). A whole forty-two inches of plasma stretched along the wall and the remote all to myself, I pulled up the solid light oak coffee table and set down my groaning plate and tea. After that, I grabbed the remote control and deftly turned on a cookery programme. Once again I chuckled to myself as I wondered what the possibilities of finding a 'cooking with dog-chocolate' programme were. I could just imagine Nigella wanting to suck her fingers after that!

Having found something halfway suitable – but not half as much fun as the 'cooking with dog-chocolate' programme I would have liked to see – on making cakes and biscuits, I picked up my busy plate and began to eat. Twenty minutes later with the plate now empty and the programme watched, I quickly drained the last of the nectar that was tea from my cup and decided it was time to start work on my baked goods. Or, in this case, 'bads'.

It was time to get into my 'zone' so I sat back onto the settee, turned off the television to make the room hollow and silent. Next I began to think dark, brooding thoughts. If I shut my eyes tightly I could raid my memory banks for images of the fights that Nick and I had and watch them play behind my eyelids.

The times he would disappear whilst we were having a quiet night in; the times he would disappear whilst we had guests for dinner; the times he would arrive late to appointments and dates armed with only some half-baked excuse. I waited as the feelings of revulsion, anger, and finally stupidity boiled to the surface.

Once I made the mistake of sharing my method for cooking revenge foods with my Wiccan friend Moonbeam (real name Moonbeam. Her mother was a Wiccan too!). She was horrified. She followed the Wiccan rede of 'An harm ye none, do what ye will' and practised only white magic. In her world, adding my ill will to food would count as a 'black magic spell', as you were feeding misfortune to another. She counselled me against it because in Wicca, as in Karma, you reap whatever you sow. I was sowing bad feelings and bad luck, so guess what I'd get in return?

I didn't tell her but, as far as I was concerned, I'd already had about as much bad luck as I could take, and was happy to pass it down to any other ill-behaved, lying, cheating, scumbag deserving of it!

Now I was in my 'zone' and ready to start work. I marched purposefully into the kitchen and banged all my used crockery and cutlery into the dishwasher. Flo knew this mood well and hung back under the kitchen table on amber alert just in case any stray foodstuffs should drop onto the floor and into her domain, the 'dog shelf'.

The dog-chocolate drops melted easily and very soon I had a couple of neat trays of Flo-rentines to show for my efforts with extra-added malice! They didn't look too bad considering what they were crafted from. In fact, if you didn't know any better, they looked quite edible and I considered for a minute that I might make some with rabbit food instead of dried fruit to see how they might look.

However, I didn't want to be the one to find out exactly how scrumptious and edible they were or weren't. So I thought that after talking to Joy, I might give Sal a call later on and see if Peter might fancy test marketing my latest batch of mouth-watering offerings. After all, it might give him a wet nose and glossy coat!

Now if I worked quickly I would just have time to make some chocolatey biscuits with what was left. Quickly I started work on my idea for the 'Bour-bones'. I aggressively poured the melted dog chocolate with rage into the biscuit mixture and beat it furiously, but drew the line at tasting it myself to check the flavour. It would be ironic to cut them into something other than oblongs though, so I settled on a heart-shaped cookie cutter from my stock of baking aids. The mixture did smell really quite chocolate-y and when cooked it smelled even more so. That had to be a good sign. Or, at least, it was for the cook, if not for the eater.

A batch of dog-chocolate cream was very quickly mixed up (with a little added vanilla and rancour to accentuate the flavour) and the appealing, rich, dark heart-shaped Bour-bones were ready to roll. Flo was now shamelessly canvassing to be the first to try one out and so I obligingly proffered one. Flo skipped merrily down the hall with her prized wage for hoovering up any spillages, and the happy sounds of crunching could be heard from the hall carpet. How many cheating spouses would soon be munching them whilst watching 'match of the day', I thought to myself.

The dishes were adeptly loaded into the dishwasher and the kitchen was hastily but thoroughly tidied. I then opened up the fridge, took a bottle of half-drunk White Grenache and poured myself a large glass as a reward. As I exited the kitchen, I deftly turned on the dishwasher and nimbly turned off the lights.

It was time to exit the poisonous and arctic 'zone' and so I took my wine and mobile phone upstairs to have a long hot soak in the bath. Maybe when my mood had lifted I would talk to my friends. I ran the taps on full and added a vanilla and spice bath bomb to the running water. I had to admit that I was pleased to see these now back in the local chemist shop, even if only for Christmas.

The scent wafted to my nostrils and I could feel my spirits lifting. To help them on their way up, I took a large slug of the sweet, summery tasting wine and sat on the downturned lid of the toilet to relax for a second and just watch the water flowing.

The bath was soon full of deliciously relaxing scent and hot water. I peeled off my messy clothes and hurriedly threw them into the laundry hamper so that I could climb in and enjoy.

I slowly eased myself in, appreciating the heat and aroma and allowed my sorry, sallow carcass to become used to the water temperature. It felt wonderful. I lounged back into the vanilla tide and began to loosen up, letting go of my anger and frustration easily as it melted away into the milky, pleasant water.

I could just about see myself in the mirror on the opposite wall. On closer inspection, my rat's nest of long mousy, brown, tangled hair appeared to be in need of a good cut. A good wash and condition would have to suffice for now. I would call my mad hairdresser tomorrow and try to arrange an appointment for Saturday afternoon, which was half-day closing at my florists.

It was interesting that most of the time, I cursed my lack of height – being only five feet three inches tall – as it meant that usually I felt overlooked. However, the one place my height had positive benefits was when I wanted a good long soak in the bath. Baths were made for people of my stature, I had always felt. It would have been better still, though, if Mother Nature had graced me with a flatter chest, because without almost filling the tub to the top it was difficult to keep mine warm below the water line.

Such were the joys of a not-so-perfect hourglass figure!

It took roughly ten minutes of soaking in the tub for my previous good humour to return, by which time I was ready to talk to Joy. It never ceased to amuse me that, until Joy had met Duncan, Joy would probably have been the perfect name for Joy. She was such a warm and positive person when I first met her. Yet life didn't appear to have been kind to her from the things she had told me. Joy – by some twist of irony – had a joyless childhood, as her mother had left early in her and her sibling's childhood. This had left Joy as the eldest of the five, with a great deal of responsibility for the care of the family on her shoulders. She quickly became one of her father's 'rocks'. His other one was alcohol. From her childhood home Joy went into a violent – and mostly turbulent – marriage with a complete waster of a husband who had fortunately smoked himself into an early grave. Then, in her late forties she had met Duncan. Given all of this and more somehow Joy had always seemed so contented and completely at ease with her life.

But lately this had not been the case. The phone calls from Joy were becoming increasingly more fraught and more frequent. Her patience with Duncan's list of things he would not or could not get to grips with was getting shorter. I had seen this pattern so often repeated with other friends' relationships, but in all fairness to Joy she had stuck with him for far longer than most would in her position. I had often marvelled that she seemed to have never-ending fortitude, but I felt fairly certain that now Joy was coming to the end of a very long tether!

I took another very large slurp of wine from the glass on the bath side then dried my hands on the towel on the table to the side of me. No sense in getting the phone all wet again. (Last time I did that by dropping it out of a top pocket into a full flower bucket. It dried out nicely if slowly in the airing cupboard luckily for me.) The number was dialled and a voice from the other end quickly answered. "Hello, Duncan speaking."

"Hi Duncan, how are you?" I questioned (I rolled my eyes impatiently as I did so, because I realised that I had just opened a floodgate that would be difficult to shut.)

"Zoe! How lovely to hear from you! Oh, same old, same old. You know me, having difficulty getting to grips with the basics in life. Employers either want cleaners or factory operatives. Joy's son offered me a little bit of work but it was in retail, of all things. I'm not really great with sales so I turned him down. I don't think he was too impressed, but there you go. I don't really 'get' children, not having any of my own. I've been telling him 'There's really nothing out there for someone with a degree in zoology in today's marketplace'. Did you know that? Jobs with animals are hard to come by. You're very lucky that you just work with flowers. People will always buy flowers, won't they? Pity they don't buy elephants, anteaters or Bengal tigers! I've not been feeling too well in the old tummy region either and I've got trouble with my left thumb again – the cold makes it so much worse – you know? Then of course the bank is after me for the money to pay a couple of standing orders that bounced, because the funds from the dogs I was walking for old Mrs Davis have now stopped. She passed away last month. You probably did some of the flowers. Anyway, how are you?" Duncan finally finished.

"Oh, I'm great, thanks," I replied in a deliberately false upbeat tone. Sometimes the easiest way with Duncan was to jolly him out of his 'downers'. 'It's a good job that he works with animals', I thought, 'at least he can't depress them'.

"And business?" Duncan continued.

"Is also on the up," I lied. "We're gearing up for Christmas now, so things are getting busier every day," I informed him, adding "Is Joy around? I was hoping for a word with her?"

"Yes, just a sec, I'll get her for you. See you soon," Duncan ended. There was a short pause.

"Hello, Zoe, thanks for getting back to me." Joy came onto the phone speaking in hushed tones.

There was the muffled sound of a door closing, and I could easily picture Joy taking the handset into the kitchen of their home. "I'm sorry to keep bothering you, but if I don't offload, I will burst," Joy began.

"Think nothing of it, that's what friends are for. What's he done now?" I asked cautiously.

"I sent him down to the shops whilst I was at work with a list and some money. He's come back with books on scuba diving, wok cookery and a jazz compilation CD. You and I both know he's afraid of even a bath full of water, and with his tummy Chinese food is right out of the question. As to the CD, if I have to listen to the dreadful cacophony once more, I'm going to break the bleeder in half and slice his head off with it!" Joy ended crossly.

"Joy! I can't believe you just *swore*!" I told her, almost completely dumbstruck by Joy's out-of-character outburst. I knew she must be extremely upset, because in the entire ten years I'd known her that was the first time I'd ever heard her swear.

"Oh, I'm sorry, I shouldn't have done that no matter how upset I am. Forgive me?" Joy was contrite.

"It's ok. I don't mind, I'm just surprised. I don't know how you have managed not to use whole strings of four letter words to his face, to be honest. I think most people would have lost the plot living with

31

Duncan for as long as you have," I returned. Then realising what I had said, quickly added "That's not to say I don't love him to bits. He's been a good friend to me down the years, but I know I could never live with him. You deserve to be sainted!"

"Well, it's not that I don't love the very bones of him too, but right now, I could cheerfully kill him. Why do you think he does such stupid things? Do you think he deliberately sets out to annoy me, or is it just that he's totally blind to the feelings of everyone else? It's like living with a teenager. In fact, my own kids weren't this impossible when they *were* teenagers! I've been seriously considering getting him committed, or at the very least checked for Alzheimer's!! He falls into the right age bracket, and he's behaving like a twat in a selfish little bubble! Oh dear, there I go again with the potty mouth! I'm sorry. You don't need this at the end of your working day, do you?" Joy stormed.

I bit hard on my lip drawing blood in a vain attempt to stifle a snigger. Her beautiful, clipped pronunciation of twat sounded just plain wrong! "Oh, don't you worry about me I'm fine. As far as anger goes its better out than in, I think. We can't have you hanging on to all this frustration. It's not good for you, as you of all people should know. So, what are you going to do with him? Does he know how upset you are with him and why?" I wondered. The irony of the situation was not lost on me, with Joy being an anger management counsellor.

"Well, I'm going to have to tell him obviously, but you know what he's like. He'll just walk away, or come over all hurt or defensive. I think I will wait until I calm down, first though. It won't be helpful if I just rage at him. I don't think, feeling the way I do now, that I will make much sense either. Funny, isn't it? I'm great at telling others how to handle their temper, but useless with my own!"

"I'm sure you'll find all the right words when the time is right for you. You are brilliant at reasoning with him. Better than anyone else. I'm certain that you can get him to understand why what he's done is out of order, too. He may be a bit thoughtless sometimes, but he's not thick," I soothed.

"Yes, you're right, of course. He's just upset at not being able to find anyone to give him the type of job he's trained for, and angry with himself because he can't help out with the bills. It was probably a low moment that made him think he needed the books and CD. He did say that the Chinese cookery book was going to be used to make me a treat, so I suppose his heart was in the right place," Joy finished, her anger spent.

"There you go then! He was trying to think of you, not of the shopping list," I ventured.

At Joy's end of the line there was the noise of the TV in the background and a door opening. I could hear Duncan now talking to Joy even through Joy's hand obviously over the receiver attempting to smother the sound. "I'm sorry Zoe, I have to go. I must have been talking to you in a louder tone than I intended because he's twigged that I'm a bit upset and he's doing his best 'hurt' act. I'll let you know what happens," Joy spoke quietly.

"Ok, speak to you soon. Hope it all goes well. Stay calm. Bye," I found myself whispering equally quietly.

Clicking the closed button on my phone, I hung up and lay back in the bath to ponder. There were many times when I felt blessed living on my own with just Flo for company, and today was one of them. Of course there were equally days when I felt lonely, but all in all, in a shocking, disgusting sort of a way, Nick had done me a huge favour. He had forced me to build a business out of the misery and suffering he had inflicted upon me. A brief memory of the day the he brought home a nurse's uniform snuck under my defences. It was obviously a second-hand uniform, and of the very tasteful sex shop type. It was well-stained and bedraggled, yet he fully expected me to put it on! In fact, looking back he'd probably taken it from someone's washing line! I remember feeling sick and humiliated that he would even expect such a thing. I now found myself wondering how and where he came by the offending article but hurriedly pushed it to the back of my mind. I was supposed to be relaxing. Even so, from those little acorns of shame and degradation had come tall oaks of empowerment; and yes, mostly now, even laughter. I laughed a lot these days.

Whoever would have guessed?

The bath was turning a little cool and so I ran yet more hot water in and took a sip at the wine. I slid down into the comforting depths of the now-temperate bath and enjoyed the warming sensation against my skin. Flo heard me sigh and stuck her head over the side. She sniffed at the water and began to slurp heartily from the bath. Vanilla Spice bath bombs were one of Flo's favourite beverages. As I began washing my hair, Flo lapped at the shampoo bubbles in the water and then the little scamp made attempts to ingest the conditioner. I had to admit that the smell of it – honey and oatmeal – was very appealing. I finished up and neatly wrung the excess water from my hair.

Next, I carefully dried my hands on the towel from the table and dialled Sal's number.

Chapter 3

It took a couple of rings for the phone to be answered, and then it was Sal's daughter Louise on the other end. "Hello?" Lou opened with.

"Hi, Lou, is your mum around" I queried.

"Oh, hi Zoe, how are you? She's around somewhere, I'll just give her a shout," Lou said, without waiting for my reply to her question.

"Hello?" This time it was Sal.

"Hi Sal, how are you all? Doesn't Lou sound so much older than twelve when she answers the phone? I hadn't noticed before."

"Hi Zo, yes, and unfortunately, she's starting to look and act much older than twelve too! We're all fine here, how about you?" Sal wanted to know.

"Oh, I'm good, thanks. I was just wondering if I could come over after work tomorrow and maybe test something out on Peter., I wondered tentatively.

"Only if it's highly poisonous and will inflict serious harm," Sal half-quipped.

"Well, I'm not sure about that, but I know he's always a willing guinea pig for my baking. Is he insured?" I returned, laughing.

"To the hilt! Yes, it will be good to see you. I could do with an ear to bend. Sometimes, I really envy you your house and life to yourself!" Sal told me.

"Oh dear, things still a bit rocky, are they?" I remembered that on my last visit to hers Peter had admitted to eating all but one wing of a cooked chicken. She had put it in the fridge for their tea for that evening. He was such a hoover! She told me after he had left the room that she had begun entertaining murderous fantasies. Mainly of Peter being choked by a supersized, one-winged chicken with a bag of elastic giblets. That thought made us both laugh, I can tell you!) "Well, it'll be good to catch up with all your news, so I'll see you at about five thirty. Will you be in from work by then?" I asked.

"Yes, easily. See you tomorrow," Sal replied.

"See you then," I said, and clicked off my mobile.

By now the water was becoming little better than tepid, my skin was turning to prunes and I was starting to feel tired. I climbed out of the bath, hurriedly dried myself and climbed into my fleecy, cream pyjamas. They didn't make me look like sex on legs, but they were cosy! And why would I need to be anything else?

I let go of the icy water and watched as it disappeared down the plughole., all the while dwelling a little too long on what Sal had said about envying me my independence and my home being my own. There were times when I envied Sal her life, her daughter, and being settled in a relationship. They weren't often, but they did exist. Sal having Louise was one of my biggest reasons to envy my friend. I thought that it would be lovely to have children with the right man, but it would have to be someone very special – and not in a window-licky sort of a way – to make me trust men again!

The bathroom light pinged off as I yanked the cord and trudged downstairs to put the wine glass into the dishwasher and start it up. After this, I let out the dog to the freezing, dark dog toilet that passed for my garden. I silently passed the time making myself some hot chocolate from real, good quality milk chocolate flakes, rather than the type of chocolate I'd been using earlier. I have always loved this stuff; it was just like broken up Cadbury's chocolate flake in a can. I casually dipped a damp finger in for my instant fix before my drink cooled.

Having let the dog back in, I then cautiously locked up. I briefly thought of switching on the TV, but with cocoa in one hand and Flo almost willing me along, I decided to 'go with the flo'.

"Well Flo, there endeth another weary day. Let's go up to bed," I told the little dog. Flo excitedly bounded up the stairs and on to my duvet, taking the lion's share of the bed as her territory, waiting for me with a smiley tongue-hanging-out face and a wagging tail.

My days were mostly like that. Tiring but running to a kind of format. No nasty shocks. No chaos. No pain. Just slipping by on well-oiled wheels. This was the way I liked it!

The following morning, I packed all of the Flo-rentines into a Tupperware box and added a couple of the Bourbones just for good measure and placed them at the bottom of my bag. The extra ones went in to an old biscuit tin and were carefully hidden at the back of a drawer full of tea towels. It wouldn't do to leave any of them lying around because my dad might decide to try one later when he came to walk Flo! The last remaining one I naughtily fed to Flo on the way out of the door.

"Stand guard, Flo, see you later," I told her.

The shop was reasonably quiet for most of the day. I watched through my steamy windows as Christmas shoppers hurried by shielded from the cold by their scarves and scowls, fighting both the weather and the premature Christmas cheer hanging from every shop window. This vacuum enabled me to get on with making some pretty silk table decorations for the Christmas display and put in an order for cards and giftware that might sell well in the shop. I always savoured ringing the stationery company due to the man in their sales department, Mr Sidebottom – strange name made even worse by the fact that he entertained delusions of grandeur. He would insist that it was pronounced Mr Siddeebottomme, and woe betide the person that didn't! He would ritually hang up on anyone failing to give it his correct pronunciation and reverence. Also he talked as if he was sucking helium between each word.

His own name wasn't the only thing he pronounced in a unique way; there were other words too. It was as though he had his own language. Also, he was so *unbelievably* grumpy that he truly could turn milk sour by just looking at it. It made me wonder how his wife could bear to converse over tea when he got home from work. I'd imagine that living with someone like that would probably make a person positively suicidal after a while, so the long, winter evenings must just fly around him!

However, to those of us who didn't have to live with him, it was just plain funny!

I spoke to Mr Siddeebottomme with relish and it

fairly brightened an otherwise dull morning. I especially enjoyed ordering the cards covered in little elves and deer. I asked for elves, Mr *Sideebottomme* told me in a forceful manner that they were in fact dwerves. Yes, *dwerves*! I asked for deer and he says *poinkydeers*!' Hillarious! What is a *poinkydeer* and are those people who dedicate their lives to cataloguing and categorizing new species even aware of them?

Later on, one of the regular customers, Miss Tibbs popped in with some of her delicious, melting, homemade scones, so I made tea hot and sweet - how I know she likes it - and thoughtfully put it in the good china cups and saucers that I knew she preferred. This china was normally saved for customers who came in to plan weddings and funerals but Miss Tibbs was a traditional kind of lady who favoured the tinkle of china on china to the sound of mug on countertop. I brought a comfy, padded chair through to the front of the shop for the elderly lady. I wanted her to be relaxed while the two of us passed the time away talking. All the while I continued to work on the orders for the following day along with my blue, white and sparkly silver Christmas preparations.

Ralph blustered in as we gossiped and was pleased to see that he had been included – as ever – in the afternoon treat of a real, homemade fresh scone. Kindly Miss Tibbs hadn't only brought one for me. She loved to treat Ralph now that old Mr Tibbs had passed away; it gave her a warm, rosy glow to listen to the praise Ralph heaped on her baking. It filled a void, I think, for both of them in different ways. Ralph explained to us that his Kerry wasn't much of a cook, and so he really missed his mother's scrumptious home baking greatly. I offered to bring him in some of mine but he seemed to have misheard it as an offer to poison him. Good job I'm thick skinned! He told us through mouthfuls of scone, "It's treats like this that take the shape off the day!"

The day passed relatively quickly and – after the shenanigans with the baby poo of the day before – without incident. The light fell away from the skies at around four, and once again I noticed how black the evening had become so suddenly. Ralph and I began the ritual of shutting up shop for the day when a flustered, slightly dishevelled man charged in through the door and stopped me in my tracks. I thought that I vaguely recognised the man's face, but in such a small town as Clagdale where everyone pretty much knew everyone it was hardly a surprise. It was quite possible he'd bought flowers from me before. I put down the dirty flower bucket I'd had started cleaning and wiped my green, slimy, slippery hands on the back of my already dirty jeans.

"Can I help you?" I politely enquired. The man blushed slightly and hopped from one foot to the other. I eyed him steadily and watched as he nervously jiggled from one foot to the other "Do you want to use our facilities?" I eventually asked.

"Erm, no but thanks for asking. No, what I'm looking for is the lady who makes 'revenge' items," he finally replied.

"Then you can stop looking, 'coz you've found her" Ralph threw in from the cold room.

"Brilliant" he cried whilst eyeing me uncertainly. "In that case, can I have one of your pies as it's my turn for making my girlfriend's dinner."

"I see." I said slowly. "You know what the filling of these pies is, I take it?

"Erm yes. They were recommended highly by one of my work colleagues. I thought I could have a bit of fun at her expense for a change and well, here I am." He answered with a smile in my direction.

Ralph ambled through from the back store room with a frozen pie in his hand. "You'll be hard pushed to identify these from any other meat pie once it's cooked. But watch out, 'coz they seem to have the unfortunate side effect of bringing misfortune to the eater... Are you having pie too?" he wanted to know.

The man stared at Ralph like he thought Ralph might be mentally deficient. "Well no, I wasn't planning to. I thought I might just feed it to her and laugh quietly to myself. Surely the laugh would be on me if I ate it too?" he finally replied, rolling his eyes slightly.

Ralph looked at me with one eyebrow raised and then at the dishevelled man "Eh? Oh, no, what I mean is, have you bought a proper, separate meat pie from somewhere for your own tea?" Ralph blustered.

"Oh, I see. No, I'm planning to tell her I've already eaten as she's working late tonight. How much is this?" he said, taking the pie from Ralph and proffering a five pound note in my direction.

"One pound ninety five, please." I snuck a glance at him from under my too-long fringe as I took his money again trying to place how I might know him. Nothing came to me, but me had a suspicion I would remember in the middle of the night, because that was Murphy's law for you.

"Would you like me to put it in a bag for you?" Ralph asked, but the man was already halfway to the door

"No, that's ok. Bye and thank you," he replied without so much as a backward glance, his raincoat flying behind him.

Ralph and I stared in unison after him as the door swung closed. Ralph was first to break the silence. "Nowt so queer as folk, as my old Nan used to say!"

"Quite." I answered, as I deftly kicked the flower bucket I had been cleaning under the counter. Then swiftly I moved to turn the sign on the door to the closed position, before anyone else could run in for service.

Ralph saw me to my car and watched as I rapidly belted up and locked the door. He smiled and waved as I pulled away, and in my mirror I watched him get into the still dirty van.

Sal and Peter only lived a short distance from the shop, and so even in the rush hour traffic I was there in fifteen minutes. I had known Sal since our earliest school days, and I still marvelled at Sal's loyalty to her husband, Peter. Peter was at best slothful, and at worst, a complete pig. They made an unlikely couple, her tall and elegant with a great sense of style and a strong work ethic. Peter was much smaller and rounder than his wife would ever be, with no redeeming characteristics at all (barring his usefulness as a guinea pig for my culinary experiments). He pretended to be a taxi driver, but would regularly be seen spending all his profits at the local kebab and pizza house, Chinese takeaway, or local chippy. He would eat it all in the car in order to avoid sharing with his family, so as a consequence no one wanted to take a ride in his particularly pungent taxi. Alarmingly he also had an aversion to bathing and this just added to his fetid problem. Many times his boss had threatened to shut down Peter's taxi on environmental grounds.

I rapped loudly on the door. As I waited I could hear Sal bellowing at Peter and Louise in the hallway beyond, telling them to take out their dirty plates and put their shoes into the hall cupboard before someone fell over them. Finally the door was flung open to reveal a fraught and frazzled-looking Sal with paint on her powder-blue bias cut skirt, and what appeared to be jam on her neat, white pintucked blouse.

"Ignore the state of me, we had the kids making bonfire pictures and jam sandwiches at work today. Although not all at the same time!" Sal worked in a school with year three children, and looked like she had been through the mill most days after work.

"What fun! You must have been very involved with it!" I laughed.

"Got to earn a crust somehow! Come on through to the kitchen where it's quiet," Sal invited.

Sal made some tea and brought a plate of biscuits to the table where we sat for some time chatting. Sal was having a difficult time helping her newly hormonal daughter through puberty, and forcing her lazy slug of a man to go out and work for a living. I smiled inwardly, suddenly remembering the purpose of my visit. "Speaking of Peter, where is he? I have a little something I'd like him to test market, if that's ok?" I asked.

"That's right, so you have! What exactly is it you'll be giving him?" Sal wanted to know.

I took the Tupperware box from the bottom of my bag and removed the lid, replying, "They're my home-made Flo-rentines and those two are Bour-bones!"

"Ohh, yum!" Sal cried, reaching into the box to take

41

one.

I quickly lightly batted her hand away, telling her, "They're not as yummy as they look. They're actually covered in and made from dog chocolate, hence the names Flo–rentines and bour-bones!"

Sal hurriedly withdrew her hand saying "Oh my God! Ha! He'll scoff those without a second thought, let's get him in here!" Sal went to the kitchen door and shouted through, "Peter, Zoe is here and she wants you to test out some Christmas chocolates she's making for the shop!"

There was a loud 'thump' followed by thick, elephantine footfalls on the hall floor, and for a man of his size Peter appeared in a matter of seconds from wherever he had been lying in wait in the house.

"Hello, Zo. How's my favourite little chef, then?" he cursorily wondered. I watched Peter's piggy blue eyes light up like Christmas trees when he caught sight of the practical Tupperware box and its velvety contents lying innocently on the table. He eyed them hungrily. I caught sight of Sal smirking, and hurriedly looked away. I didn't want to laugh and spoil the moment. "Oooh, are these little beauties all for me?" Peter wanted to know.

"Yes, but you have to tell me honestly what you think of them!" I cautioned him.

Peter reached in with his pudgy hands, took a Flo-rentine out with his fat, sausage-like fingers and examined it briefly before cramming it whole into his mouth. "This is lovely, very buttery! I like the plain chocolate too!" Peter mumbled through a mouthful of food. "Can I eat them all?" he asked, picking up the canine-treat-filled box without waiting for a reply.

"Oh yes, we can't eat them, they're full of calories and bad for our figures!" Sal replied hurriedly with a giveaway smirk. Peter's bulk was already halfway down the hall by this time. We watched him through the glass panel in the kitchen door shovelling them hungrily into his mouth (lest Louise should appear and ask to try one) as he disappeared into his lair.

Once the two of us were sure that his door was firmly closed, both of us began to chortle. "Did you see the delight on his face when he crammed the first one in? I haven't enjoyed anything so much since he test marketed the pies!" giggled Sal.

"It was pretty funny!" I replied, and then added more seriously "He must be really winding you up at the moment!" This last statement hung like a gradually deflating helium balloon in the air for a moment.

Sal stopped laughing and looked at me dejectedly, "Yes, I am pretty fed up. He eats everything we earn, and leaves nothing in either the cupboards or the bank for Louise or myself. Sometimes I wish he'd just explode like Mr Creosote then at least I could claim the insurance and live a happy life," she mused.

"Are you serious? Does he really get on your last nerve?" I queried.

"Often, yes! But it'll pass." Sal tried to sound jovial, but I could see through the falsely blithe tones of my long-time friend. It worried me a little that Sal should feel that way, but it wasn't the first time. Maybe Sal was right and it would pass.

I gently patted Sal's arm "Well you know where I am if you want to talk or if you feel the need to escape for a few hours." I told her, and then, looking at my watch, added, "I'd better be making tracks, Flo will have crossed paws and be desperate to be let out."

Sal stood up to see me out but as she did she reached out and put her hand on my arm lightly, remembering something "Before you go, I thought you ought to know something. Louise swears blind that she saw Knickerless when she was on the way home from school yesterday. I know his mum told you that he was living down south - and I hope for all our sakes that's the truth - but Lou said it was definitely him. She said he was wearing dirty council overalls and working on a border near the College. I think he's back in town and I want you to be careful."

I sat back down heavily in the chair, suddenly deflated like a burst helium balloon after a large prick (and believe me large prick doesn't begin to cover what I think of Nick). "Oh no! Why now after all this time? I thought he'd at least have the decency after everything he put me through to stay away! So much for serving a

43

three year sentence!" I let all the old feelings of resentment, disgust, and revulsion take me violently and shake me heartily until I felt sick.

"I'm so sorry to be the one to tell you, but I thought someone should forewarn you. And I hate to point out the obvious, Zoe, but he did. He served all of it because he got into a fight with another inmate. Do you not remember his brother telling your sister about it? " Sal said quietly.

I regarded my friend for a long moment and eventually (when I could swallow the bile now forcing its way up) replied, "Yes, yes of course. Where does all the time go? Thanks for not just letting me run into him. That would have been far worse a shock. I'd better go." I could feel the large salty tears already stinging away behind my eyes.

Sal led me down the long and dingy hall and as she passed the cheery pink, welcoming living room where Louise could be heard laughing with her friends. It's such a heart-warming sound, children's laughter. I decided to hang onto that and let go of the black hurt for now. Hurt would come in useful when I needed to whip up another batch of the seemingly successful Florentines.

As we passed the office a pudgy hand came shooting from round the door, the sensible but now empty Tupperware box was thrust into Sal's face. "Ooof, thanks! I take it you've eaten the contents and they were ok, then?" she questioned as Peter's face hovered into view around the now open door.

He nodded briefly in my direction and said "Scrumptious, thanks, darl! If ever you need me to test some more, let me know! See you later, ladies." and so saying, he once again shut the world and us out of his hideout by closing the door to his domain.

Sal and I exchanged glances and then laughed loudly.

"I'll let you know if they have any ill effects tomorrow!" Sal told me quietly. "Meantime, I hope I haven't ruined your evening, and that you have a pleasant one."

"Thanks for the tea, and the warning... and the use

of your husband. That sounded quite bad, didn't it? Still, you know what I mean. See you soon." I thanked Sal and as an afterthought added, "by the way, I'm thinking of setting up a girls' night out. Would you be interested?"

"Would I ever! Let me know when and where and I'll be there with bells on! I could do with a good night out!" Sal smiled. I climbed into the well-worn safety of my car. I exchanged a wave with my friend, and the gangly vision that is Louise appeared at the door to join her mother in waving me off.

As I drove away, fleetingly it occurred to me that very soon, Peter and Sal would no longer be together. I hurriedly shook this black thought off and, ridiculously, made a conscious decision to make a detour around the college grounds on the way home.

I knew in all fairness that it was foolish, since it was by now pitch black and gone seven. The chances of any council workers still working anywhere were highly unlikely, let alone groundsmen and gardeners. If it was true – and he was now working as some class of groundsman – I felt it was even more anomalous. The Nick I knew had always gone to great lengths to avoid the gardening – or any kind of work about the house, for that matter – when we had been together. In fact, he had always gone to great lengths to avoid every room inside and out except for the bedroom and the room where he kept a locked gun cabinet. What was he playing at now? It made me feel sick to the pit of my stomach to think that he was back in town!

There was no way I could breathe the same air as him knowing what I knew!

This last thought was the one which made me think again and take yet another detour from my route. Giving him space in my head was a bad enough waste of my thoughts, but I decided that passing the college was not only futile, it was also a waste of my good petrol. When I really stopped to consider it I genuinely didn't want to see him ever again if I could help it. Just the thought was enough to put me off my dinner. And it had! Straight home and an early night was the order of the day!

45

I congratulated myself at being so grown up and making such a sensible, adult decision. I showed the world by blasting my horn in celebration of the fact.

That felt good!

Chapter 4

Two days later on November fifth, as I was tidying up the rotting remnants after a particularly satisfying revenge bouquet, the speedy man who had called in for a pie two days previously was back in the shop. I saw him milling outside the door for a few moments out of the corner of my eye and smiled to myself. He was looking much less dishevelled and hurried than the last time he visited the shop. I straightened up and pushed a stray lock of hair back from my face as the man came in. Once again I had the suspicion that we had met before somewhere and may already know each other.

As he came in he pushed his floppy, thick black hair back from his eyes and smiled sheepishly at me, only narrowly missing having to duck to get into the door. He gave no clue himself that he recognised *me*.

"Hi... again!" he said, almost embarrassed. I moved from where I had been placing the unhappy, offensive little floral tribute on the floor, noticing as I did that there was a look of sheer horror on the man's once smiling features. His soft brown eyes were glazed and his mouth was set in a perfect O. I followed his gaze, realising that he was staring at the freshly made, rotting pile of dead flowers in the chipped blue vase which I had just lovingly placed carefully on the floor (amongst the beautiful orders for real tributes and bouquets). I couldn't help but laugh at his contorted features, whilst as I did he stared open mouthed at the arrangement then back at me as though admonishing me for my poor floristry.

"Surely you can't seriously send that out? I don't mean to be rude, but it's gross!" he finally bristled. "You'll bankrupt yourself!" he added quickly, seeing me double up with mirth.

When I could finally draw breath, I explained, "It's ok, it's meant to look like that. It's a revenge bouquet!".

Slowly a look of comprehension crossed his features, and then he began to laugh himself. "Oh, that's excellent! That's very cool!" he laughingly said, screwing up his nose slightly. "I especially like the putrid, rotting smell. It really adds to the sensuous quality of the overall picture!" he added.

"I'm glad that it now meets with your approval!" I smiled, and then as an afterthought added, "what can I do for you today?"

"Well, I was wondering if you had any other revenge foods up your sleeve – or in your freezer, as it were – as the pie slipped in really easily. It gave me a great laugh watching her gobble it down. Likes a good gobble, does my girlfriend, but unfortunately that pleasure isn't usually one she saves for me." He realised that there was probably too much information in the last sentence, so quickly added, "I can't believe I said that aloud! I'm so sorry! Anyway, do you have anything else I can feed her?" He finished somewhat breathlessly with a hundred watt smile.

I regarded him for a long moment. He was really quite attractive and I couldn't help wondering what sort of person would cheat on him. "How do you feel about giving your girlfriend some scrumptious, rich chilli chocolate ice cream?" I finally asked.

"As wonderful as that sounds, she hates chilli..." he replied.

"Well then, how about some delicious hand-made chocolates?" I wondered.

"That sounds interesting, what's in them?" he wanted to know.

"Not in, but on. They're Florentines with a twist. They're covered in dog chocolate. I recently tested them out on one of my friend's hungry husband and he described them as deliciously buttery! It's a pity that dog chocolate has mild laxative properties to humans, not that we realised this until the next day. Still, he probably shouldn't have eaten an entire box in one sitting. Still, I can always take him some more when he goes 'down'. His wife called yesterday to say that he'd been caught doing a hundred and ten miles an hour in a seventy zone. The police mentioned a custodial sentence and his boss mentioned the sack," I replied.

"Funny you should say that, my girlfriend got a speeding ticket yesterday too. They must be having a purge on bad drivers around here! The choccies sound like just the job though, I'll take them!" he agreed without missing a beat.

"You might want to ration them if you don't want to give her the runs," I cautioned. Then I had to admit, "I don't have any here with me right now, but if you have time to pop back in tomorrow, I can have some ready for you. Is that going to be ok, or did you specifically need them today?"

"I was specifically looking for something I could serve up for dinner as it's my turn in the kitchen, but as you are offering chocolates they can be given any time as a 'gift'! No, tomorrow will be fine," he agreed.

"Great! Then if I could just take your name in case I'm not around and my assistant serves you..." I knew that there was no chance that I wouldn't be in and that Ralph would have to serve him. I was starting to realise that I found this man quite attractive and amusing. I wanted to know more about him and his need to feed my revenge comestibles to his 'gobbling' girlfriend...

"Mr Gelder. Will to my friends," he replied, smiling down at me.

"Well, Mr Gelder..." I started to speak.

"*Will* to my friends. And I think I would prefer to think of you as a friend, now that you know so much about my strategy for taking revenge on my so-called girlfriend!" he interjected.

I stopped writing and smiled at him, "Ok, *Will*, I have your name and I'll make sure that my assistant knows that the Florentines are spoken for when he comes in tomorrow just in case I'm not around. We'll see you then."

"Great," Will responded with another big smile. "See you tomorrow."

As he left he stopped beside the vile revenge bouquet, and turning back to me he quipped with a killer smile and a wink, "I can't wait to get her out of my life so I can send her one of these as a parting shot." With that he was gone.

Ralph came through the door as Will was leaving and clearly noticed the look on my face as I watched him go out. "Someone's made your day! I haven't seen you glow that much since... well... ever! What's been happening?" he enquired. I was interrupted from my wicked musings and naughty thoughts as I watched the retreating back of Mr Will Gelder.

"Sorry? Oh, nothing, just thinking, that's all. What do you mean, glowing?" I quickly recovered my poise.

"Was that bloke chatting you up? He poisoned his girlfriend with the pie he came in for the other night, and now he wants to replace her with you?" Ralph asked knowingly, but sounding – to me, at least – a little worried.

I snorted. "Of course not! He came in to buy something else to give her for dinner this evening, but I had to send him away empty handed. It'd be a bit suspicious having pie two nights in a week. She might start thinking that he wanted to fatten her up. I sold him some Flo-rentines instead. He's coming in tomorrow to collect them. So, guess what I'm doing tonight!"

"Couldn't you have made him some extra special Bonfire Chilli, with extra added Schmako or something?" Ralph offered.

"If I had thought of it, I might have. Although he did tell me that she hates chilli 'coz I tried to sell him some ice-cream. Actually that's a pretty good idea you have there with the chilli though, Ralph. I might have to try it out," I mused.

Ralph began to ferry out the remaining deliveries and stopped short when he saw the revenge arrangement wilting in it's cracked, chipped and damaged pot. "Will this get there in one piece, do you think?" he queried.

"Do we care if it doesn't? It'll all add to the overall shabby-chic charm of the thing," I countered. With a sharp knowing nod he picked it up and placed it more carefully than it deserved in the back of the van.

The rest of the day was pretty busy. I had to empty the window of the Halloween display: pumpkins filled with floral arrangements – beautiful when fresh, but a bit rank when they start to deteriorate. I looked through the order book and found that I had another revenge arrangement for the morning. One of the pumpkins would be wonderful for this, so I put the most pungent and rotten one of the bunch to one side. Such a delight!

I spent much of the rest of the time whilst I started on the window thinking about my new 'friend' Will. In between I served customers with bright coloured blooms of all kinds and orders for displays, fruit baskets and tributes. It kept the wolf from the door and brought all kinds of fascinating and interesting new folk into my life, and heaven knew I had no other outlet at the moment by which to meet other humans.

Just into the afternoon, the telephone rang and I spoke to my culinary friend and guru Ros. She owned a magnificent restaurant just outside the town in the nearby village of Clagdale. It was built in a refurbished mill, and the builders and she had done a stunning job of the refurbishment. It was very contemporary inside with minimalist but extremely comfortable decoration, and Mediterranean food to die for. Ros was doing a monochrome wedding for a flustered 'bridezilla' and needed some tasteful, minimalist table decorations for the coming weekend.

She explained that the colour scheme for the wedding was all black and white and that the bride was hoping for anthurium lilies and black bamboo in elegant tall vases for the tables. I had to be honest with her and admit that I had reservations on this. I knew first hand that tall vases were more easily knocked over by people who had imbibed too much. Also they weren't terribly conducive to conversation, as they were a devil to see around when you were trying to speak to the person opposite you on the table. Though they could be quite handy if you were sat across from someone you didn't want to converse with, such as if you found yourself sitting across from your new mother-in-law on the top table. Stick one in between and effectively ignore her for the entire afternoon. *Very useful*!

I helpfully suggested instead that they go for smaller pots with Star-of-Bethlehem, white spray roses and black beregrass. Ros could see the sense in this, but felt that it may lack the impact of the tall, elegant and more structural arrangements. I disagreed and promised to come up with something small and beautiful. I would drop something in via Ralph for Ros to show to the bride this very afternoon.

As soon as I'd put down the receiver, I picked it up again to speak to the flower wholesaler. He agreed to drop in immediately with some Star-of-Bethlehem, black beregrass, white spray roses, and a couple of white anthuriums. I also asked for some black bamboo. I wanted to play around with the ideas doing circuits in my head and make up a couple of arrangements for the desperate bride's perusal.

Immediately following this the phone rang again. (This wasn't getting my window dressed). This time it was my father telling me that he had walked the dog and patched the two big, open gouges in the skirting rail of the hall in my house. He also suggested that it would be best if I didn't try dragging items of heavy furniture down the hall in future, but instead asked for help to lift it in order to spare my poor house more scars. I explained to him that I would feel awkward expecting yet more help, since my parents were always on hand to rescue me from all kinds of situations already, but dad wouldn't hear of it. He insisted that in future I should call him for help with heavy lifting. Eventually I agreed, but only because I knew that if I didn't I would never get him off the phone. I also added that I would cook dinner on Sunday by way of a thank you for all his help. He said that he and mum would look forward to it. Then he ruined the conversation and my day completely by tentatively asking if the invitation was to be extended to Saiorse.

I hesitated. It's not that I don't love or enjoy the company of my sister, but Saiorse was apt to conveniently forget arrangements like Sunday lunch. It would annoy me if I cooked for someone who would be too hung over, or too forgetful to bother to turn up. Dad must have noticed the brief hesitation, and because he's used to being let down by her in so many ways also. He recognised my reticence without me having to say anything. Spending several minutes, he went to great lengths to promise that he would make sure that Saiorse was there and ready to eat on time. Eventually, and somewhat aggrieved, I capitulated. I felt I had been pushed into agreeing to extend the invitation to Saiorse, though. I knew that my dad's motives were reasonable. If I didn't feed Saiorse, mum would be foolish enough to feel like she had to cook for her regardless of whether she and dad had already eaten, negating the benefits of me making dinner for them. Saiorse was just selfish enough to let mum do that, too, I knew from experience.

It rankled slightly to have to extend the invite but for the sake of peace and quiet I would just have to put up with it.

Half an hour later, I was putting on the kettle and counting my blessings – to make myself feel less annoyed – when Len turned up with the flowers I had ordered for the wedding at Ros's. Len was small with thinning brown hair and kind green eyes. Despite the thinning hair he still had a sort of boyish face and figure, and he was easily one of the kindest and most helpful people I knew.

I saw his big, green, daisy-patterned van arrive and went outside to greet him. I wanted to raid his van for attractive, tall, glass vases. As luck would have it, there were some. They were shaped almost like 'yard of ale' glasses with a small glass bubble at one end and a stem which was long and thin but slightly flared at its opening. I took one and also a small, round, black glass vase for the smaller arrangements. Len brought in the flowers, and in return I made us both coffee. As we drank, we spent a further half hour gossiping like old ladies at a tea party about our own and other people's businesses (in a not unkind way) before Len realised the time, and announced that he had to dash.

It didn't take me too long after that before I had both styles of arrangement ready for delivery to Ros. Ralph declared them fit for purpose and loaded them into the van, waving cheerily as he went.

The day was pretty much over when I next had time to glance at the clock. I had already begun the ritual of closing up when Ralph reappeared with a neat little package of silver cartons from Ros for me. He explained that they contained some Chicken Diablo, sautéed potatoes, and green beans as a thank you.

Ros was pleased that I'd been able to sort out the floral arrangements so readily at such short notice. He explained that Ros had originally been told that the floral decorations for the tables were being brought in by the bride's own florist; but this had turned out not to be the case. The bride's florist then had a drama queen moment to Ros over the phone about the lack of organisation by the bride's family. He said that it was now too short notice for his firm to sort out the table arrangements as well as the bridal flowers. The flowers for the bride's bouquet, etc. had now already been ordered from their wholesaler, so it was now too late to amend this to take in the equipment for the table arrangements. It was one large mix-up, and in the finish Ros had told the tearful, anxious bride not to worry because the restaurant could easily provide something beautiful and practical for her tables.

Ralph then admitted sheepishly that he'd stayed a little longer at Ros's than he intended as she'd offered him coffee and home made pastries. As if he could ever refuse an offer like that!

We set to and closed up shop for the night, then as ever Ralph saw me safely to my car. On the way home I decided to stop off to buy everything I would need for the Flo-rentine order, but I determined to do it as fast as I could because a) the sound of fireworks going off all around me was starting to grate, and b) more importantly, the smell of the food in the foil containers was now permeating the car and making me feel ravenous.

Before too long I was back home, tucked up with Flo. I'd put the TV on good and loud to blot out the sound of the fireworks outside, and was enjoying the dinner that Ros had thoughtfully provided for me as a thank you for the flowers. It was delicious. To top it all off I had found a velvety, rich, chocolate mousse in the fridge for dessert.

Result!

After dinner, I fussed Flo for a while whilst watching the news, took out my pots, expertly loaded the dishwasher and began to prepare the ingredients for the Flo-rentines. As I did so, I reflected on Nick being back in town and how wretched it made me feel.

All the pain, disgust and loathing came flooding back in an instant. For some reason I found myself thinking about his victims. I could remember their faces and even some of their names as they stood outside the court that warm and overcast July day. The pain seared into me like a white-hot poker stabbing away deep in my heart and guts. I threw all of my black feelings into the mix. It felt good to be rid of them, But I knew what Moonbeam would say if she were here instead of in Ibiza...

I spent the time while the Flo-rentines cooled off in the kitchen dressing a small, pretty box I had in my 'findings' drawer in ribbon and popping a bed of tissue paper inside it. Once the chocolates were ready I placed them carefully and neatly into the waiting box and tied them up – gently but tightly – picturing the ribbon around Nick's neck as I did so. This was new. I had never felt so bad as to want to strangle him before! Maybe it was time to seek help...

I sited them carefully at the bottom of my work-bag ready for the following day ready for collection by Will. It was easy to dwell on Will, I found. My curiosity ran a little wild when I considered what his life must be like and why he didn't just leave the woman he believed to be cheating on him.

I mentally shook myself. It really was none of my business...

After a tidy round, bath and double-checking that everywhere was locked up I was relieved to at last find myself in bed with my book and my customary hot chocolate. It didn't take long before the light was out and I was dozing. Before I finally made my foray into the land of zeds, I made a note to myself to test out Ralph's chilli idea on Peter.

With Sal's kind permission, of course!

Chapter 5

I unexpectedly found myself wide-awake at six thirty in the morning the following day, feeling quite refreshed and as though I'd had a very long lie in. The heating hadn't been on very long so the room was still quite nippy. A symptom of the approaching winter!

I got up quickly, throwing on my fleeciest dressing gown, zipping along down the stairs to the kitchen. Flo followed in my wake, tail wagging as though we were playing some kind of game. I let her out and fixed us both breakfast – Flo having dog biscuits and me having porridge and coffee – then took mine back upstairs with the paper so that I could sit in bed in the warm under the cover of my duvet to eat it. Flo ate hers in the quiet of the kitchen, joining me only when every last biscuit was gone from the dog bowl.

After having read the paper I took a great deal more care than normal over getting ready for work. I straightened and brushed my long (and still slightly straggly) brown hair until it shone and then carefully bound it up into a French plait. Then I put on a thin screeding of foundation and the slightest hint of blue eye shadow round my (quite tired-looking) grey-blue eyes. Next, I added just the merest hint of soft pink blusher and lip-gloss, and squirted myself with the faintest spray of perfume. It was a bit of a treat to have made the time to make an effort, I thought to myself. But worth the energy expended!

From here I took myself to the wardrobe. Normally it would be scruffy old jeans and a jumper, but today didn't feel like jeans and jumper day, it felt like... grey flannel pinstripes, navy blouse and pale grey cardigan day. A bit smarter than usual, but again it felt good to be presentable.

Lastly I dug out some gunmetal grey leather boots and deep blue Murano glass jewellery to accessorise the ensemble. There was no doubt about it; this presented a much better image than my normal workaday clothing. I decided I would have to try to do this more often. Getting up a little earlier seemed (aesthetically, at least) to suit me!

By the time I arrived at work it was a little earlier than usual, as I had managed to miss all the early morning rush-hour traffic. This gave me time to rearrange part of the window that I didn't think looked the best it could. I was also able to give the flower buckets a good scour, ready to take the new order that Len would be dropping off any time soon. There was a message on the answer phone from Ros to say that 'bridezilla' had agreed with me, and the smaller arrangements were much more congenial to sociable conversation. The long vases were more elegant but totally impractical. I'm almost ashamed to say that this made me smile a bit of a smug smile.

I was able to catch a flustered Len before he left his vast warehouse and get him to add the flowers for the twenty small arrangements along with the small black glass vases to the order. I'd be able to get quite a few of those out of the way today with luck! Of course I'd need to clear a shelf in the cool room to keep them on until Saturday. Two days away... they should survive until then! From looking at my order book there were only eight other orders to fill and they wouldn't take too long if the shop didn't get too busy. I could have a nice, easy day.

I put on the radio and began to hum quietly with the tunes whilst keeping an ear out for the wind chime at the door – announcing the arrival of customers, Ralph, or hopefully Len – from the back of the shop where I deftly worked at the sink emptying and cleaning the slimy buckets. The telephone rang and I dashed through to answer it taking an order for some buttonholes for Saturday. More monochrome! Possibly they were guests at the Wedding Ros was catering? Still, they were simple enough; I'd have enough flowers left from the Wedding order and they wouldn't take too long to put together. I could easily make those up nice and early on Saturday morning.

As I was writing the order out into the book, Len breezed into the shop, his arms full of white Iceberg roses and black beregrass. I looked up and smiled.

"Good morning, how is life treating you, Len?" I

asked.

"Oh, you know, so-so," he replied, moving through the counter gate to the back of the shop. He set the flowers down and looked up from where he was placing them on the back room work surface. "Are you going somewhere today then, Zoe? You're looking very smart for a frosty Thursday morning!"

I grinned widely, saying, "No, just working in the shop, but I was up earlier than usual so I thought I might treat myself and make a bit of an effort, you know? Can I get you a drink?"

"Much as I would love to pass the time with you – lovely as you're looking – I can't stop this morning. Seems everyone needs orders delivering early today. It's funny, but time was when weddings at this end of the year were unpopular. Now they seem to be all the go. I can't work it out... why would you want to stand in a church yard and freeze your bits off, while some whippersnapper with a David Bailey complex poses you into awkward pictures with relatives you never see and friends you only hear from once in a blue moon – and all the while it howls a gale and slings down rain in stair rods – when instead you could have a wedding on a beach somewhere for far less, and make all the guests pay their own way? Makes no sense to me. Still, it brings in the money, so I shouldn't whinge," Len finished.

"Much as I agree with you, I won't be pointing that out to my customers!" I laughed.

Len disappeared out to his van, and several minutes later all of the vases and flowers for the orders littered the shop surfaces and floor.

I began to unpack them, and was soon joined by Ralph. Between us the flowers were soon ready to work with, the kettle was boiling for the first drink of the day, and the orders for that morning were safely packed into the mud-spattered van, ready for delivery.

Ralph appraised me as I came in from the cold room as if seeing me for the first time. "You're looking very lovely today Zoe, what's the occasion?" he finally asked me.

"What is it with my appearance? Am I normally

such a tramp? I was up a bit earlier than normal and decided to treat myself to a bit of make-up and clothes that aren't jeans. That's all," I responded, a touch more irritably than I probably should have.

"If you say so," Ralph smiled knowingly.

A couple of hours later I found myself watching both the shiny, open clock face and the door to the shop. I realised with mild shock that it I was looking forward to seeing the vengeful Mr Gelder, but I wasn't really sure why. I thought it might partly be due to his looks – he was really quite attractive in a Colin Firth sort of a way – and partly down to his fascinating (if sad) story. Although I realised that, in all honesty, his story should really set alarm bells going in my head, I wondered what his partner had done that could be so bad as to elicit the response he was giving. After all, why did he not just leave her? He didn't look like money was the issue. He had made no mention of there being any children – and I would hope that there were none to watch whilst daddy fed mummy dog food pies. That scenario was even too vengeful and twisted for my head to deal with, and I quite enjoyed a bit of cold, hard vengeance, so I was happy to think it unlikely that that could be why he had chosen to stay with her either. It intrigued, me truth be told. Fascinated me in a black way. What would make someone stay to deliberately extract a long revenge in such a covert way? Maybe I could tease a little more of his story out of him today?

I tucked a stray strand of hair behind my ear and forced a rose into the oasis of the arrangement I was working on. The shop did eventually open, and Saiorse came gushing in, cheeks pink from the November cold. She carried several bags from local high-end clothes shops and perfumeries so I knew that it could only mean one thing. Saiorse had been hitting her credit card again but hard! I was only too aware that this would entail our parents bailing her out again eventually, as Saiorse had an inability to hold down a job for more than a couple of months at a time.

"Hi Sis, put the kettle on, I'm parched!" Saiorse requested on entering the shop. "I've had a bit of a morning in Langdon scouting for some much-needed

Winter woollies!" she added by way of explanation for the bags. She held them up and waved them cheerily smiling broadly at me as she did so.

"Yes, so I can see." I hoped I didn't sound too annoyed but continued, "I take it you're working at the moment if you can afford all that lot?"

"Don't be such a killjoy, Zo! Yes, I'm waiting tables at The Slug and Sofa if you must know. I'm surprised mum hasn't mentioned it. She was quite pleased when I managed to get Uncle Alex a good discount for his birthday party in January. Dave and June are very generous employers. I'm having a terrific time working for them," Saiorse gushed.

"Hmm, well, good for you. I hope this job lasts longer than the last one at Mayples. I'm surprised Mrs Mayple gave you a reference, let alone one that got you in at the Slug. You're going to need to hang on to this job if you've been throwing your money around on clothes." Inwardly I was cursing myself for sounding bitter, but Saiorse's selfish attitude really rankled sometimes.

I knew that Saiorse gave no thought to tomorrow. She never had. Her attitude to tomorrow would run in line with whichever mood she woke up in. Having said that, Saiorse had been known not to wake up at all sometimes. She would just sleep the day away if she was in the fug of a depression. Which she was... frequently. This had been the straw that broke the camel's back and lost her the job at Mayples. Saiorse refused to see a doctor because she said she couldn't stand the idea of being on medication. No surprises there, since taking regular medication was a commitment of sorts and Saiorse wasn't particularly good with commitment. So, no doctor's certificate, no taking three weeks off sick because you don't feel up to working!

My friend Karin was a mental health nurse and, worryingly, had pointed out to me on more than one occasion that Saiorse displayed symptoms of being bipolar. Karin had also volunteered this information to mum and dad and recommended that they try and get Saiorse to the doctor for a full and proper diagnosis.

My folks were wary of this, saying that because Saiorse was twenty-nine they didn't feel able to tell her what to do and that advice was always wasted on her unless she had sought it from you in the first place (which I had to admit was true). I had given it some thought myself and eventually offered to step into the breach to try and help her, but it was made very clear that they thought it would only disturb Saiorse more being told by her younger sister that she had mental health issues.

I had a sneaking suspicion that the real reason that they refused to sort out Saiorse's problem was because they were old-school and didn't want the stigma of having someone with mental health issues under their roof, and so openly sharing from their gene pool. If it went undiagnosed then it wasn't happening! It was a difficult mindset to break!

I grudgingly made Saiorse some coffee and put the biscuit tin in front of her. She was in an upbeat frame of mind and refused the offer of biscuits on the grounds of watching her weight. Saiorse had a perfect hourglass figure, in complete contrast to my lumpy, dumpy, sack-of-spuds hourglass. At a height of five feet six tall, with natural white blonde hair and glacial blue eyes, I had seen her devour an entire tin of chocolate biscuits (you know the type, those big, fancy Cadbury Christmas tins) when she'd been on a 'downer' on more than one occasion (Saiorse found Christmas depressing because it was a family time, and she found being with us all for more than a couple of hours at a stretch too much like hard work) and not put an ounce of weight on. It was almost laughable.

I, on the other hand, only had to sniff sugar to put on five pounds. Not that I had ever sniffed sugar, you understand.

On the rare occasion that we went out together Saiorse would always end up with a string of smart, (actually they couldn't be that smart to get sucked in by Saorse) handsome men vying for her attention. I have watched time after time as men swarmed over her like bees around a honey pot. However, once she actually became involved with any of them, they never lasted more than a couple of weeks. Saiorse was hell on wheels to be around for any longer. She could give a three-year old child a run for their money in the demanding stakes.

It's really not that I dislike her, although it may seem that way (ok, so I'm a little jealous!). No, truthfully all of this saddens me. I would really like to see my sister settled and living a contented existence with any one of the men she had dated. They had all been hard-working, solvent, generous, new-men and any one of them would have given anything to have Saiorse as their life partner if she were only more mature. As she was Saiorse was given to bouts of low lows, high highs, and being just too wild... with the attention span of an amoeba!

I watched my sister and listened to her chatter animatedly about the regulars of the Slug and Sofa, the tips she had earned since she'd been there, and the numerous offers of dates she'd refused. She knew how to spin a tale and make her audience laugh, did Saiorse. She was so bright, funny and *alive*, and in this frame of mind she was a genuine tonic for the soul. My sides ached from laughing by the time Saiorse had finished sharing her stories from the Slug.

Eventually, though the real purpose of her visit was revealed. She couldn't make Sunday lunch as she had a date. I couldn't help but feel relieved, as Sunday lunch would be a sedate, quiet affair. The relief of this news only served to make me feel even guiltier than I already did for biting Saiorse's head off over the shopping trip.

I finally saw Saiorse off with a wave and some not inconsiderable relief forty-five minutes later.

During the course of the morning I realised that I had managed to make all of the table decorations for the wedding at Ros's. As I stacked them neatly on the shelf in the cold room I was stopped by the sound of the door being opened. I climbed carefully down from the steps and went out to the counter. As I did so, I noticed a large green stain at the bottom of the right leg of my trousers. I cursed under my breath and looked up to see Will Gelder smiling at me.

I smiled back, asking, "Good afternoon Will, are you here for your goodies?"

"Yes, I certainly am! I'm so looking forward to watching her devour them. She's such a chocaholic!" he responded excitedly.

I giggled nervously. "Goodness, what can this woman have done to make you want to feed her laxative Flo-rentines? It must be pretty terrible."

Will pondered the question and then supplied "It depends what you call terrible. In my case I would call sleeping first with my brother – and promising never to be unfaithful again; and then with our painter and decorator – and promising never ever to be unfaithful again; and finally – or at least I think he's the last one – the defendant of a case I tried a while back – terrible, then yes, it is pretty terrible." He looked away, and then added, "I suppose you're wondering why I don't just leave?"

My eyes wide with shock I recounted "Oh dear, that is quite a catalogue! I must admit as you were listing your reasons there it did occur that it might be simpler for you to just go... or just throw her out if the possibility were there. Most people might well have given up on her well before now. Though of course it's none of my business really." Inside I was now mentally kicking myself for delving into his private affairs.

His eyes darkened slightly and he complained "I would love to just walk, or kick her into the gutter where she belongs. The problem is that we have tied everything we have up financially in ridiculously ostentatious house on Knob Hill. Knob Hill! Even the name is ridiculous! I can't afford to buy her out, and even less can she afford to buy me out. Neither of us has parents we can go home to, and I can no longer stand the sight of Ed so I can't live with him – Ed's my brother – and every time I have threatened to leave her she threatens to do away with herself if we split up. It's pure madness, of course. She can't be in love with me, because actions speak louder than words and so her actions speak volumes. I think she just can't bear the idea of having to change her lifestyle. Not that we have much of one after we've paid the bills! I daren't call her bluff because she's just cracked enough to do something stupid just to prove her point if I do leave her. So, for now, feeding her these little treats is my only way of getting a little bit of my own back without her realizing that I'm laughing at her expense. I am hoping against all hope that the schmuck she is seeing now isn't just doing it to get his own back on me for getting him sent down, but he might actually fall for her. From the things our friends have told me she seems very taken with him. It would be wonderful if they would just clear off together! However she's such a gold digger that I don't know if being with him on a permanent basis will hold enough kudos for her!"

I picked up my bag from under the counter and removed the beautifully packaged Flo-rentines from it. Handing them over I ventured, "Well, I'll keep my fingers crossed for you that they do. It's either that or she'll have to stay and risk the slow rotting of her digestive system if you carry on feeding her my treats! Knob Hill eh? I have always loved the look of the Georgian properties up there. Could you not just sell it?"

"We could, but due to what we paid for it and the state of the market at present – added to the fact that it's a half finished project – we'd end up in negative equity. Doesn't bode well if you're looking for somewhere to live. On top of that, I've got to consider that we'll have a mountain of debt from all the furniture and carpets and things we bought for the damn place. Believe me, I have considered all my options, and it could be better!" he finished.

"So, the best scenario for you would be for her to be true to her word? That way, just as she does herself in because you've told her you're off, the market explodes giving you top dollar for your house?" I attempted to quip. It took several seconds for the weight of what I had said to sink in, after which I apologised profusely.

Will only laughed and said that apologies were not necessary, and that he knew I had not meant it in any serious way. He did add that it might be quicker to simply poison her – with anything I could concoct – when the market showed signs of recovery, as they had both taken out large insurances on each other. I chided him mildly, and further to that said that I hoped the man his partner was seeing wasn't sent down on any class of murder or GBH charge, or else the boot might be on the other foot with regards to whom would be claiming the insurance!

Some twenty-five minutes later Will left the shop with his parcel of treats neatly hidden in his raincoat pocket, and me smiling wistfully from my shop doorway. As he left he asked, "Why do I feel so comfortable telling you my woes, Miss Parsons? You are very easy to talk to. I'd like to come and talk to you again soon if that's ok?"

Without hesitation (and possibly a bit too quickly for decorum's sake) I told him, "Please call me Zoe, and you're not alone. Most people tell me things that they wouldn't necessarily want to tell their nearest and dearest. I would look forward to seeing you again."

So, now I knew why Will Gelder was so comfortable feeding his partner my baked goods and sweets. She was a serial sleep-around, and they had bitten off more than they could chew with their mortgage. Strangely it was pretty much all down to money. "Well, they say never judge a book by its cover and you've done just that, Zo!" I told myself. I would have sworn he was comfortably off. His clothes and shoes didn't look cheap and he was always well turned out. Not a pinch of plaster dust or a paint splatter anywhere! Maybe he didn't do the house up himself. "Maybe he's hopeless at DIY... " I thought to myself. "Maybe he's so busy with his work that he doesn't have time to do it himself?"

As I pondered on what he had said, I began to think that his partner sounded like a bit of a tart to be honest. And not one with a heart, either! 'Maybe she's a bit psycho. .?' I deliberated. Although I wasn't so blinkered by lust as to think that Will would be perfect – which of us is? – I believed it would take a particularly selfish mare to wilfully and repeatedly hurt someone in the way this woman had set out to do. Hell, I couldn't even think of Saiorse as that ignorant and spiteful; and generally she took the cake when the mood was on her for being a handful. Saiorse was nothing if not honest, so if she had fallen out of love with someone I was sure she'd be straight with them and leave. At least I would hope.

This led me to wonder which one of the Slug's customers Saiorse was planning to meet on Sunday? I knew there were some of those kind, solvent, stable types of men who drank in there. It would be good if she could land on her feet, find someone who understood her and could help sort her out. I was far-sighted enough to know that mum and dad wouldn't always be around to clean up our mess. I certainly didn't want to find myself at some point in the distant future inheriting Saiorse in her present state. My nerves wouldn't take it!

This made me think about my parents, and that mum and dad could do with some time to themselves. Have a break from the two of us, and our messy, tangled lives. Maybe I could see about sending them somewhere for a holiday as a Christmas present...

And the subject of Christmas led me to realise that I ought to finish off the half started window. Finish getting some silk arrangements and gifts together for the season. Firstly, though, I'd decided I would shut the shop and get myself to the buttie shop next door for some lunch.

I made for the door but, as I reached for the handle one of my more unwelcome customers came in. I was forced to go back behind the counter to serve. Mrs Edwood was a formidable character and known to all of the shop owners on the block as 'a little bit of a difficult customer'.

"I'd like to order a floral tribute to go on Monday," she almost barked.

I smiled politely and proffered the book of tributes. "Of course. Here's the book; if you'd like to select something we can make it up and deliver it for you." No, no, no! I don't have time for that. I just want a simple spray – the cheapest – in whites and green for my father-in-law.

"It's to go to Pott's funeral home and his name is Graham Edwood. The funeral is at the Crem at ten fifteen, so you'll be needing to get it there sharpish on Monday morning," Mrs Edwood almost shouted. I had already grabbed a pen and the book and was jotting the order down.

"Certainly, how would you like to pay?" I asked politely when I had finished noting the order down. Generally with funeral work I would just bill it out and the customer could pay when they were ready, but not Mrs Edwood, she was 'special'! She didn't like to pay without being chased.

"What? I'm in mourning for my father-in-law! I can't think about money at a time like this! You can send me in a bill. You have my address from previous orders. I will pay when I get it." Mrs Edwood spat the words at me whilst almost foaming at the mouth. Turning abruptly she stomped out.

I watched, relieved, as the large frame of the other woman disappeared in a fug of anger from my shop, and couldn't help wishing I'd had a box of Flo-rentines handy so that I could have offered one to her. Grief struck people in many ways but that was the first time I had seen it strike so cheaply and nastily!

Chapter 6

By Friday at five o'clock I was starting to feel ratty and tired. It had been a busy but interesting week and I was ready for the weekend. After a full day with several table arrangements for the wedding at Ros's, a mountain of buttonholes, a revenge arrangement, and three bouquets, Ralph and I had tidied, cleaned and locked up. Exhausted, I decided to call in at the takeaway and the shop on my way home. A delicious bowl of Chicken Passanda and Pilau rice along with a glass or three of rosé would help start the weekend off just right.

My friend Dannie had called earlier in the day, and after a general chat had said that she might call by for a drink and a chat later, so I was feeling a little apprehensive. The wine would certainly be of help on that score as it would relax me. Dannie had been having some relationship issues of her own and I knew where the answer lay but was unsure of how to break the truth to my friend. I hoped that the wine *wouldn't* help on that score and relax my tongue!

I could do without breaking the truth to Dannie if I were anything less than stone cold sober!

Before long, I was sitting in front of the television with curry and wine to hand, and Flora contentedly gnawing at a pig's ear at my feet. I had lit some of my favourite little Jo Malone wild fig and cassis candles (one of my little extravagances. Worth every penny) and put the fire on so it all felt very snug and wintry. Outside I could hear the strident wind caterwauling like a football fan whose team had just lost an important match as the weighty rain launched itself with habitual gusto at the windows. I ate slowly, savouring my food, and sipped at the wine, feeling ever more mellow as each sip slipped passed my lips. Sometimes it felt good just to *be*.

Dannie turned up at a little before eight, and despite being in the car she was quite bedraggled. "Look at the state of me! This weather is atrocious! Who'd believe you could get so wet just going from the drive to the door!" Dannie blustered.

"I'll fetch you a towel for your hair. Take your wet coat off and hang it up on that peg over the radiator, then get yourself parked by the fire," I ordered.

In no time at all the pair of us were sat beside the fire with rosé wine in hand and chocolate on the table, dissecting the various happenings of our week. Dannie had recently 'come out' and had left her fifteen-year marriage to run off with a woman four years her junior and ten inches taller than her. At five feet, five inches, Dannie wasn't exactly on the short side of short for a woman herself, but Georgina was positively mountainous. I was pondering this last point whilst Dannie spoke,

"And she keeps leaving the top off the toothpaste and clothes all over the bedroom. It's like living with Brendan all over again. I thought if I moved in with a woman I could at least expect a tidy house! Though that's not why I moved in with a woman, of course," Dannie complained.

"Hmm, well maybe she wasn't brought up to look after herself. You did say she is an only child. Maybe she was spoiled in that way by her mum?" I volunteered.

"And that's another thing, her mum doesn't have a single picture of Georgie out on view anywhere in the house. Georgie reckons it's because she hasn't come to terms with her only daughter being gay, but there's not a single print anywhere! That's a bit odd, don't you think? That a mother would destroy every single childhood picture of her only child just because she disagreed with that child's lifestyle choices?" Dannie was so upset that she was barely stopping for breath.

"Well, not being a mother myself, it's hard for me to know how she'd react, to be fair. And everyone handles situations differently, don't they?" I tried.

"And if her mother is *so* against Georgie being gay, how come she extends the invitation to me go round there every Sunday for tea *with* Georgie? Doesn't make sense, does it? I'm convinced that there's something I'm missing about Georgie, but I'm not sure what that something is." Dannie was nonplussed.

I was almost certain that the thing that Georgie was missing was her manhood! Meanwhile I was debating whether there would be any good in telling Dannie the truth. I knew if I did it would end in tears and anyway I wasn't sure how best to broach it. The other problem was that I had no absolute proof that Georgie wasn't Georgie. I was really only going on rumour and that wasn't sound enough basis for blowing your friend's life apart.

We talked long into the evening and finally at two I asked if I should make up a bed in the spare room for Dannie. Georgie was out of town buying stock for her equestrian shop at a trade fair, and so I didn't imagine that Dannie would be missed at home.

"Oh, why not? She doesn't need to know where I am and I don't need to be at her beck and call! Can you handle the scandal of me being under your roof alone with you now that I'm 'out'?" Dannie joked.

"Ha! You've stayed here a million times before in the past, and since when did I care what people thought of me? I'd be glad to have you stay if you can handle the backlash when and if Georgie does find out." I replied.

"Death holds no fear for me!" Dannie threw back with a dramatic flourish. And off we went to lock up and make up a bed in the spare room for Dannie.

The following morning I had to leave for work at eight thirty. I left a note on the kitchen table telling Dannie to help herself to the contents of the cupboards and fridge (not that there was loads of choice in there) and generally make herself at home. I explained in the note that I would be going straight to town after work, but that Dannie would be welcome to join me for lunch if she chose and if she was still a free agent.

Saturday was my half-day and I had managed to make an appointment with my hairdresser for later on in the day. I thought I might even go mad and treat myself to something new to wear. That was if there was anything left in my kitty after I had done a bit of Christmas shopping.

Ralph was already loading up the sea of

monochrome table decorations from the cold room for Ros's when I parked outside the shop twenty minutes later. There were the bouquets and a balloon to go too. I blew up the balloon whilst Ralph whistled tunelessly as he expertly loaded everything into the van.

"Alright darlin'," he shouted over to me with a wink. "Sleep well, did you? You're looking a bit pale," he told me.

"I'm fine, just a bit too much wine and a bit less sleep than I would have liked last night," I replied, somewhat irritably.

"Wild night, was it? Ooooh, who was the lucky fella?" he questioned, smirking lasciviously.

"There wasn't one, since you asked. Dannie came round and we got talking. We didn't realise how late it was until two this morning," I divulged.

"Dannie? Is there something you want to tell us? Have you got an announcement to make?" he asked, only half joking.

"Of course not! You should know better than to ask that!" I bit.

"Alright, alright I'm only teasing. Don't get your knickers in a knot!" He laughed. Then added "Get the kettle on, this lot won't take me long and you can tell me all about it."

I waved my middle finger at him playfully as I disappeared into the shop.

I knew that having Dannie stay over in such a small town would provoke a reaction, but I have to admit that I hadn't expected it to start so quickly and with Ralph, who should know both of us better. It riled me somewhat to think that people (particularly people I counted as friends) could be so narrow-minded. Dannie and I had been friends for years. She was the same Dannie as she'd always been! She would often stay over at mine before she came out, when Brendan was working out of town. Funny how no one ever read anything into it then! Had people nothing better to do than speculate on my life?

Mind you, after what Nick did, should I be surprised that people would so readily think I'd turned gay myself? In fairness and looking at it from the outside,

71

Nick ought to have been enough to put me off men for life by rights. He hadn't, though, I knew, because I couldn't stop thinking about Will Gelder.

The shop was busy until eleven fifteen, so as soon as it went quiet I had the opportunity to start cleaning up. Ralph returned rather later than he had hoped and his reason was that he'd been sampling some canapés for Ros. He brought a small paper plate with one or two on for me and I enjoyed nibbling at them while I worked. It made me vow to visit Ros's for a meal in the very near future. I paid Ralph in cash (as this was his preferred medium) from the till and he wished me a pleasant weekend after asking as to my plans. I returned the gesture and enquired as to his.

"Rugby, beer, and putting my feet up," he grinned.

"Kerry ought to be sainted," I muttered, shaking my head at his retreating bulk.

At eleven thirty Mr Bartlett – one of our regulars – called as he always did and bought one of the ready-made bouquets of carnations for Mrs Bartlett. He was a lovely old-fashioned gentleman and it was a great shame that there weren't more like him. My profits would double if there were for a start! Moreover it might help to renew my long-lost faith in male human behaviour!

At eleven forty-five Dannie called to tell me that she was unable to make lunch due to the early return of Georgie. Dannie had just spent a fraught half hour trying to pacify a livid Georgie who it transpired had tried to call Dannie at home at eleven the previous night. Due to the fact that Dannie wasn't home, Georgie had her down as having run away with their perfectly formed postwoman (apparently their postie was just Dannie's type and yes, Georgie was *that* insecure). Dannie was going to have to get round to their home pretty quickly if she was going to beat Georgie back in. Georgie was only now a short ten minutes away from their front door.

I thought Georgie sly to try and catch Dannie out like that, but Dannie was so in love with Georgie that I couldn't bring myself to tell her that. Dannie wasn't ready to see Georgie's clay feet quite yet. Nor was I really ready yet to be the one to tell Dannie that they weren't so much clay as size twelve and safety boot clad.

I got Dannie off the phone in the end by promising her that it honestly didn't matter that she couldn't make it for lunch. I told her that I had enjoyed our cosy evening in with a bottle and a gossip-fest and hoped that Dannie did too. Dannie had enjoyed our time together until then. Now Dannie was just plain scared and worried. She told me that if everything went badly she'd be back on my doorstep with a suitcase later! I told her to make sure that she also brought at least one very large bottle of wine if she was going to do that.

Putting the receiver back into its cradle I announced to the world at large and no one in particular, "Well, Zo... A whole afternoon practically to myself, so what to do first?" I had left the door to the shop open whilst the floor was drying, and at this point I had my back to it. I hadn't seen Will Gelder come in through it.

"Really? How about lunch?" he suggested.

I made a mental note that I *really had* to stop talking to myself!

Chapter 7

"Will! You gave me a fright!" I breathed. I turned around to see Will with a look upon his face that rather suggested I might be his lunch if I wasn't careful! On balance I wasn't sure that I minded all that much if I was.

"Sorry, I didn't mean to creep up on you. But you did just say you were at a loose end?" he questioned.

"Yes, sort of," I slowly replied.

"So... " He continued. I took a minute to think about the implications of this. Will Gelder was living with someone – albeit in a rocky and unstable way – and this would make me his bit on the side! Actually that might be overplaying my hand. He had only suggested a spot of lunch. It was his features that were suggesting something else, but that might just be a combination of my rather fertile and overactive imagination and wishful thinking. A roll on a plate (maybe with soup), not a roll in the hay, was what was on the table here!

"That would be lovely," I eventually replied.

I locked up the shop and as I did I explained that I had a hair appointment at three thirty with Xavier (actual name Collin) so it would be best if he went in his car and I in mine and we could meet somewhere mutually agreeable. Then I dug my once-cream-but-now-faded-and-greying-gloves from deep inside my messy, battered bag. The weather definitely felt colder by a few degrees now than it had when I came into work. We hurriedly made a decision (I told you it was cold) to meet at Brown's bistro in the town centre and went our own separate ways.

On the drive over I had thought about how best to approach things with Will so as not to blur the lines of propriety. Pity I wasn't Saiorse, because then I wouldn't have given a second thought to what was decent behaviour, I would just have 'gone for it' and jumped on him between the soup and the main course!

I decided that it would be best to maybe establish some ground rules. Start by insisting that I pay for my own lunch and drinks. Then I could be careful to open my own doors and pull out my own chair etc. That way my independence and a very firm, straight line would be established from the first.

Thirty minutes later on my arrival at Brown's I found him sitting in the brightness of the window at a cosy table for two. With menu in his hand and waitress dancing attendance, ready to take our drinks order, he was perusing the list before him slowly to keep her there until I arrived (or maybe he was just enjoying keeping her there for his amusement and interest. Maybe I had better get this cynicism of mine into check!)

Before sitting down I pointedly and discreetly told him that I would only partake of the meal if we were going Dutch. The waitress stood by uncomfortably, rocking from foot to foot and picking invisible lint from her blouse. As I explained that I didn't want to get into anything I might not be able to get out of later, she reddened and wandered over to the people on the next table to enquire as to whether their food was ok. I didn't blame her – I was probably being rather too forward whilst also making an idiot of myself – but I had to keep things on a 'friendship' grounding, so I continued by explaining that I didn't yet know him well enough to know if he was the type of man to buy dinner for a woman and then expect 'payment in kind' later. (Such was my distrust of all men!) All of this was probably too much of a statement for just a quiet lunch and a bit ... bold! Anyway, it was hurriedly garbled and I couldn't take it back now that it was out and running free all over the Bistro.

He laughed gently and gave me the sort of look that made me feel like I had just let my last brightly coloured marble glide into the nearest drain. Then he chivalrously accepted my offer to pay for my own lunch and so I accepted the seat that he had by now pulled out for me. So much for establishing my independence! This was actually quite pleasant in all honesty ... a man with good, old-fashioned manners! I could get to like this! Then I caught up with the fact that I was running away with myself again. It was just lunch, that was all! I would have to keep reminding myself firmly of that.

The waitress turned her attention back to us and quickly took our drinks order, then disappeared to fill it whilst we made our choice over the food. I really wanted the carbonara, but I knew that this would in all probability necessitate some slurping and messy eating, so I plumped for spicy prawns in a chilli and lime batter with a sweet chilli dipping sauce and a side order of wedges. (The cold weather always makes me feel hungry). Will ordered beef and vegetable soup and a baguette with warmed beef and onion. 'Soup,' I thought, 'what a brave choice'. I'd have to slurp that too, to an extent. Yes, it was really quite brave for a first date.

But then again, this wasn't a date, was it? Maybe I could have gone for the carbonara after all...

We made small talk whilst we waited for our food to arrive, and this flowed easily. Will told me that following her ingestion of the Flo-rentines his girlfriend had needed a day off from work due to their laxative effects. I had warned him, but he said he'd been hoping for that to happen because he knew her boss was growing weary of her taking time off sick. She'd also been given another ticket. This time for parking in a disabled bay while she called in at the chemist to get something for her upset stomach. It really hadn't been her day! It had made Will laugh though.

We people-watched (a sport, it transpired, that we both excelled at and enjoyed) and occasionally assassinated the odd passer by with our suppositions and theses as to why they were dressed as they were or why they walked as they did or why they were carrying whatever they may have been carrying. There was an endless ebbing and flowing tide of human flotsam for our dissection drifting past our pleasant little island in the cheery, well-lit window.

Eventually the food arrived on satellite dish sized plates and we were quiet for a short (shock at the portion sizes, surprise at the delicious flavours) while each of us concentrated on our repasts. And in so doing we were adeptly managing to ignore the elephant in the room. This was the frisson now running between us.

Will was first to break the silence. "So Zoe, you know all about my home life – or lack of – but I know nothing of yours. You're a mystery to me. What do you do outside of the shop?" he probed.

"I live a quiet and blameless existence," I joked.

He laughed lightly, saying, "Come on, you run a revenge business! Blameless... you? Tell me, what's the real Zoe like?"

I put down my knife and fork and thought for a second. "Well, I live with my dog Flo in a little three bedroomed cottage in Thumpington village, and I have quite a wide and eclectic circle of friends. My parents live in Clagdale and my older sister Saiorse still lives with them." I paused and then carried on "She's a bit of a case but not one I want to get into right now. The florist shop is my own business that I bought with money from a property I owned jointly from a failed relationship, and money I was left by my grandfather, as is the cottage." I held up my fork as if to bar his way as he made to ask about that one. "Before you ask, I don't want to talk about the failed relationship either. It's in the past for a reason, and that's where I like it to be left. Apart from that, I'm twenty-eight years old have a penchant for anything sweet and my worst habit is eating biscuits in bed. Crumbs can be devious little devils, don't you think? A little like sand in that respect. Other than that, there's not a lot to tell. I'm a bit of a beige personality, I'm afraid."

Little did I know that this last sentence was going to be the one to wake the elephant up, open it's pen and set it free to crash wildly over the little wooden table with humongous grey hooves...

"Beige person?" he quizzed.

"Yes, as in I fade into the background. I don't stand out in any way and people don't tend to remember me." I explained. "My sister got the 'all shades of red and all manner of sparkly' gene. I got the leftovers." I smiled.

He put down his spoon and the bread he had torn from his sandwich. His face unreadable, he began, "I beg to differ! I think you are very memorable. In fact I'm having a hard time forgetting you," he volunteered with just a little more honesty than was required given the situation. We both reddened. He looked away as he added quickly, "I'm sorry I should never have said that. I don't want to put you in an awkward situation, nor do I want you to think I pick up women as a regular thing. But you should know that you are the first one I've felt drawn to in a very long time. Not even Wendy Wide-legs had me so firmly hooked in such a short time. I find you very ... intriguing."

I snorted a little too loudly at the Wendy-wide-legs moniker. What a way to address your beloved! On top of this... so much for keeping things on a friendship level! This was rapidly turning into an untenable position to be in. I squirmed in my seat. "Nice one!" I snapped a little more testily than I had intended. What I had been trying to convince myself in a not too convincing manner was that we were simply two new friends meeting for a light bite. Now the light conversation I had been hoping for was becoming heavy and ungainly.

He continued, unabashed. "What I mean is that I find you fascinating and physically very attractive. In fact I'd go so far as to say that there is something magnetic about you that draws me in a way that no one else ever has. Far from being 'beige' as you so neatly put it I would describe you as the deepest, warmest shade of iridescent I have ever come across." He drew breath and smiled meltingly, then after a moment's thought added, "I have no rights, in fairness, telling you any of this, and I don't want to put you in a difficult position, but I would love to see much more of you if I were free."

I suddenly no longer felt hungry. I stared at my half-full plate, wondering how to swallow the very chewed, spicy prawn now positioned at the back of my mouth, then I looked into the eyes of Will Gelder.

It was the dumbest thing I could have done.

I was lost to all reason in that one tiny movement. I had to fight hard with my conscience and all my power of reasoning (not that there was much of either). Eventually I told him "It would be very easy for me to throw caution to the winds and just go with this. But you *are* with someone and I have always promised myself that I would never settle for just being someone else's 'bit on the side'. I'm not sure where this really leaves us other than in what could be a very long and happy friendship."

Both of us sat with my last statement hanging thick in the air between us. "You do understand that I don't want to be with Wendy? It's purely fiscal, I can assure you," he pressed.

"Yes, you did mention it. It's not that I don't believe you but I can't be in a relationship where there are three of us – having a Princess Diana moment there! I'm not prepared to put myself through that kind of agony playing those kinds of games. I've been on the receiving end of something similar and I know how it feels. Can *you* understand?" I returned.

He thought for a second and then, returning to his (probably lukewarm) soup, told me quietly, "Yes. I'm in such a position myself as you know, so I do understand. I can also see that two wrongs don't make a right and all that!"

"Exactly. I'm not trying to hurt you. Nor am I trying to let you down. I simply don't want to condone that kind of thing by being party to it." Then, having thought for a moment, I added, " I would have hoped that you wouldn't either, to be frank!" I pushed my plate away. He pushed his hair back from his eyes and looked down into his soup bowl as if expecting to find a large shark hiding in there. His face was fearful!

Eventually, with hurt in his voice, he answered quietly "I invited you here on the spur of the moment. It seemed like a gift from the gods, finding you alone in your shop with nothing else to do for the afternoon. I even managed to convince myself it was all fate at work on the way over here. Stupid, eh? Then I told myself that I just wanted to be friends because that would be enough. I would consider myself *fortunate* if you were prepared to be my friend. Given the mess that my life is in you are probably wise not to get too involved. Who knows? Maybe your friendship will be the thing that saves me from the madness and chaos that is my domestic setup." His eyes crinkled into a smile as they searched mine, as if hoping to find some kind of shelter from the storm we had created with our words. We both knew we were whipping up a potential tornado here.

I thought carefully. I didn't want to be inflammatory. Well actually, I did. I really, really wanted to be completely contrary and run naked through his bowl of beefy vegetably goodness and then prostrate myself willingly on his baguette so it took loads of self control to say what I said next.

"I'm relieved that you can see it from my point of view. That's not to say that if things change in future, and we are both free, I wouldn't be interested, because I would. In the meantime, I promise to do my best to 'save you from your madness and chaos' in any way I can. So long as it's not in a sexual way. If we're going to be friends you need to know that I'm a bit of a chicken, you see. I just don't want to end up in a messy situation I might not later be able to get myself out of. Been there and done that, got the scars to prove it!" I finished, flashing him one of my most dazzling smiles (but wanting to flash him *so* much more). He returned the smile and I had to battle with the urge to mess up his latte by dipping in my finger into it and thrusting a perfect, foamy finger fully between his perfect, kissable lips.

I was so close to going back on what I'd just told him! It would be so easy to fall hook, line and sinker for Will Gelder, but I'd made up my mind to find the strength not to so somehow I wouldn't be going there! At least not today!

He reached across the table and put his hand gently on mine. "I will take any time you are prepared to spare me and be grateful for it. I'm sure that we can have a lot of fun together. You certainly seem to have a wicked sense of humour, if the revenge business is anything to go by. I hope that I haven't put you in a difficult position by telling you how I really feel?" he asked.

"No; I'm flattered, if you want the truth. But that's as far as it goes for now. And since you understand, you'll agree we can be just good fronds as we florists say. Shall we not mention it again?" I tried.

"We shan't mention it again, if you'll leave out the awful florist jokes," he agreed.

And we didn't! Will ate the remainder of his lunch while I shuffled mine slowly around the plate, my appetite having packed its bags left for far off lands earlier. It never ceases to amaze me that males can always eat regardless of the situation and in such vast quantities too. As he ate and I shuffled food we told each other stories of our past and dreams for our future.

All the while we were both very much aware that the big, ardent, electrically charged elephant sat firmly back in his pen but still waiting for his chance to pounce again... if something as ungainly as an elephant could ever pounce.

Chapter 8

I had to work hard to tear myself away from his delicious company at three fifteen, as we were having such a fantastic, fun time. Will was interesting and he made me laugh easily with his tales of life, the universe and everything. However hard I tried it was difficult not to *like* him, *like* him.

Before I left we made tentative plans to meet for lunch the following Saturday too. I felt fairly certain that since we were meeting in such an open way – in full view of the world and his wife – then our meetings couldn't be misconstrued as anything other than just two friends meeting for a spot of lunch and a catch-up. Also I thought I wouldn't be tempted to tear open his shirt with my teeth and bite him instead of my food if we were in public (though even this was very tempting!). I felt it was the *safest* option barring complete self-deprivation.

It was a short, and by now almost icy – the temperature was plummeting with the wintry sun from the flaming sky – walk through town to the hairdressers, and I arrived on the dot of three thirty. I was pretty much unaware of anything as I walked because my head was full of Will. I had to admit I was smitten and it was going to be a tormenting, difficult, uphill battle to just remain friends (or even fronds!). I was almost daring myself in my desperation to consider the option of us becoming 'shag buddies' (a term I'd heard my friend Bel mention recently. Apparently it was the modern way to go because it was guilt-free, pain–free, harmless but fun sex. I can't imagine it though somehow!), when I caught hold of myself and realised that in order to have any class of guilt-free sex you'd be needing to have a wild and uninhibited nature. That wasn't me at all! I was sensible, level-headed, and, well, beige! Even so, I couldn't stop myself from considering what it would be like to be with Will. Who was it that said 'a man and a woman can never just be friends. Sex always gets in the way'? With the way I was going on, I had a feeling that their statement was going to be hard to refute.

Once he'd got me in the chair, my hairdresser tried long and hard to persuade me that I needed the rare treat of a retro eighties mullet with a few crimson highlights to boot. The only way open to convince him otherwise was to forcefully explain that if I ended up with a mullet he'd end up with a lawsuit (and that I'd be taking a full-page ad in the local rag to announce to everyone that didn't already know that his real name was Collin!) He pathetically feigned hurt and tried to sell the point that he (as a hairdresser) was a master of his craft and would therefore know much better than I (a florist) what would best suit me. He suggested that he wouldn't tell me how to make up a bouquet because he wouldn't know where to start, and therefore I should leave the hair to him.

In principle I could have agreed, but in practice I've had enough bad haircuts through the years to know that some hairdressers have a very skewed view of what suits a client. I then respectfully reiterated my firm warning that I wasn't ready to revisit the eighties and certainly not in any way with anything as radical as a red mullet. It would make me look like a short, angry, lumpy toilet brush! Not great or easy to carry off! (I know I said I needed to sort out my image, but that was a biscuit I would not take.) I patiently explained that I had a new friend who is a solicitor and for the correct reward would sue his sorry ass for free and that another of my friends was a sub editor on the afore-mentioned local rag who would also do it for free. So, in effect, it wouldn't cost me a penny to get my revenge and Xavier knows how I love to get revenge!

He knew he was beat then, and not wanting to lose everything he'd worked for capitulated, eventually just trimming off the ends as instructed and cutting in a few layers to 'give it movement and reduce the bulk' (not only did I have frizzy hair, I had fat, bulky hair!) I have to admit as he chopped in with those layers, I was more than a little concerned that by the time he was done I wouldn't be looking at myself with something resembling a mullet anyway.

Xavier (Collin) was as good as his word though and

when he had done cutting in the layers and luckily the effect wasn't half bad (shame in some ways, because suing him would have given me an excuse to see Will sooner!). So, then it was my turn to capitulate. He was determined to inject a little colour into my locks somewhere so I let him put a brown rinse through it to 'bring out the natural chestnut tones in my hair'. I scoffed that if ever I had heard it, *that* was nonsense because my hair is and always has been mousy brown in my book. Still that's artistic licence for you!

Either way, when he had finished I had to admit that the change was quite dramatic in a positive sort of way. I was almost happy to part with my hard-earned cash to pay the exorbitant price for my new look.

On the way out I asked on a whim if the beautician could maybe squeeze me in for a quick facial, and found that I was in luck! They'd had a cancellation due to a client slipping over on some ice very early this morning and breaking her nose. Apparently the broken nose put her off having a facial (and I could well see how it could be construed as a waste of money sorting out your skin when your nose looks like it's having an argument and going off in two directions). So, by the time I left the hairdressers, at almost six, the town centre was quiet as all the shoppers had left to make way for Saturday night revellers and I was primped, pampered and ready for some action. Pity, really... all done up with nowhere to go!

I made my way back to the car and by the time I reached it my now plumped up skin was starting to look a little pinched from the cold and my hair was everywhere from the positively Arctic wind (yes, I'm a bit of a drama queen) that had swooped into town whilst I had been sitting in the (relatively – mullet crazed hairdressers notwithstanding) safe haven of the hairdresser. C'est la vie!

As I drove at a snail's pace – the traffic was still quite thick even though the pavements and paths were quiet; people leaving work from the town centre/people heading back into it for a night on the razz – towards home my mobile began to ring and so I took the call through the Bluetooth in my dashboard.

"Hello," I began.

"Zoe, is that you?" returned a tearful Dannie.

"Dee… what's wrong?" I tentatively asked (knowing that the answer was obviously going to be bad and would most likely have to have something to do with her staying over at my place).

"Zoe, does the offer of a bed tonight still stand? I've left Georgie. There are things that she won't tell me. There are issues that we seem to have that I can't begin to understand. And her jealousy is just out of control," she wailed.

"Where are you? I can meet you at mine in twenty minutes if the traffic picks up its feet in town," I assured her.

"I'm on your doorstep in my car. I'll wait here for you." She said through sniffles.

"On my doorstep? How long have you been waiting there?" I questioned. I also questioned – but to myself - what my neighbours would be thinking *now*. Not that I could care less what they thought, but I'd be willing to bet that it had piqued their curiosity. At least it would with the nosier ones (like old Mrs Mack) of which there were quite a few!

Just under twenty minutes later I was opening the door for my new 'lodger' and myself. Dannie was in a terrible state and so I took off my coat and poured us both a glass of wine.

Dannie had gulped hers down within minutes. She didn't say a word until her glass was empty (which didn't take long) and then she burst out tearfully, "When I got home Georgie was already waiting for me. She was in an evil, black temper. She'd smashed up half the furniture and was sitting in a pile of my winter clothes. She'd torn them all to shreds! She'd spent the time it took her to drive home convincing herself that I'd spent the night with our postwoman – as if I'd be so clichéd! The postwoman, I ask you! – so I thought she'd be quite relieved when I told her that I was here having a drink and a gossip with you last night.

"I was wrong! She accused us of having spent the night together in a 'more than friends' sort of a way and then told me that staying up all night drinking had made me look tired and old! She also added that because I was unable to sleep in my own bed without her to anchor me there, that she could see me for the 'slut' I was. Also that without the blinkers of love she could see that I was also overweight and a bit of a troll. She was so *hurtful!* I tried to explain that you and I were just old friends and no more and that she was barking up the wrong tree if she thought anything else, but she wouldn't have it! I had no idea that her temper could be so vile or that she was prone to such jealousy! I can't go back. I'm living with a woman that I don't know at all!" she finally finished.

I picked up the tray I had been preparing as she talked and we took our drinks through into the living room. We set ourselves out at each end of the big, black, squashy sofa, our legs curled under us, the security of a furry throw over us, the now fire lit and an array of munchies from the tray I had made up on the coffee table in front of us.

I refilled our glasses to the brim from the bottle, sat back and then squirmed slightly as I assessed Dannie's predicament. I idly wondered if now would be a good time to tell her that she *didn't* know the person with whom she was living at all. Would there ever be a good time to break this to her? What if I told her what I knew and she went back to Georgie? They'd both hate me and I'd lose one of my best friends. What if Dannie found out what the rumour mill was putting out through another, less sympathetic source and *then* she found out that I'd known all along? Again I'd lose one of my best friends. Damn I hate being stuck between craggy, impenetrable rocks and implacable hard places...

She turned her face to me and then a look of recognition passed through her eyes. In that split second I knew the game was up...

"I have to say that you don't seem very surprised by any of the things I've told you about Georgie. Why is that, I wonder?" she finally asked.

I cast my eyes around the room so that she couldn't 'read' me as she obviously had been. "Not sure what you're getting at," I gamely tried.

"I've known you a long time, Zo; your face is an

open book for what's going on in your head. Always has been. I have to say that I'm a bit worried that I didn't notice it before, but I think you know something. Something about Georgie... " she tailed.

"Like what?" I asked. Maybe if we could turn this into a bit of a game it wouldn't sound quite so bad when the truth (and I'm using this word loosely) came out. Also, I was buying time, I realised. Or possibly that was just wishful thinking on my part. I knew that if she asked me any direct questions I'd have to give her direct answers because we both knew that I was the world's worst liar. (As in I could never lie properly to save my life.)

"Come on, spill it Zo. I know you're hiding something," she pushed.

"What could I possibly know about Georgie that you don't? You live with her!" I said with mock incredulity whilst trying not to meet her eyes.

"Lived," she corrected "And I told you yesterday that her life is full of little anomalies that I can't get to the bottom of. So, stop stalling... *what* do you *know*?" she pressed.

"Everyone's life is full of little holes if you look hard enough! I don't think you want to read too much into stuff, or overthink things Dannie. That way trouble lies... " I appeased (whilst still managing to stall and buy me some time).

However, Dannie could smell a rat, and she wasn't willing to let go until she had it by the tail. "Don't you think it's a little late for that? I'm here and Georgie is wherever she is and we're not together any more. It doesn't matter what she may or may not have done in her past, or what you know, or think you know. You won't change that one simple fact. We're *over*. But it would help me immensely if I could understand why we're over. This was my first real gay relationship. I need to understand how it failed and I can't because the argument that finished us... well, it makes no sense!" she exploded.

"Do you really think that this is you finished with Georgie? Don't you think it's just a lovers' spat and you'll be back with her by tomorrow?" I tried.

"Don't be ridiculous, she's cut up all my clothes, smashed up the house and won't tell me what's in her head. She's a bunny boiler, Zo! I've been living with a bunny boiler and now that I've recognised that little fact I can't go back to pretending that she's the mild-mannered, loveable dote that I fell for! The basic building blocks of trust and love are all missing because she's been wearing a big, over-made-up mask! Whatever she says now, there's no disguising what she really is. She'll never be able to persuade me that this relationship is anything but a sham built on half-truths at best and lies at worst. Would you go back to that?" she tried.

I thought for a moment (and still said the wrong thing) and replied "No, but then I'm a different animal to you Dee. I would never have been able to spend fifteen years with a man in a relationship that was all built on a lie."

She looked wounded. The tears sprang forth running like rivers from her eyes and she recounted "Thanks for reminding me about that. It was good of you to point out that this was probably karma for what I did to Brendan."

Bugger! Now I had done some real damage to our friendship without meaning to. See I'm far too honest for my own good. And I suffer badly from 'foot-in-mouth' disease. "No Dee you're missing the point. I wasn't trying to remind you of the past, nor am I trying to say that this is your karma, silly! In my own tactless way I'm just trying to say that you are much more stoic and self-sacrificing than I could ever be! I'm a much more selfish person than you so no, I definitely wouldn't go back to Georgie. But you might!" I attempted to placate her and had my fingers crossed that it would work. I didn't want storming off in a huff in the state she was in. Where would she go? Her parents lived in a nursing home, so that wasn't an option, and her sister's house would be packed to the rafters with her lovely, lively, ever-expanding, ever-extending family. I certainly didn't want her proving me right and going back to Georgie just because she felt she had nowhere else to go!

She stared blankly at the television (that wasn't turned on) and after a moment she said, " Of course. You're right – brutally honest – but right. I won't go back to her now because the damage is done and I can't live with someone with her temper. It'd drive me round the bend." She shot me a sidelong glance and then added, "So come on, out with it!"

I thought I had managed to successfully steer her off the subject for a minute there! Oh well if she was sure there really was no going back... I sighed wearily. "Are you sure you want to know what I've heard? It's only rumour and you might hate me once I tell you for not mentioning it two weeks ago when I first heard it?"

Without hesitation she returned, "I'm positive. Now get on with it before I rip out my hair and bite my nails to nothing!"

I searched her face for some clue as to whether she meant it. She seemed to be fairly earnest, so I began. "Ok, well, two weeks ago Mrs Drummond was in buying flowers for her friend who was sick. She started to tell me that there was no wonder her friend was sick given that her only son – who had not long undergone a sex change – was now in a relationship with a lovely woman but wouldn't come clean and tell this woman his whole story. Mrs Drummond said that it was shameful because this new woman had recently left a fifteen year marriage thinking she was gay because she was attracted to her friend's son but his mother – her friend – and Mrs Drummond didn't see how she could really be gay being as her friend's son – *George* – was in truth a man!" I again searched her face for signs of shock but found only bewilderment.

"I don't understand what it is you're saying." she eventually said.

"*George... Georgina*? Anyway, I finally got Mrs Drummond to tell me that her friend's name was Mrs Weaver. Margaret *Weaver*... " I let her digest this last bit whilst I peered into the fire for confirmation that I had done the right thing. Unfortunately the fire fairies were out on call appearing at random weekend bonfire parties or not answering their doorbell due to too many late nights in the week, because I got nothing from

89

there. We sat in painful and never-ending silence for the time it took Dannie – a good ten minutes – to piece together all of the information I had just given her and digest it. At length she asked "Why do you think that this is all speculation or rumour?"

I chose my words carefully. "Because Mrs Drummond often likes to 'information share,' but she does it in a Chinese whispers sort of a way. She doesn't always get the information she's sharing right, and occasionally – but only very occasionally – she likes to embroider it a little bit. Just for shock value, and to inflate her own self-importance. She doesn't mean any harm and ninety-nine percent of the time I wouldn't repeat any of what she tells me for the reasons I've just outlined. I can never be certain of their correctness. Otherwise I might have told you sooner."

Dannie gulped back her wine and refilled her glass quickly. Then she began to make short work of that one too. Her face was ashen and her eyes red. I was starting to think that I should be shot for telling her what I knew. She was my friend and I had hurt her.

"Well," she said at last, "that makes sense of a lot of things." She sounded a little deflated and a lot relieved. Maybe I didn't deserve to be shot then? "I always thought she had big hands, and was really very messy for a woman. The pills she takes for her 'heart condition' plainly must be some kind of hormones. She can't possibly *have* a heart after what she's done to me! The weirdest thing is that I'm not at all surprised," she told me.

Dannie was taking this very badly whilst pretending that she wasn't! She had taken to referring to Georgie as 'she'. Her overall assessment was that this wasn't much of a shock, but her words were conveying a different message. The term 'she' could not be said to be very polite or correct however you viewed it …

"I'm so sorry to have been the one to tell you. But please remember that it might not be correct. Or bits of it might be wrong. You really need to ask Georgie for yourself," I tried.

"What? Huh! I won't bother, if it's all the same to you. She tells too many lies! I can't believe that I've been so duped by her! I should feel so betrayed but I don't. I feel … empty! I can't understand why she wouldn't see fit to tell me!" she sniffed.

Gingerly I moved over toward her side of the sofa and hugged her. "That'll be the shock. We all thought Georgie had been born female, but even if she wasn't, it wouldn't affect us. We liked her for who she was. Because you fell so spectacularly for her, I agree that she should have been honest about her past. When the two of you got together you'd been through enough just coming out; you didn't need the added confusion of Georgie's condition. But that's probably why she felt unable to tell you. She could see you were still raw from your self-discovery. Georgie perhaps didn't want to burden you with her problems. You shouldn't be so hard on yourself, or Georgie. On the upside, whoever did her op did a pretty neat job - apart from the hands, obviously," I soothed. Unfortunately for poor Georgie, she had hands like Spear and Jackson super-sized shovels and every one of us had commented on that – including Dannie.

She sniggered through her snotfest. "And her bloody big, ugly, sweaty feet. They should have alerted me to her birth gender, don't you think?"

I hooted with laughter. "Really? Ok yes and the bloody big, ugly, sweaty feet."

She snorted, giggled, and added, "And the way she would sit with her hands on what were her crown jewels on an evening when she was relaxing! That's a very 'bloke' way to unwind, and yet I still didn't realise."

I snorted loudly. "Oh my God, what a giveaway! Ok yes. And the hands on the 'crown jewels' relaxed position".

She chortled as she told me, "Oh yes, and let's not forget her preoccupation with owning the TV remote. That's blokey too."

"Very!" I confirmed. "And so we'll add owning the TV remote to the list."

By now she was hysterical, wheezing and having difficulty spitting out the words for laughing. " And high heels were always a *major* challenge. She always walked like a lame pantomime giraffe – with rickets – in heels. Could never seem to gracefully sashay, no matter how she tried. I used to insist that if we went out she wore flats. I would pretend that it was a height issue, but … really I couldn't bear to be seen out with a woman who walked like she'd polished off the contents of the drinks cupboard before we left the house!"

We were clinging to each other and rolling with mirth, our faces wet with tears. Eventually I was able to stop laughing so hard and add, "Ok yes. And maybe the lame pantomime giraffe with rickets walk thing might have given it away. But – and I stress that this is a very big but… "

"Like mine! Mine's an enormous butt!" she interjected, self-effacing as ever.

I ignored her. " I also walk like a lame pantomime giraffe – ok, not exactly giraffe because I'm too short; maybe more heifer – in high heels and I was definitely born a woman," I finished. By now tears of laughter rolled down our helpless faces.

Twenty minutes later Dannie was guffawing again. "I'm so confused!" she wailed in mock bewilderment whilst more tears of mirth streamed down her face.

"What is it?" I questioned, a smile on my lips.

Finally she was able to squeeze out the words, "Does this mean I'm not gay?" from between guffawing hiccups. "God, I sound like George's horse. Maybe that's why she was really attracted to me?"

The evening had turned a corner never to return!

I decided to share the news of Nick's return with Dannie then. I needed to let out my angst somewhere and I trusted Dee. "You know that Nick is back in town?" I asked.

"Oh no! Not Nick the knicker nicker? I thought he'd promised not to come back here?" She looked aghast.

"He lied. *Again!* Lou saw him tending that roundabout thing near the college," I slurred.

"Tending? How so? Has he moved on from knickers and into road signs, or traffic islands? Was he really just an objectophile all the time?" she guffawed.

"Ha! I don't know but he's pretending he can keep gardens these days," I giggled.

"Better than keeping knickers!" she grinned. We discussed how he had managed to keep his secret perversion secret for so long, and the comedy the local paper had made from his case. He had become known as 'Nick the knicker nicker' after Chronicle had got hold of the facts relating to his crime. And then later, after he'd been put away, the headline read 'Nick, Knickerless.'

He'd been stealing women's underwear from their washing lines, abusing it and then keeping it in a locked gun cabinet (he apparently didn't have a gun either, but being so gullible and trusting I had no idea.) Occasionally, if he really found himself attracted to the woman he'd stolen from (yes he stalked them all too) he'd hang them back on the line with a filthy love-note attached. In one particularly memorable incident he even went so far as to assault one lady as she unsuspectingly hung her smalls out to dry.

At the time, I'd been heartbroken both for myself, and his victims. Now - though I found it difficult to think about what had happened – I could just about see the humour in it.

Two bottles of wine and an Irish coffee later, as all good girly evenings should, it gradually declined into raucous, snot-fuelled, tear-stained, tuneless singing. It started with 'The Killing of Georgie' (predictably), moved to 'Lucky Stars' (always laughable), and ended on the chorus of that anthem for the broken hearted 'I Will Survive'. We weaved our way precariously upstairs and we impetuously hugged on the landing, with me promising Dannie that she would come out of this whole, sorry mess a stronger person. Both of us fell into our respective rooms on the high note of that timeless love song 'Classic' by Adrian Gurvitz (never heard of it? No most people haven't but if you had you'd know that ignorance was bliss. It's about a man writing his lover a song in an attic. In all fairness there's not much else you can rhyme with the word 'Classic' is there?) Mrs Mack, my friendly neighbourhood witch, kindly added in a little drum beat and bass for us by hammering loudly on the paper-thin adjoining wall and yelling through it so we both screamed our thanks out to her as we prostrated ourselves on our beds in readiness for the coming of the sandman.

Always end on a song, as they say in showbusiness!

Chapter 9

After an appalling night's sleep (I was either running to the loo or getting yet more water to sip at) I finally gave in and decided to get up at nine thirty. The house was almost as cold and quiet as the grave. So, I put the oven on in readiness for the Sunday roast I was going to be cooking for my parents for lunch and then stuck the heating back on just for good measure. There was a carton of fresh orange juice in my fridge that called far too loudly to me when I opened the fridge door. Normally I would never do such a thing, but I was so parched from the previous evening's alcohol-fuelled singing session that I drank straight from the waxy, cardboard carton. Before too long the carton was empty and I was feeling a little bit sick. Carton poisoning! I knew I should've fetched a glass!

I stuck the large silverside joint of beef onto some foil in my roasting pan, carefully scoring the outer edge of the meat as I went and rubbing on some garlic oil and cracked black pepper for extra flavour, then I folded the foil around it into a neat package and stuck it on its tray into the oven. 'There! That's the thing that takes the longest to cook out of the way', I said to myself. I didn't pay much attention to it after that ... at least not until fifteen minutes later when I could smell something burning. I had been in such a hurry to turn my back on it that I didn't notice that I had the oven set to gas mark eight and that the roasting pan was badly positioned partially off the oven shelf and into the flame!

'I ought to give up drinking, it renders me useless for a whole day afterwards,' I was telling myself as Dannie put in her first appearance of the day.

"What's that burning smell?" she asked wrinkling up her nose.

"Don't panic, it's just me," I replied.

"What! You've set yourself on fire now?" she said incredulously.

"Eh? No, I've set the Sunday roast on fire. Well, almost. I positioned it so that it was overhanging the flame and not completely on the shelf in the oven," I explained.

"Oh good," she said, not really taking it in. "Can we have breakfast before dinner, d'you think?" she continued.

"Of course, what shall we have?" I mused with my head already in the fridge again.

"Erm, how about eggs? They're supposed to be good for unsettled stomachs," she helpfully supplied.

"Why not? How d'you want them?" I asked, turning to look at her. Dannie was eyeing the empty orange carton on the counter top hopefully by now. She turned to look at me the unasked question hanging in the air. "I'm sorry, but it's all gone," I provided before she asked. "I was so dry that I finished it earlier," I admitted, slightly ashamed of my greed.

"Aha! So you're going to be the kind of self-centred, thoughtless landlady who sneaks down first and drinks everything without a 'don't drink me' label on, are you?" she asked smiling. "I'd better stock up on sticky labels then," she added, coming over to inspect the contents of the fridge. "That's if I'm ok to stay for a while?" she cautiously finished.

"You know you are!" I told her, "but don't bother with the sticky labels, we'll just have a food kitty and a cooking rota. If it gets too much for you to deal with me taking all the good stuff first you can learn to get up earlier," I smiled.

We made soft poached eggs and quite well browned toast (this time it was deliberate. No, really! Charcoal is supposed to help with nausea too and neither of us was free of that), which we ate sitting congenially at the kitchen table with the Sunday papers to hand. By ten forty-five we were working as a team to clear away the wreckage from our previous evening's binge from the living room and getting the vegetables prepared for dinner. By ten forty-seven I was fielding the first of many calls from Georgie to Dannie!

"Hello," I tentatively answered the ringing phone. iI truth I was wondering how long it would be before Georgie came a-calling.

"Hello, Zoe. It's Georgie here," she replied firmly.

My eyes opened like saucers in surprise and I frantically began to windmill my arms to catch Dannie's attention but with no joy. She either couldn't see me, or was deliberately ignoring me. So the only way to alert her was ... "Oh, Georgie, what a surprise. What can I do for you?" I bellowed just a little too loudly into the receiver.

Dannie's head snapped up and she swung round from the kitchen counter where she was menacingly chopping the carrots in a purposeful fashion. She began making a motion with her arms and silently but emphatically (if you know what I mean) mouthing the words 'No, I don't want to speak to her yet!'

Too late! Georgie was too fast for us.

"Given the way you've just almost deafened me, I'm going to take it that Dannie is within earshot but she doesn't want me to know that, yes? Can you please tell her that I want to speak to her?" she tried.

"I'm sorry, Georgie," I lied; badly, as usual. But at least she couldn't see my face. "I don't know what you are talking about. Why would Dannie be with me? She was here on Friday night, but I haven't seen her since then." I hoped I sounded convincing.

"Nice try, but I know that she has nowhere else to go. And as you'll no doubt know by now, know we've had a fight over her spending Friday night with you. So, now can I speak to her?" She was trying to push my guilt buttons now.

'Well good luck with that one' I thought 'I've done nothing to feel guilty for.'

"I didn't know that, since you asked. If she was here, you probably could speak to her, but as she isn't, no, you can't," I forcefully reiterated. "But if she does turn up here I'll be sure to tell her you called looking for her. How's that?" I conceded.

There was a deflated sigh from the other end. "I know that she's with you, I'm not stupid!" she angled. "But if Dannie really won't come to the phone, then I guess I'll have to hope that you can persuade her to call me back later," she said hopefully; a bit too hopefully, as it went.

"She *isn't* with me, but if I see her, like I said, I'll

get her to call you," I repeated firmly whilst watching my nose with crossed eyes. (It ought to be five feet long by now, didn't it?) "Bye, George" I finished without thinking. I didn't wait for her to make her goodbyes, I hurriedly threw the handset back into the cradle as if it had scalded me.

Dannie was laughing! I looked up from where I had just pelted the phone receiver and she was laughing at me. "What's so funny?" I demanded.

"You really are the world's most unconvincing liar! People even know when you're phone lying! That's how bad you are! I suppose it's on she's way over here now, is she?" she asked.

"I don't think so. I think that either way she must have realised that you aren't ready to have anything to do with her yet. And if you don't like my rubbish lying you can always lie for yourself!" I exploded, full of mock indignation and hurt.

We got on and fixed a banquet of a Sunday lunch for my folks and ourselves; the table fairly groaned with food. (And later on so would we!) As we worked, I fended off George's calls because he knew with certainty from my hopeless lying that Dannie was here.

We started with homemade carrot and coriander soup. Dannie had gone a bit mad with the carrots and prepared too many of them. I think she was just taking out her anger and frustration on the unlucky vegetables, but anyway they made great soup.

George called again.

Then we moved onto traditional roast beef with all the trimmings, right down to the horseradish sauce; queue more jokes about the horse-yness of George!

I took another call from George – God, she was desperate! – and then finished with sherry trifle, heavy on the sherry. By now I'll have you thinking that I'm some class of raging alcoholic, but I'm not! I can go without alcohol anytime, but I'd be hard-pressed to give up trifle. As I've said before, I've got a terrible sweet tooth. Anyway, if George kept calling like this, I'd need more than just a little drop of sherry in a trifle to get through it!

As we sat around afterwards, contemplating the

coffee and chocolate mints I'd put out, the telephone rang again. I picked it up with quite an aggressive movement and was poised to bellow into the receiver, "Go to Hell, George" when I heard a beautifully manicured Irish voice saying, "Good afternoon, I have a Miss Saiorse Parsons on the line. Will you take this call reverse charges?"

I sighed. Did I really have a choice? What had she done with her mobile this time? "Yes, that's fine," I said at length.

Saiorse came onto the line in a highly agitated state. "Zo, oh Zo, is that you? Are mum and dad still at your house?"

I would hate myself for what I was about to say, but, "Yes, it's me, yes they're still here and whatever's wrong now?"

"I've got myself into a bit of hot water," she garbled. "You know that date I was going on that meant I couldn't be there with you all for lunch? Well, he took me to Dublin for the weekend and now he's dumped me here with no way of paying the bill" she wailed.

"Who is '*he*'?" I asked, dreading the answer.

"Oh God, you're going to go nuts... it's Major Tomm!" she finally admitted.

I narrowed my eyes so hard that I could feel a harsh furrow being carved on my brow and dug deeply into the recesses of my head for an answer as to where I had heard that name before. Then it hit me and I wished that it had not. Major Tomm was actually a local farmer, and rather a good-looking piece of farm kit if memory served. He was a local, *married* farmer who drank *locally* (and liberally, considering he had a farm to run) in the Slug, and was well-known *locally* as a bit of a philanderer. He should really have been called Farmer Tomm, but everyone knew him as Major Tomm after the David Bowie song.

"Oh, for heaven's sake Saiorse! How do you get yourself into these messes? Tomm is a married man, and his wife is built like a sumo! She'll crush you with one blow! Are you insane? *Why* hasn't he paid the bill? It's not as if he's hard-up," I raged.

"There was a bit of a disagreement last night

between us and he stormed off and left me," she sobbed.

"What on earth were you disagreeing about?" I wanted to know.

"Well, we went to this place called The Arlington for a drink before heading back to our hotel for the night, and there were these Australian blokes stood at the bar. One of them, Miles, took a bit of a shine to me, and we got into quite a deep conversation. Tomm saw his arse and took off without a word. I just turned around and he was gone!" she sniffled.

"So him – a married man, and all – took offence at you having a lengthy conversation with another man?" I repeated, adding "You literally went for Miles?" (I didn't add not for the first time, although I wanted to!) I just wanted to be certain of the facts here because they sounded a little sketchy, shall we say.

"More or less, yes," she answered.

"How much more or less, Sairs? This is important. Also it's costing me money since it's reverse charge. Tell me the truth." I was becoming exasperated.

"Well, I might have been a bit tipsy, and this might have led me to kiss him a bit," she grudgingly admitted.

"Kiss who? Tomm or this Aussie?" I was becoming crabby, and very un-PC.

"Miles, his name is Miles!" She retaliated by becoming angry.

"So, you were all over Miles like a rash and Tomm stormed off! Why are you surprised? A man – a *married man* – goes to all the trouble of whisking you away for the weekend to Dublin, and so what do you do? You bag off and leave him so that when he should be stroking your arm, he's left there stroking his pint! Nice one Saiorse! You are truly priceless, you know?" I sneered.

"Oh, he didn't just bring me to Dublin, he bought me a three grand Rolex too," she bragged.

"This just gets *worse!*" I was practically yelling by now. "You could try showing a little contrition! How could you let him, Sairs? You know he's married with kids. Where are your morals? Where's your self-respect? Where's this Miles character?" I stormed.

"I brought Miles back with me but the concierge wouldn't let him in because it was after eleven, and guests aren't allowed after eleven," she explained, slightly more meekly.

"You brought him back? You're incredible! How much after eleven?" I prodded.

"It was about two am," she sniffed.

"And what time did Tomm leave this Arlington place?" I wanted to know.

"Er, about midnight, I guess," she confessed quietly.

"So you ran after him? You did try and catch him, then? Make some sort of effort to sort it out? Did he leave the hotel as well as the Arlington?" I wondered.

"No, I couldn't see any point, really, and I was having such a lovely time with Miles. And yes, he must have, because he wasn't here when I finally found my way back to our room," she told me.

"Found your way back to your room? How big is the hotel, for heaven's sake? So I take it Miles is gone but not forgotten. And the same goes for Tomm? He's gone but not forgotten due to the bill you're left holding?" I asked snidely.

"The hotel is quite large… and either way, both of them are gone, but I'm left here with this bill. The hotel won't let me leave until it's paid. Can you help me, Zo? I haven't got anywhere near the kind of money they are asking for," she asked.

"Well, I don't suppose I've got much choice, have I, because I can't take this to mum and dad. They despair of you at the best of times. This will just kill them. How much?" I spat.

"It's one thousand, two hundred and twenty Euros," she squeaked.

"Bloody hell, Sairs! I'm not made of money! This'll have to come out of my rainy day fund, so I'm going to want every penny back," I raged.

"Come on Zo, you know me! I will pay you back!" she tried. Oh yes, I knew her, alright, and that was why I was so sure that she *wouldn't* pay me back.

An idea hit me… "I know you will, because you are going to sell that watch he gave you to do it. Then you can pay mum and dad what you owe them too!" I suddenly and out of nowhere ordered her.

After a few seconds digesting this, she asked, "Are you serious?"

"*Never been more so!*" I returned, a touch too sharply. "What you've never had, you'll never miss, Saiorse! You're not going to be able to go out for a while, because you won't be able to hold your head up in polite company after this little episode, so you'll have nowhere to wear it anyway! And you can always get some other poor, deluded sucker to replace it for you at a later date. Furthermore, you can get some bloody therapy for your whacky behaviour!" I boldly ventured (since I was now on a bit of a roll in the 'speaking my mind' stakes and seemingly unable to stop myself.)

"What! Now you're just being... " She began. But I was in no mood to let her finish.

"I mean it, Saiorse!" I told her, brooking no argument on the subject. "Do you need me to bail you out, or not? If not, get off the line and stop wrecking my Sunday lunch, and if you do, you'll have to agree to my terms and conditions!" I pushed.

"Well, I can hardly refuse, then, can I?" she tried. "I'll agree, if you'll just get on with it! You can save your rant until I get home, because I'm sure you'll be dying to make up the welcoming committee. If you don't I'm going to miss my flight as well so it'll cost you even more!" she told me aggressively.

"It won't cost me anything, because you're paying every cent back! And as for forming a welcoming committee ... oh, you can be sure of it! How are you getting back from the airport? Should I have a black Mariah on the airfield for you? Or are you expecting a lift in an ambulance after Mrs Tomm is finished?" I fumed.

"I can get the rest of the way home on the train. I can just about afford that from what's left in my purse!" she told me.

She handed the phone over to the receptionist and I grudgingly covered her bill, as promised, with my debit card. It almost made me cry to think of all those pound notes wafting away over to Ireland just to save

Saiorse's elegant, dove-white neck. She had really overstepped the mark this time, and I was going to not only get my money back, but I was determined to get her sorted out once and for all so that she would stop and think about the mad consequences of her stupid actions!

I turned back to my lunch guests to find them all sat in stupefied silence. They had heard every loud, angry word.

I should have known that Saiorse could ruin our lunch without even being present!

Before I could even reach the decimated Sunday table I was bombarded with questions from my parents, and they made it abundantly clear that they were none too happy about the way I'd handled things. No matter! It was time someone sorted Saiorse out for her own sake and safety. They left pretty quickly after the call, thanking me for lunch but telling me firmly to go easy on my sister. There was no chance of that, but I decided that it would be best not to tell them so.

Sometimes ignorance was bliss!

As we were clearing up the mess from lunch Georgie called to nuisance us yet again. This time, having given Dannie a warning that this would be the last time I'd be covering for her, I picked up the phone and very strongly told her that Dannie was definitely not with me and to stop calling because I was going to be forced to stop answering! I didn't think that it could honestly have any real effect on her, but my Sunday buzz was already wrecked, and I didn't see why everyone else shouldn't suffer because of it.

We managed to get tidied up and the dishwasher loaded with pots before she was back on the line, but this time Dannie could see I'd had enough so she took the call herself. By the time the call was over, Dannie had organised for Georgie to come over with some of Dannie's things (the ones she hadn't ruined) and they were going to discuss the state of their relationship. Dannie strongly tried to notify her that this was in no way a reconciliation talk – she wouldn't even be considering that as an option – but she wanted to understand what had gone wrong (she wasn't supposed to know that Georgie had been George, remember?).

They were *both* in agreement that they wanted me to mediate. I wasn't sure that I wanted to, but I agreed because I couldn't see Dannie left on her own with Georgie and her foul temper. This time it might not be just Dannie's clothes that got torn!

We spent the rest of the afternoon walking Flo in the crisp winter air, lounging around, watching dross on the TV, talking over Dannie's situation and sleeping off the oversized Sunday lunch, so that by seven, when Georgie knocked at the door, we were both feeling much more human.

Dannie nervously answered Georgie's knock and tentatively invited her in. Georgie's six feet four frame dwarfed my hallway, which, with only eight feet high ceilings, meant that she had to duck so as not to hit her head on the pendant light fittings. She was also quite broad-shouldered and so this meant that she had to hunch herself up to get through and into my living room.

I politely asked if she would like a drink and she accepted a cup of coffee. three sugars, so no, she obviously didn't consider herself sweet enough already. But then neither did we. We considered her an overly aggressive, lying, shovel-handed bully.

Then, we sat opposite each other on the sofas waiting for someone to break the silence.

After a minute (which felt more like a lifetime) I grew a little bit bored and decided to kick the riot off. "So, Georgie, have you always had problems controlling your jealousy?" I began.

"What? What has Dannie been saying?" She glared at Dannie whilst addressing me.

"Only that you insisted she and I had been up to something, and that to illustrate how you felt about that you'd cut up all her winter clothes. That sounds like you have a few jealousy and anger issues to me," I explained.

"Well, I admit that I was a bit shocked that she'd stayed out all night, because she didn't tell me that she was going to. How was I supposed to know that she was only here and I could have called her on your landline? But as for thinking that the two of you were up to something, surely that's just preposterous, isn't it?" she asked.

"Yes, it is preposterous, but why would you have needed to call her here? It sounds like you also have a problem trusting her," I wondered.

"Of course I trust her, but it would have been good to have been able to wish her goodnight, and just to have heard her voice," Georgie tried.

"I don't buy that!" Dannie chipped in. I thought she had fallen asleep for a minute there, but no. She was just biding her time to make an entrance!

"What do you mean by that? You know I can't go for more than a couple of hours without speaking to you! So knowing that, you went out and didn't take your mobile so that I wouldn't be able to get hold of you easily. You must have known that it would raise my suspicions when you did it," Georgie snorted, her unusually large emerald eyes like slits in her now-red face.

"I already told you... my mobile was out of charge, so I left it plugged in to recharge and forgot to bring it out with me. The weather was so foul that I wasn't going back for it when I realised I'd forgotten it. It was never part of the plan for me to stay overnight here, but we had such a great time just talking, laughing and drinking, and so when Zoe offered me her spare room I thought it'd save a taxi fare. I threw caution to the winds and said yes. I didn't think for one minute that you expected me to clock in with you! I wouldn't have expected you to clock in with me. I'd guessed that you'd not sit alone in your hotel room all night, but would go out for dinner with your horsey mates; but that wasn't a problem for me. You are entitled to a life outside of us, as far as I am concerned!" Dannie fumed.

You could have cut the air with a knife!

"I'm not saying that I mind that you were out, but if there's nothing to hide why didn't you tell me you were coming here?" Georgie said in an ominously quiet tone.

"Oh, for heaven's sake!" Dannie shouted. "For precisely that reason! I had nothing to hide. It's not out of the ordinary for me to either drop in on or stay over at Zoe's! I stayed over here plenty of times when I was with Brendan, so I wouldn't have mentioned it on account of that. To us, it's just something that happens occasionally. You have a girly night in, and it ends in crashing out wherever you are sitting. No big deal!"

"That's right, drag the saintly Brendan into it! Pity you didn't stay with him if you thought so much of him!" Georgie cried (in a very jealous and angry fashion for someone with no jealousy or anger issues).

"Well, now that you come to mention it, I'm beginning to think that way myself!" Dannie seethed.

"Could it be because you discovered a fondness for women?" I threw in.

"That's right! I did! So what the hell am I doing with this piece of creation?" Dannie was practically foaming at the mouth and hadn't stopped to think before she said that. This was my hope. I knew Dannie well enough to know that if she had stopped to think she probably would have kept quiet and made up some polite reason for not wanting to be with Georgie. ('It's not you it's me', or 'I need some space'. You know the kind of thing.) To be fair, and to stop Georgie making the same mistake again, she really did need to know that the game was up. She'd been caught out in her deception by omission.

"Creation? Its one thing to tell me that I was never physically attractive to you, but 'creation?' What do you mean by that, exactly?" Georgie barked crossly.

"Ooh, come on! You weren't always a woman, were you? Not from birth!" Dannie retaliated. (This was rowdy and vicious and had all the hallmarks of an episode of Jeremy Kyle in my own front room! It would have been almost entertaining if one of my best friends hadn't been cast in one of the starring roles.)

Georgie's face fell. She crumpled, defeated, into the sofa like a pricked balloon (if you'll forgive the analogy) and stared blankly at the wall.

"Well? Say something." Dannie said softly, realizing size of the wound that she had just inflicted.

"How long have you known?" Georgie finally asked resignedly.

"That's not important. What does matter is that you

didn't feel you could tell me yourself. Why didn't you?" she returned acidly.

"You think you are gay. You thought I was a woman. You obviously couldn't tell that I was previously not, and I am now by all *but* birth, anyway. I thought I was the luckiest woman alive when you fell for me. The timing was never right to tell you, and I could never find the best way to say it," Georgie finished.

"Right. Let's get one thing straight. I *am* gay. I have only ever really fancied women, and I was wrong to marry Brendan knowing that, so that makes me less than a saint. I can sort of understand how you let it go on without telling me the truth, then. However, it's only fair to tell you now that you were never physically all that attractive to me, but we hit it off in every other way. We had some great times and some laughs together. That said, we've had even more lousy times of late, and I'm sick of all the back-biting and arguing we do. You have to get your temper and jealous nature sorted out and into some kind of perspective because if you don't it'll wreck every relationship you ever have! Also, it would help if you were honest about who you are. You've had me doubting my sanity for the last couple of months due to your lying and no one likes to think they're going round the bend." Dannie smiled a sad little smile at the memory of it as she said this.

"So, there's no chance of you coming home with me, then?" Georgie tried.

"No, there's no chance of me coming back with you. My home is here, now," Dannie replied.

"So there is something going on between you?" Georgie asked curiously.

I watched as the stones set in Dannie's eyes. "Please go now, before I rip off your head and boil and eat it! This conversation is at an end."

"What about the rest of your stuff?" Georgie asked.

"I'll get a small van and collect it. Thanks for bringing my work clothes. I'll see you out," Dannie finished.

Dannie saw Georgie to the door and a minor scuffle kind of broke out when Georgie tried to hug Dannie. A photograph frame was smashed in the skirmish but I didn't mind too much because it wasn't a favourite.

Dannie took herself off to her room pretty early, complaining that she was feeling her age and she needed to lie down in a darkened room to contemplate the husk that was her life now. I made her some of my favourite hot chocolate and packed her off to her room with a hot water bottle. Sometimes a little quiet time can make a lot of difference.

After the last twenty-four hours I was ready for some myself!

Chapter 10

After a good night's sleep both Dannie and I felt much better and in a more positive frame of mind. Dannie ran her plans for the week past me over breakfast because she intended to start finding a place of her own as soon as she could and she wanted to start getting back out 'onto the scene'. I had to say that she was getting over Georgie very quickly. She pointed out that from her perspective the breakup had been a long time coming. She had known for a while that there was something Georgie wasn't telling her, and the relationship was becoming more claustrophobic by the day.

After an amicable tussle between us for the bathroom (it's been a while since I had to share my space), and a light breakfast, Dannie went on her merry and bright way a little after eight am. I wasn't all that far behind her. It was still not fully light as I locked up and told Flo to watch the house. We were at that point in the year where we were going to work in the dark and coming home in the dark, and it was all rather bleak! This led me to start thinking about all the positive things in my life, which then led me to thinking of Will.

The last twenty-four hours had been so busy that I hadn't had time to moon over our lunch dates. The previous one had been highly enjoyable and the coming one would give me something to look forward to for the rest of what I was certain was going to be a very long week.

I had also decided on my way to work that it was high time to chase up my sister and a) get my money back before she spent it, and b) get her to keep her word and go to a therapist or a doctor. I let myself in to the shop and completed all the usual chores and tasks, then after a brief conversation with Mr Siddeebottomme (that's Sidebottom to you and I) to order 'fifty 'angle' (that's angel to you and I) card hangers and some of his cute little 'dwerf' hats (that's dwarf to you and I), I moved on to the heavy business of the day.

I took my flower order from Len, made up all the orders, made a drink for a sniffly Ralph and I – he was coming down with 'man flu', which is to say a cold – and loaded the orders carefully into the by now extremely grubby van. I chided Ralph mildly on the state of it, because it was so bad that you could no longer read the signwriting on the van side. Instead of 'Scents of Humour Florists of Distinction' it now read 'Scent of our Florist stinc'.

Whilst this could be said to be true of the revenge bouquets, I didn't think it was fair to say it of all our products, so it was a bit unreasonable of Mother Nature and all her little elements to muddy the van up to read as such (quite apart from the fact that they are obviously all dyslexic!). Ralph apologised and said that if he were feeling better by the weekend he would clean it up. Although he was very quick to add that he didn't hold out much hope of being better because 'everyone knew that man flu was worse than swine flu – and a killer – and it took ages to get back to full strength if you'd had it.'

I briefly glanced through the diary before waving him off, and upon finding that there was nothing to go out for the afternoon, I ordered him to go home to bed after he'd delivered the contents of the van. He didn't argue. He hadn't the strength! Man flu is a real drain both on the sufferer and those around them!

I ate a quiet lunch from the sandwich shop next door while watching the hefty, bulbous raindrops heave themselves with a mammoth effort against the window. It was a misty, dirty day, alright; the sort that made a person feel like they should be wrapping themselves up in the duvet and snuggling in for a film-a-thon. Even the rain was having a hard time being bothered today. The few people brave enough to venture out were scurrying around like woolly, well-wrapped-up ants at a 'there's sugar on this path' party.

The shop was toasty warm (if I didn't count the cold room – and I was happy not to for the moment) and I was happy to spend a little time indulging my lazy, dreamy side for a change.

Whilst I sat, I noticed a large, rotund man in a black

hoodie and barbour coat talking to a small, rotund, grubby-looking woman wearing a Hackett jacket, her hair clinging to her wet face like dirty bedsprings. Her backside was Thelwellian! She was almost as unkempt as me (that would be the 'me' before I started to care that I looked like a bag lady.) He was cramming some class of pastry into his mouth with one hand and what appeared to be a burger with his other. That was when I realised that I knew him.

It was Peter. I leant forward on my stool to get a closer view and watched agape as he hurriedly crammed the food into his enormous gob, and then – and I swear he was still chewing his last mouthful of food. Eurgh! – swept the lardy lady into his arms, covering her with his blubbery, greasy lips!

I felt sick! Not just because I was sure that he was French kissing her with a mouthful of food, not just because she looked like something that the cat had dragged in, but mostly because he was married to my oldest, closest friend and this put me into yet another treacle-sticky situation with someone I care about.

The lardy lady seemed to be enjoying it immensely. This was no surprise, because looking at her I would doubt that chances for her to go at that sort of carry on were few and far between! That is to say that she made no move to kick him between the legs and whack him about the head with her shopping bag (she'd been to the greengrocers, as it was one of his bags she carried. I'm very observant!) Quite the contrary … she was clinging to him for dear life, and seemed to be actively encouraging him to suffocate her.

I had to look away because it showed no sign of abating, and I was now in grave danger of throwing up my lunch. It put me right off the finger of fudge I had been happily sucking!

I was going to have to decide how best to tell Sal. I had only just got over having to break things to Dannie, and now here I was in the same position all over again, but this time with Sal. I would have to think about this and tread softly.

Thinking of treading softly led me neatly into Saoirse. Another woman that didn't mind messing with

111

a married man! Was there no one left in the world with any scruples? I glanced out of the window again and saw with relief that Peter and the wolf had gone. What a relief, not to have to look at that any more. I would really enjoy making chilli with extra added Schmako for him now.

I tried phoning my mum's again, but when there was no reply I gave in and phoned Dannie at work. "Don't cook anything for tea, we're going out!" I told her.

"Great! Where?" she asked.

"The Slug," I said simply.

"Oh, any reason?" she questioned, knowing that Saiorse worked there and that we had unfinished business.

"Just because it'll cheer up a miserable Monday," I tried.

"Ok, and?" she pushed.

"And I want to get my money out of my sister and/or that slimeball Tomm. I'm in just the right mood to do it, so I've decided to strike while the iron's hot," I finished.

"So you want me along to keep you out of a fight? Or am I going to play referee?" she asked.

"Neither. We are going to get the girls together and have a night out. I'm going to conduct my business so quickly and quietly that you won't even notice that I'm missing from the table," I promised.

"Huh! I know you better than that, Zoe Parsons, and you'll do it loud, noticeably and noisily in order to make a point! But let's throw caution to the winds and do it anyway!" she laughed.

"You're on. See you at home!" I returned.

"Later!" She countered.

By the end of the afternoon I had a girl's night to be proud of in the offing. Sal couldn't wait to escape Peter (if only she knew that it was so easily within her grasp!), Karin was happy to tag along once she knew that Dannie was coming along as a single woman again, (Karin was also gay and for the moment single. How handy!), and Joy was in the mood for a bit of time away from Duncan and his DHSS gripes.

We had all agreed to meet in the lounge of the Slug at seven thirty pm, and first one in was to get the first round. So seven thirty saw Dannie and I squabbling over who was getting the first one in. Dannie won by a small margin (elbow to my ribs to get to the bar first) and by seven thirty-five the two of us were sitting in a quiet nook nursing our drinks and scanning the room for signs of Tomm and his cronies.

Sal was next to arrive. She'd had to argue her way out of the house due to the fact that Peter hated her going out without him. (Didn't want her himself, but didn't want her to be with anyone else either more like.) She was a little red eyed but made it clear that she just wanted to forget about home and enjoy being out with us. We therefore didn't try and question her too closely or pry out information she wasn't ready to give. However, it was noticeable that she kept checking her text messages, so she was obviously having some sort of text was with him during the evening.

To distract her, we filled her in on the wonderful adventures of Saiorse in Dublin, the price I'd had to pay to bail her out. Then speculated what the outcome would be if I got my hands on Tomm during the course of the evening. At the mention of revenge taking the form of two bricks and a meat cleaver, she laughed delightedly. No doubt this momentarily took her mind off what she'd had to fight in order to have a night out, instead of the usual night at home in front of the TV. It would maybe even have given her some ideas for her own escape in future.

Karin and Joy arrived together in a taxi a little before eight, looking as though they had something to get off their chests. I was to find out later that this was very much the case! Speaking in hushed tones so as not to be overheard by the rest of our little group, they explained that their taxi driver knew all about Peter and his lardy lady friend, but he also knew Sal. He wondered what on earth Peter was doing throwing away his marriage with Sal for such a grubby old boot as the lardster, and pointed out that it was like watching 'Charlie leave Di for that trout that he married!'

I must have looked a little shifty when they were

recounting their tale, because they knew from the look on my face that I already knew something about Peter's venture into Cheatsville. Their next question was, how would I break it to Sal? My question was 'why does it have to be me?'

I knew very well why it had to be me. I was her oldest friend. Theirs was an excellent question, though, and one that I'd been asking myself for most of the day. How *would* I tell her? I had however been hoping to put thoughts of the unpleasant task out of my head for the evening, and just deal with Saiorse's little problem for now. 'One thing at a time!' I told myself.

We ate, drank, and were merry by about nine thirty, which made a mellow evening for a Monday! Saiorse had come on duty behind the bar at eight and had been eyeing us coolly and cautiously through glittering, glacial blue eyes ever since. Periodically I waved and smiled to attempt to put her at ease, but I fear that this only unsettled her more. She knew me of old, and she knew I wanted my pound of flesh!

It was eventually my round again, so I dutifully went off to the bar. There she cornered me and quietly explained that the watch was waiting for me at mum's. She wanted me to collect it, sell it, and use any proceeds to pay myself off. The remainder could then be passed on to mum and dad, because she owed them plenty too.

I replied that she had no cause to worry. I would be round to collect my dues and take her to the doctor's just as soon as she made an appointment, which should be at her very earliest convenience. To ensure compliance, I would be letting the happenings of the weekend be known to her bosses if the appointment wasn't forthcoming within the week. I was fairly certain that they wouldn't be pleased that she was using her job to better get to know married punters, then clean out their bank accounts. Just a precaution, lest she decide to renege on our agreement! I knew her of old too...

Saiorse turned an unbecoming shade of puce at the mention of this. It was clear that she enjoyed working at the Slug, in a way that she had never enjoyed working at Mayples. The Slug was an upcoming gastropub with contemporary décor and a strong line in moneyed clientele, where Mayples had a stronghold in pensioner market. I smiled to myself as I turned from the bar bearing a tray laden with cutlery, condiments, serviettes and alcohol. Better make sure that I kept my eye on those knives, lest one ended up in my back!

By nine forty-five as I was tottering crab-like through the lounge to the loo (told you I walked badly in high heels; like a lame heifer with a bad case of vertigo), I spied Tomm and his cronies over by the dartboard. I would deal with him on my way back, through, with an empty bladder and a fresh coat of lippy. Lippy arms a girl against the deadliest of foes, I find.

Ten minutes later I ambled as gracefully as I could manage, given the heels and a fair bit of wine, over in his direction in what I hoped was a nonchalant way. (I was later told that I actually strutted over like a crustacean on a mission! Just shows what alcohol does to your perception though, doesn't it, eh?). I wedged myself in to his small circle of friends, pulled myself up to my full height and fronted him directly.

"You're Tomm, aren't you?" I addressed him. The monster in my head told me that I hated him before he even opened his mouth. He was obviously good looking in a swaggery, George Clooney (without the class, only much more rugged) sort of a way. It was fairly obvious that no matter how much anyone else loved him, they could never love him as much as he loved himself.

He looked me up and down as if imagining me with no clothes on (yup, one of those blokes!), raised one eyebrow, and asked cockily, "Who wants to know?"

"I'm Zoe. Zoe Parsons and that gorgeous but outrageous blonde behind the bar is my big sister!" I purred. His features changed instantly. They rearranged themselves from interested to horrified immediately. I smiled inwardly and had to stifle an evil 'mwoh, mwoh, mwoh!' type of laugh out loud on seeing this because he really deserved to look horrified. "I'm the poor mug who was forced to rescue her from the predicament you left her in at the weekend. I can see that you're a little shocked that there's been any comeback on this, but you're going to feel even worse when I tell you that if I don't recoup what it cost me to bring Saiorse home for you, I'm going to tell your wife all about it." I threw the 'verbal grenade' and then waited for the blast to hit.

There was an embarrassed silence within his group of friends and they all looked away in different directions. I knew from his reputation Tomm was a man used to getting his own way and never having to apologise for however ill his behaviour may be to get it. He began to laugh quietly, his grey-green eyes almost disappearing into the creases around them. 'Here was a man who laughed a lot and mostly at other peoples' expense,' I thought. "You find that amusing?" I asked.

"My wife is well aware of my little dalliances, she's been turning a blind eye for years. Do your worst, little Miss Parsons. I'll have fun watching you try," he told me, puffing out his overstuffed, he-man chest and grinning lasciviously.

Funnily enough I was prepared for this! A bit of a gamble was in order now. If she knew about his little flings, I was willing to bet that she didn't know he was taking them away and buying them jewellery. Not just any jewellery, either; Rolex type jewellery.

I cleared my throat as he began to turn away and added, "Oh, I just bet! But I'd be willing to bet even more that she doesn't know that you've been buying them expensive gifts, *and* whisking them off on weekends away!" I smiled my best sweet and innocent smile as I finished. Bingo! I had struck paydirt big time here!

He swung round quickly and grabbed me by the arm, frog marching me into a vacant seat in the corner.

"Take your hands off me now!" I shouted. You could see tumbleweed rolling across the bar floor (or at least I could in my mind's eye) as everyone stopped to look. Tomm instantly dropped my arm and politely invited me to sit down. I eyeballed him, my eyes burning with anger, to let him know that I meant business, whilst acquiescing and lowering myself into the vacant chair at which he was now gesturing.

He sat down opposite me sheepishly and after a minute of apparently admiring the dirt ingrained in his hands, began. "Ok, you've obviously heard your sister's side of things, and she's clearly made it sound as if the debacle at the weekend was all my fault. But she was the one who ditched me! I paid for a romantic weekend – through the nose, I might add – and she spoilt it all by picking up some Aussie in a pub! I think she got what she deserved, don't you? She also came out of the deal with a three-grand Rolex, so in the scheme of things, she should count herself fortunate!" he spat.

"Oh, I know that she got her just desserts on that score, believe me! I'm used to my sister and her tricks, and I'm willing to bet you there that half the men in this pub could tell you a similar – if not quite as costly – tale. However, it wasn't her who paid the price, it was me! I paid your hotel bill and your enormous bar bill. I paid her taxi fares and brought her back to my parents in one piece without them knowing what had happened. You should be thanking me for that, by the way, because my dad wouldn't have bothered discussing it with you, oh no; he would've gone straight to your wife for recompense and then given you a sound kicking into the bargain! So I'm giving you the opportunity to pay up first. I want it in cash, because I don't trust you in any way with a cheque – you seem good at evading your responsibilities – and I want it by tomorrow evening, or you'll regret my actions," I finished, hoping that he'd never get the opportunity to find out that my parents had known all along and that my dad's fighting days were well and truly over.

"Right, so I just pay up and Saiorse gets off Scott free does she? I don't think so," he began.

I held up my hand to stop him. "No, she damned well doesn't, since you ask! She's going to get some serious help for her erratic, outrageous and quite frankly dangerous behaviour. It's not a prospect she relishes, and believe me, she isn't likely to come quietly. But if I don't make her do this now, she's going to spend the rest of her life jumping from one unsuitable man's bed to another, getting herself in fixes that she can't get out of, and waiting for idiots like me to rescue her! As for you, you just might learn to keep it in your pants, save it for your wife, or find someone less volatile and more malleable for your 'flings' in future! Now stop arguing the toss and get your hand in your pocket. Give me my savings back, because I blew them sorting out the chaos the pair of you whipped up!" I explained aggressively.

I could see the cogs whirring away in his head as he scowled at me, but this only served to harden my resolve. He thought he would be the one to get away with it 'Scott free' as he put it. Not whilst I had breath in my body!

"How do I know that once I've paid you, you won't come back for more?" he tried.

"Because unlike you, I'm honourable! I'm not here to screw you; I'll leave that sort of carry-on for my lovely sister, a mistress of that particular dark art! Like I said, I just want my savings back, then you and yours won't hear from me again. Don't you think I've got enough on trying to sort out Saiorse's messes, thanks, without creating any of my own?" I questioned.

He mulled it over for a minute and then threatened me, "If you do, I will take action of my own and it won't be of the legal type. Do you understand?"

"Oh, I understand alright, Mr Tomm, but there really is no need to compound your mistakes by adding threats to them. Like I said, I only want what you owe me," I countered brazenly. I didn't actually feel brazen, though, it had to be said. Inside, I was by now feeling the surge of adrenaline, and had to fight to remain seated. My only hope was that outwardly, my face and body language wouldn't betray me.

"How much did it come to?" he asked tentatively.

"One thousand, two hundred and twenty euros, but as the pound and the euro are pretty much on parity with each other at the moment, we can call it one thousand two hundred and twenty pounds," I told him.

"Bloody hell! That's the last time I take one of my tarts away to anything more fancy than the local steak house!" he said, frowning. "Wait there, I can get it from the bank ... but I want to see the receipt from the hotel!" he added.

I had very sensibly had the hotel email me the bill. By lucky chance, it was safely stashed in my bag for such an eventuality, though admittedly I thought I'd have to wait for the money if I managed to squeeze it out of him at all!

"No problem; I have it right here, and many more copies where that came from." I took it out, neatly unfolded it, and waved it in his general direction. He plucked it quickly from my hand and sharply sucked in his breath at the figures on the paper. "That might teach you not to spend your money knocking back magnums of quality champagne with substandard women!" I said ruefully with a small smile.

"Don't hold your breath." He smiled what was obviously his best, triple-strength, mega-beguiling smile, in an attempt to turn his charm on to me. I had big news for him; I liked my men a bit more... Colin Firth than George Clooney without the class, thank you very much!

"Wait here and I'll see what I can do," he told me.

"Going nowhere!" I promised. "I'm on a girls' night out, so I'm sat down there with my friends." I pointed to our table and he nodded, already turning and walking away.

" Won't be long," he threw as he retreated ... and somehow I knew he wouldn't!

I tottered back to where my friends were sitting and heavily plonked myself onto my vacant seat. Sighing, I took a long sip from my glass and pulled myself together. If only I was as assertive as I pretended to be! I listened to the girls all chattering, and waited for my heart to resume its normal steady rhythm. I wanted it to desist from samba-ing all around my chest like Anton DuBeke on speed.

Dannie noticed my agitation and moved in for a hug. "You ok?" she questioned. Sapped from the effort to stay strong and self-assured in the face of the errant farm boy, I simply nodded.

It had been a trying evening, but then I had known in my heart of hearts that it would be. Now I just had to hang around for him to bring my cash and then I would have two main choices: stay and get wasted – but this would mean taking money from my hard earned savings when I got it back – or go home and go to bed. My head was in it for the second choice right now.

Ten minutes later, Tomm came sailing through the door of The Slug and motioned with his head for me to follow him. I could see that Saiorse had noticed this, and she stared at me quizzically as we passed the end of the bar where she stood talking to her next 'victim'. I gave her my best Mona Lisa smile and she frowned so hard that she looked a bit like a Shar-pei dog.. I could see that she from the furrows and hard stares she cast our way that she was trying to work out what the deal was between Tomm and I. She needn't worry. He was one smelly bottom-feeder of a fish that could stay grovelling around in the sea as far as I was concerned.

We found a quiet spot near the toilets (classy) and conducted our business there. "Here it is. You can count it if you like." He proffered the wad of cash.

"I will, thanks," I told him as I took the cash from him. Strange how small the pile of notes looked for a pile bearing one thousand two hundred and twenty pounds! Nevertheless it was all there and he watched whilst I deftly checked it.

"Debt satisfied?" he asked.

"Well and truly. But let that be a lesson to you," I admonished with a rueful smile.

"Will I see you around?" he ventured gamely.

I smiled widely and smugly. "Not if I see you first. Now scram and keep it in your trousers or for your wife," I told him.

"No amount of money in the world could induce me to that," he laughed with a wink as he walked away.

I had to wonder about those people staying in relationships that didn't make them happy. Surely no amount of money in the world should be enough to make someone do *that*. Life was just too short!

I popped the money safely into my little black purse and made to walk confidently back to my seat. Saiorse headed me off at the pass. "What were you doing hiding out round there with Tomm?" she questioned, the Shar-pei furrows still firmly riding her brow.

"Just making sure that he won't do to anyone else what he did to you at the weekend. The next woman he leaves in a far-off land with no means of returning might not be as lucky as you. They might not have anyone to rescue them!" I returned, beginning to walk away.

"And just how did you do that, may I ask?" she wanted to know.

I stopped and looked her full in the face. "I just pointed out that if it happened again, his wife might hear about it. I doubt she'd be too pleased to find that her husband had been taking his 'squeezes' on pricey weekends away and buying them expensive high-end jewellery!"

"Well, thanks for that!" she blustered. "I'm sure, though, that I don't need you to fight my battles or hold my hand. I could have sorted things out for myself!"

"Yes, I'm quite certain you could have continued to bury your head in the sand and say nothing. Waited for the next willing victim to come along in the meantime..." I laughed. "Yes, that would really have put him in his place and told him what was what!" I laughed.

"It's not funny!" she ranted. "I'm warning you; stop poking your bored, no-life little snubby nose into my business, Zoe! I am grateful for your helping me to get home, but that doesn't mean that you have earned the right to interfere in my affairs!" she spat as she walked away. Affairs were the correct word!

I watched her storm off back to her pitch behind the bar, all smiles and sweetness and light for the punters she'd been talking to previously. Suddenly, I felt about ninety years old and completely drained. She was right; I was snub-nosed, and I didn't really have a life... still, if in order to have a life I'd have to act like Saiorse, I would really rather be bored!

Time to go home!

121

Chapter 11

A couple of days later I was working away industriously in the shop, when my mother stalked into the shop in a menacing mood. She had with her the shiny, high-priced, high-class Rolex watch.

On her way through to the counter she cast a quick if critical eye over the work on the 'outgoing' shelf. She couldn't stop herself from remarking on a particularly nasty revenge bouquet and 'salty sponge' cake I had made. This last was a trial run for a customer and iced lovingly with the words 'Arsey Birthday Bitchface'. Raising an eyebrow she admonished that the flowers were hardly my best work, and did I think that they should be allowed to leave the shop in such an appalling state. I patiently explained about the blossoming revenge arm of my little empire, which seemed to satiate her curiosity with my lack of floral finesse on this item.

She approached the counter brandishing the watch. "Saiorse has asked me to leave this with you. She says you'll know what to do with it," she said, uncomfortable and slightly embarrassed, whilst waving the timepiece through the ether like a low-budget hypnotist (with expensive props) in front of me.

Suddenly, she abruptly stopped waving it and gazed at it thoughtfully, as though seeing it for the first time. "It seems a shame to sell such a liberal gift though. It's rather lovely, don't you think?"

I deliberately didn't give eye contact to either the reassuringly expensive offending article, or my aggrieved mother. "Great. Let's hope that someone else thinks it's rather lovely! We can all get our dues from her once I sell it on. She must owe you and dad an arm and a leg by now. She might have been out of work for a while, but I noticed that it didn't curb her spending!" I pointed out matter-of-factly.

"Well, you know, Zoe, we do give you help in other ways… " Mum began irritably.

I hurriedly interjected, "I wasn't saying that I feel hard-done by, far from it! Just that I think it's time she stopped treating the pair of you – and everyone else she knows – like door mats with endless supplies of cash, and stood on her own two feet instead of other peoples'. This last 'adventure' of hers was the living end, mum, and well you know it. I'm just trying to help her realise her personal responsibilities."

"Hmm, well, that's as may be, but you can be a bit hard on her. She's not as worldly-wise and sensible as you – never was – she's always been a bit of a dreamer. That's no reason to bully her into growing up on your terms," she admonished.

I relented a little. "Well maybe I won't take everything she borrowed from me out of the proceeds of the sale from the Rolex. Maybe I'll let her off some of it. But she has to get help for her erratic moods and behaviour, mum. It makes her hell on wheels to be around! You should know!" I wasn't about to tell my mum that I'd already got my money out of Tomm. I was planning to use some of the money from the Rolex to fund a little weekend away for her and my father. If she knew that, she'd find a reason to stop me, so that Saiorse got all the money for the sale, barring what she actually owed our parents. This I *would not* have. There was no lesson for Saiorse in that!

"Admittedly she can be a handful when she's in one of her fugs, but that's Saiorse. I can't honestly see what the doctor can do to help her!" she finished.

I didn't want to frighten her with talk of medication and anti-depressants or counsellors, so instead I gently said, "We'll see. Did she make an appointment like I told her to?"

"That's the other reason I'm here. She asked me to tell you that it's tomorrow morning at eleven thirty. You won't be available to go with her, though, will you? You'll have to be here to man the shop," she said, sounding sneakily triumphant.

"That's ok, I'll ask Alli if she can come and mind things for a couple of hours. I said I'd go with her and I will. Besides, it'll give me a reason to take a day off. I could do with that," I answered brightly.

"Oh!" she answered, now simply knowing that I meant business and would not be put off.

After a little small talk, she went on her way to pass on the 'good news' to Saiorse. So! It seemed that Saiorse had shrewdly decided I wouldn't be able to go and keep tabs on her if she made her doctor's appointment during my normal working hours. She should have known better; I'm far more resourceful than that!

I would have to speak to Alli. She was a friend from my days at Alwin's Florists. She liked to do the odd day here and there, since packing in work to have children, just to keep her hand in with all the latest floristry techniques and designs. She had also admitted to me that she loved the contact it gave her with other adults. (This I think is a very loose term for describing my customers.) I was sure it would be fine with her, she rarely said no.

I meant to sort Saiorse out once and for all and she wasn't going to get away that easily! It wasn't all for altruistic reasons though...

This would be my best ever opportunity to sort out another one of life's small problems, and hopefully give myself the sister I had always wanted. The pleasant, affable, good-humoured, kind and loving Saiorse I knew she could be! As opposed to the man-hungry, gold-digging, difficult, depressive and deceitful one we'd all been treated to for the last ten years or so instead.

Mid afternoon and Dannie phoned to tell me that she wouldn't be in for tea. This was music to my ears since it was my turn to cook, and I could find neither the inclination nor the energy. She explained that she was going out with Karin for tea and then on to 'Flights of Fancy', a gay club that had recently opened up in town.

The invitation was there for me to join them, but somehow I just wasn't in the mood for fun and jollification. I was feeling all hardnosed, purposeful and serious. A night in alone would probably do me the world of good. I could spend a little time reflecting on all the changes going on around me (brooding, more like) and then spend an hour wallowing in the bath with a good book, some good wine and some chocolate for afters! Perfect!

As I sat with a cup of coffee (I fancied ringing the changes. Oh, the excitement!), putting the finishing touches to a silk Christmas arrangement at the counter in the last dregs of the gloomy winter afternoon, I noticed something under the streetlamp (dark. So soon! Again!). It was over the road by the hairdressers. Peter rolled (literally) into view with his lardy lady friend, but as they stood talking I saw him do something that was as rare as seeing a rocking horse poo. He reached slowly into his jacket and withdrew his wallet.

This was made even more notable because he spent so much time complaining that he was not earning enough to give any to Sal. Therefore there was never any need to get out his wallet. Consequently it was something he never did. Sal paid for everything (in every possible way) and Peter, due to his 'lack of earnings', made sure to pay nothing into their household economy. Yet here he was, in broad daylight (alright, maybe not broad daylight. Maybe I mean vaguely orange streetlight breaking the velvet, indigo, afternoon of winter light), removing and brandishing his wallet meaningfully in a public place. What could induce him to do such a thing, I wondered incredulously. I couldn't recall ever seeing him do it before!

I watched in stupefied and fascinated wonder as he removed a wad of notes so large you could use it as a pouffe, and shove them deep into the pocket of his dirty-looking 'friend'. Hmm; so now he was paying for sex? Or maybe it was drugs. Except if it was, I didn't see her hand them over. In fact I didn't see her pudgy hands come out of her filthy pockets until he kissed her again! They were grappling with each other in the street like two elephantine hippos in a major, world-class mud-wrestling competition. So that was how whales mated! My coffee was now threatening to swiftly make for the exit so I averted my eyes and went back to my arrangement.

It dawned on me as I did so that he must be desperate to get caught, because he must have realised that I would be able to see him rendezvousing with his

Soiled Cynthia from my window. I'd never done anything that would leave him in any doubt my loyalties lie with Sal. He was clearly waiting for me to do his dirty work! I fumed silently, and cruelly stabbed a silver bow into the innocent, cheery, little festive arrangement I was working on. All the while I was wishing it was piercing the nether regions of Penury Peter, the petty pervert, and doing him serious and grave injury!

When I next looked they were gone.

I felt now that I was being pushed by the fates (and Peter of course) into being the one to tell Sal. I honestly didn't know how best to do it, or whether now was the right time. And I didn't like this one iota! When I came to really think about it, could there ever really be a 'right' time? Sal had stood by him through thick (which he undoubtedly was) and thin (their financial situation; his hair and intellect), and I was sure that this humiliation would be just too much for her to take. I made a mental note to myself to get through tomorrow with Saiorse, then I would find a way to tell my oldest, closest friend what I had seen. Let the greased piggy Peter slide his way out of that!

Mind you, if they split up I'd no longer have a guinea pig for my revenge foods!

Now was *no time* to be selfish! I chided myself for that and began clearing away to go home. Ah! Home... to peace quiet, and a long, hot, soak in the bath. Heaven!

Ralph had gone home earlier in the day. I chased him out of the shop at two thirty, as all his deliveries were done and dusted. I shut up shop alone, anxious to get away from my life's work and just chill out. Not only did I have a night in alone to look forward to, but thanks to Saiorse and Alli I could lay in bed until ten tomorrow, because Ralph was opening up the shop and Alli (good old dependable Alli) was coming in to work to give me a free day! Life didn't get better than this!

I drove carefully home through the mounting rush-hour traffic, my mind not fully on the job in hand. My thoughts flittered from Saiorse to Sal, to Peter and that greasy muck-tub I had seen him with, to Dannie and then to my own situation with Will. Just thinking about him made me smile. This was not good. He was with someone else and I shouldn't be smiling. I had accepted his friendship but still in my heart I wanted something more...

Mentally I shook myself as I let myself into the warmth and sanctuary of my home. I carefully locked myself in and prayed that Dannie had taken the key I had given her, otherwise I might be getting a rude awakening later on, and I really didn't want that! Before long, Flo and I were ensconced in the bathroom, me up to my eyes in bubbles with a glass of Prosecco to mirror the contents of the tub, and Flo with a pig's ear to chew. Luckily the smell of the bath bomb (lemon) overrode the smell of half-chewed, soggy pig skin and I sunk low into the suds, closing my eyes and soaking up the tranquillity and the silence – save for the crunch of dog-teeth on hide – that was mine for tonight.

I must have drifted off for a short while. I awoke with a jolt to the sound of what seemed – to my anaesthetised senses – to be a battering ram hitting my front door.

I quickly sat bolt upright. This caused a tidal wave in my seriously overfilled bathtub, sending water crashing like an angry tsunami all over the bathroom floor. Flo hurriedly grabbed her pig's ear and scooted deftly out of the path of the main body of oncoming surf, but in so doing knocked over the table I'd put beside me bearing the wine and my towel.

Damn!

I carefully stood up and reached for my robe from the back of the door. I knew I quickly had to answer whoever was attempting to smash their way through my front door come – literally – hell or high water! I wiped my feet on the sodden bath mat – I don't know why; it was futile, but there you go. I still wasn't really completely awake – and wetly squelched my way down the stairs towards the front door, ignoring the 'sea of tranquillity' on the bathroom floor. On reaching the front door I could just about make out the figure of a woman through the obscure glass.

"Who's there?' I tried tentatively.

"Zo, it's me! Sal! Can I come in?" she replied urgently. I located my keys from my coat pocket and quickly opened the door, pulling her inside as I did so. "Oh, you're all wet!" she exclaimed.

"Yes, you got me out of the bath!" I answered, unable to disguise that I was slightly annoyed.

If she picked up on the annoyed tone in my voice, she didn't acknowledge it. "Zo, I didn't know where else to come. I need to talk," she supplied hurriedly.

I held up my hand to stop her because if this was going to be about what I had a horrible feeling it might be about, I needed to at least get dried and throw on some clothes. I was feeling exposed and vulnerable, and not just physically. I honestly didn't need to be questioned on what I knew about her adulterous husband in my semi-clothed and soaking wet state! I sat her in the living room with a glass of the Prosecco (no mean feat for wet feet on a laminated floor, I can tell you!) I had been drinking, before my glass had ended up drifting in the ocean that was once my bathroom. Then I carefully went upstairs to sort my mess and myself out.

I decided to take my time. It would give me breathing space enough to think what to say to the excitable Sal now enthroned in my living room. Now that I thought about it, it was curious that she was excitable. I would have expected her to be angry. Or maybe devastated. Or possibly bewildered. Or very hurt. Or even all of the above, or a combination of it. But somehow excitable hadn't appeared on my radar of Sal's feelings towards what was going on with her two-timing spouse. You could never gauge how people would react to bad news. Not even the people you think you know well...

Eventually I plodded my way back into the living room, new glass in hand (but this time containing elderflower cordial and soda water. I wanted to keep a clear head for this!), and sat heavily down opposite Sal on my sofa. I observed her for a second or two and realised that she didn't look like a woman who'd found out that her porker of a husband had been telling her porkies for months. She looked more like a woman who'd won the lottery! Her eyes were bright and clear and her skin was peachy and glowing. Glowing! I could now smell a very large, brown, slippery rodent in the room.

"Well? To what do I owe the honour of your visit?" I asked cautiously.

"I'm leaving him! I'm getting out! I've been seeing someone at work for the last five months, and he's asked us to move in with him!" she blurted animatedly. "I've been desperate to tell you for ages, but I haven't dared in case I jinxed things!"

I shook my head a little, smiled and asked her "What took you so long? You should have done this many years ago. He was never right for you and you've always deserved so much more than he's given. Not so sure you should be running straight to the arms of another man, though. Tell me more."

"He's thirty-five, never been married, no kids of his own, and the deputy head of the school. He's tallish, with dirty blonde hair and a dirty, imaginative mind..." she started.

"Noooo! Too much information! Just keep to the relevant facts!" I interjected quickly, screwing up my eyes and blocking my ears.

"Sorry, it's just that things have never been so good," she apologised, red-faced. "He's quite thick-set, with deep, grey eyes – like the colour of a velvet elephant – and open features. He's got a great sense of humour – he makes me laugh all the time – and he's so caring, Zoe. He's always asking me what I want or how I feel, and goes to such pains to get things right for me!"

I was aghast. It had been a long time since I had seen my best friend so animated. He certainly sounded like a gem (if you ignored the fact that he had a thing for a married woman. And obviously it was important to Sal for me to ignore this.) On the other hand, compared to Peter, Adolf Hitler would sound like Don Juan! I watched Sal as she picked up her glass, sipped at the contents and then nursed it like a crystal ball.

Still grinning broadly at her 'velvet elephant' analogy (poetry and flowery speech never was part of her repertoire), I wondered, "So how have you been fitting him into your busy schedule?"

"We've been going out for lunch a lot. I've also been working here and there after hours – if you get my drift – and then there's the PGL trip that we did together. That was difficult, I can tell you, with all the kids around. We had to be really careful. We have been really careful. But now we've decided we just want to be together," she finished.

"What about Lou? Does he know that she's part of your 'deal'? I can't imagine her wanting to stay with Piggy – I mean Peter – and I can't imagine that you'd want her to either," I pointed out.

"He knows about her, and he's willing to take us both. I think she'll get on well with him once she's used to him. You're right, though; I definitely don't want her staying with 'Piggy', as you so lovingly named him. I always knew you didn't like him. I always had this feeling that he got on your nerves. Hopefully you'll like Johnathan a lot more," she explained.

"So his name's Johnathan, is it? I'm sure he'll be a lot more personable than Peter. I don't think there's anyone on earth who isn't! I'm sorry, I didn't do a very neat job of hiding my dislike, did I? I did try to take to him, but every time I found something positive in him, he'd do something either stupid or evil to you or Lou and I'd end up hating him again," I told her forlornly.

"S'ok, you're not on your own. I realise that most people dislike him. He's got one of those faces! And one of those personalities! In fact even I can't remember why I married him any more," she placated me.

"Well, when do we get to meet this Johnathan, then?" I asked.

"I'm going to introduce him to Lou at the weekend at my mum's – yes she's in on it too – and then I'll bring him here to meet you afterwards if you like. I'm taking Lou tomorrow to mum's with her and my stuff, and we're going to stay there for a while until the dust settles. It'll give Johnathan and I a bit of time to do normal 'couple' things and adjust to one another properly before we take the next step." She explained elatedly.

I smiled "I can't believe your mum's involved in this. I never knew she could do 'devious'!"

"She's made an exception, because she's so relieved that I'm getting away from Peter," she replied guiltily.

"Hmmm, have you thought about how you're going to tell him?" I wondered.

"I'm taking the coward's way. I'm leaving him a letter," she replied. "I couldn't be doing with the argument. Or worse still the begging or bullying."

"I think you might be in for a surprise!" I told her. "I think he might have a secret of his own to spill," I began. "You see, I've seen him with a large, grubby and rather unkempt woman outside my shop. The sight of them locked at the lips nearly made me gag on my lunch, and the fact that he's been walking her up and down outside my shop tells me that he wants me to catch him so that I can tell you!" I gabbled without really thinking about it.

For a split second Sal looked shocked, and then disappointment crossed her features. "How long have you known about this?" she asked dangerously quietly.

"Not long, a couple of days, but I didn't know how to tell you. I was going to invite you round tomorrow evening and tell you. That's what I was doing in the bath... meditating on how best to break it to you," I explained. (This was not quite a lie. I had spent some of the moments before I drifted off thinking about Sal and Peter and how best to break the news.) "He started walking up and down past the shop with her a couple of days ago, but I gave him the benefit of the doubt thinking that she might be just a business associate or a friend. Then he did it again today, and they somehow got tangled up and lip-locked. That was the crunch for me. I knew I had to tell you." (Ok, so maybe this wasn't quite the way it happened, but she was my oldest friend and I wanted to cushion the blow at least a little bit.)

Sal took a couple of minutes to digest what I had told her. "I see. I don't know why I should, but I feel, well, betrayed," she told me finally.

"Oh, Sal. I had no intention of betraying you. I swear to you I had every intention of telling you as soon as... " I started.

"Not by you, you dolt!" she smiled. "By Piggy! It makes me wonder how long he's been at it! And, also, if he knows what I've been up to and he isn't doing it just to get his own back on me."

I thought about what I had seen that afternoon as he passed the grubby woman a wad of notes. Had he been paying her for her services in order to wind Sal up via me? It was possible. Anything was possible with Peter. "I suppose it could be a pre-emptive strike if he knew you were seeing someone else. I wouldn't put it past him, and I did notice that he passed her some money today. He never parts with his cash usually, so maybe he was paying her for 'services rendered'?" I said.

"God! How pathetic! And how like him if that's what he was doing! No, I'm not going to change my plans, I'll do it by letter and then go to mum's. The solicitor can do the rest. If I never see or hear from him again after that it'll be too soon!" she fumed determinedly, adding, "I wonder where he got the money from? He hasn't worked for weeks."

During the course of the evening, I promised to help Sal after I'd taken Saiorse to the doctor's. She had to move some of Lou's and her things round to her mum's. It seemed like a small gesture, but I knew that in truth it would mean giving up a little more of the precious day off I had planned. I'd sort of had it in mind to take Saiorse's ill-gotten watch and sell it, then maybe sort out a surprise break as a Christmas gift from us both for my parents. Perhaps if I was quick and I didn't hang around too much at Sal's parents', I could still find enough daylight hours to shoehorn it all in somehow.

Tomorrow was, after all, another day!

Chapter 12

The following day I woke up to discover that Dannie's bed had not been slept in. Also that I had woken up at my usual time of seven on a day off without the aid of an alarm clock! Infuriating!

I tried gamely to get back to knocking out a few zeds for a good half hour, but then decided that I was wasting my time and I would be better employed getting up and walking the dog. Flo seemed to have somehow gauged psychically that this was my intention and had begun dancing all over the bed, tail wagging, eyes sparkling at the prospect of an early morning commune with nature and the claggy, boggy mud in the fields at the back of the house.

After my customary cuppa I donned my flowery, pink wellies (a gift from my mother who thought their theme would be exactly to my taste), thick coat, scarf and gloves then began to steel myself for the blast of cold air that I knew would hit me when I opened the front door. As I did, I was met with the sight of Dannie – complete with bed hair, and last night's smudged and therefore slightly slutty makeup – emerging from her car.

"Someone had a good night, and it wasn't me!" I grinned as she came through the door.

"Don't! I never want to drink again!" she told me, rubbing at her forehead as she passed. I noticed she was limping and wondered to myself whether I dare ask why.

"See you soon and you can tell me all about it!" I replied instead. My life was rapidly turning into an episode of EastEnders!

An hour later I let myself back in, feeling windswept, cold, pinched, and blanched, but somehow refreshed from our early morning trot through the mire. Now I was facing a trot through the mire of a whole different kind. Once again I braced myself, but this time for the tales of the further adventures of Dannie.

She was propped up against the cushions on the sofa in her brown furry house-coat with a large steaming mug of hot chocolate when I entered the room. She gazed admiringly at Lorraine Kelly on GMTV and stroked her fingers slowly along her cup as she did so.

I slumped wearily into the chair opposite, bit into the cinnamon and raisin toast I had brought in with me, and after careful thought and chewing, said, " Come on then. Spill the beans!"

She grinned like a Cheshire cat, stopped stroking the mug, folded her hands closer around it, and replied, "It was the best night ever. I drank and danced myself dizzy and spoke to lots of different like-minded individuals! Is that raisin toast?"

I proffered my plate and she took a piece of the toast. "And you did that all night, did you?" I pressed.

"Until about two thirty, yes," she gave through a mouthful of bread.

"And after?" I pushed.

"And after I went back to Karin's," she told me, smiling quietly.

"I see. So, will you be going back to Karin's tonight too?" I probed.

She went back to paying a little too much attention to Lorraine, finished the toast, and began once again caressing her mug for a moment. I noticed a trace of a Mona Lisa smile on her face that hadn't been there a second or two before and knew before she replied that the answer was going to be... "Quite possibly, yes."

Dannie didn't look at me as she told me this, so I went further... "So, are you limping because you danced yourself dizzy, or because you stayed over at Karin's?"

As I finished my question, I made for the door with my now-empty plate, and was treated to a flying cushion to the head and being told, "You're a bit nosy, aren't you?"

I would take that to mean that Dannie and Karin were now on their way to being 'an item'!

I tidied the house, did a bit of vacuuming and dusting, being almost ably assisted by the hung-over Dannie who grinned to herself like an idiot the whole time we were working. I filled her in on Sal's visit and what had transpired during my 'quiet evening in', and to be fair she didn't seem at all surprised. Just like the rest of us, it was only surprising to Dannie that Sal had withstood Peter the Porker for so long.

In no time at all through our diligent efforts the house was like a new pin, so I was able to go upstairs and start plastering makeup on my face in readiness for my jaunt to the doctor's with my big sis. I managed to unearth some black wide-leg trousers, a black jumper with large lime-green button detailing, and a black and green beaded scarf out of my wardrobe, along with my long black boots. Now that I was suited and booted, I hadn't scrubbed up too badly. I pinned up my newly straightened hair and found some small silver and jet ear rings in my jewellery box that went perfectly with my garb. To finish the ensemble I added one clear quartz and one haematite bracelet, and a quick squirt of Jo Malone Raspberry cologne. There! Good to go!

Set for anything. Well, nearly anything!

I rolled up at eleven outside mum's, and Saiorse quickly appeared beside me in the passenger side of my car. She looked tired, pinched and somehow frail. She told me that she had been awake for most of the night thinking about her appointment with the doctor. So she was pretty quiet and thoughtful during our short journey.

I decided that it would be easiest if she set the pace and so therefore I should let her lead any conversation. We ended up just talking pretty much about mundane generalities; like the exceptionally cold start to the winter weather and what we should do for our parents for Christmas.

I was secretly pleased to have the chance to discuss this with her, as I had been wondering how best to ask if she wanted to help pay for a short trip for them. She jumped at the chance, much to my surprise, and even had some suggestions of her own. We quickly managed to agree on something!

It was decided that a trip to Rome would be a good idea during early April and that we should make Christmas dinner between us at my house to give mum a well earned break. (I'd have to admit that I wasn't expecting too much help from Saiorse with this last treat, going on past form. She was big on gestures but not on actual effort.)

I was already on the lookout for a suitable city break. Hopefully I could use part of my day to go and book something for them, but this would have to be after I had helped Sal, then sold the watch. Saiorse made no mention the watch at all so I was careful not to bring up the subject. It would keep for another time.

Once at the doctor's, I asked if she'd like me to go in with her or if she'd prefer to be alone for the consultation. As I would have expected, she chose to go the lone route, but only after promising me faithfully that she would be completely honest about her symptoms and feelings. I still wasn't sure that I trusted her truth to tell, but what else could I do? I could hardly force my way in, could I?

I watched nervously as she disappeared into the doctor's office. I eventually picked up a five-year old magazine on wine to distract myself from watching the clock ticking out the time. It did little to help my jangling nerves, but there were some lovely arty pictures of Italy in it.

I so desperately wanted Saiorse to be okay. But if they could find nothing wrong with her, it would mean that she was naturally difficult and self-centred, manic and moody.

She was with the doctor for a good half hour before she emerged from his office. She looked tense, drawn, and as if she had been crying, which made me wonder what had been said.

I quickly stood up and went over to where she now stood fiddling with her phone and seemingly looking in her bag for something. "Are you ok?" I tried tentatively.

"Nope, but I will be," was all the reply she gave, dragging out a tissue.

We walked to the car in silence and just before I could open the doors she told me, "I think I'd like to walk. I might go into town and meet Rebecca, maybe have some lunch."

"Ok. Before you do, tell me what the doctor had to say and put me out of my misery, will you?"

"He's referring me to a consultant at the hospital because bipolar is difficult to diagnose. He wants the word of a specialist. Are you happy now?" she finished tetchily, sniffing into her tissue.

"Oh, Sas, I'm truly sorry! At least you know now that there may be a reason for some of your irrational behaviour," I placated.

"Yes, I'm a nut-job just like you thought! Big help, that is! This has all done wonders for my self-esteem, I can tell you," she began to rant whilst snorting into her now slightly raggy tissue.

"I don't think you're a 'nut-job' at all! I do think that you've been well out of order recently, and your manner is starting to be a concern. Picking up unsuitable men and falling into bed with them, drinking too much and losing your job, staying in bed because you're down and losing your job! Borrowing money that you know you won't pay back so that you can go on a clothing and shoe splurge, not paying your debts, putting yourself in that talent contest as a 'singing banshee' and backing yourself with 'singing strippers' because your friends told you they thought it would be amusing; and then not sleeping for a week at a time because you are somehow high as a kite, is all not normal. Getting yourself trapped in Ireland was the last straw! What if mum, dad, and I had all been away or unable to help you? Where would you have been then? You're becoming a danger to yourself, Sas, and it's a real worry to all of us because we care about you!" I snapped.

She hurriedly looked away, sniffing quietly, but I noticed as she did that there were tears coursing down her cheeks, fully and properly. I hadn't intended to upset her, but she had to see that the pattern she was getting herself caught up in was spiralling out of control, and obviously – since he had seen fit to refer her – the doctor had in some way agreed with me.

"So maybe I'm not a 'nut-job', but there is something not right, isn't there? Like you said, I've been doing some odd things recently; I just haven't stopped to think about any of them. Perhaps if I had, I would have realised that there was something out of kilter. Why didn't you say something to me sooner, though, Zo?" she asked quietly.

"I wanted to say something after you lost your job at Mayples. I told mum then that I thought you were depressed, but she didn't want to hear it. She's a whole different generation and mental illness to them is still something that gets you locked in a sanatorium for the rest of your days. The main thing is that you know now, and it's going to get sorted. You never know, I might be very wide of the mark and you might be in good mental health. After everything that's happened to me, I could be the one that's got behavioural issues and your conduct might be fine!" I smiled.

She laughed through her tears, telling me, "Even to me the tuneless Banshee and the singing stripper debacle now sounds insane, so I doubt that it's you that's got the problem! What was I thinking? I never could carry a tune in a basket!"

"Who knows, and who's to say what 'normal' is? The strippers didn't think it was so mad, did they? They agreed to it. Shall we agree not to worry over this until we find out from a consultant what, if anything, the diagnosis is?" I said, now more sympathetically.

"They didn't think it was so mad because I paid them for their time, but I still owe money to mum for that one because she lent me it thinking I had a catalogue bill to pay. See, the story just gets worse and worse, doesn't it?" she smiled through her tears. The tissue had now given up and lay dying on the floor – Sas the litterbug! – but she realised she needed to pick it up when she noticed the horrified look on my face.

"Oh Sas! I'll grant you that it does look a bit, well, odd, that you paid the strippers, and especially because you used borrowed money. Hopefully there'll be enough from the sale of the watch to pay it all back. Never mind! Like I said, all we can do now is wait for the consultant to give his verdict. I think we should cross each bridge as we get to it, since we're on the right road, so to speak. And don't leave that tissue on the floor," I said, as calmly as I could manage.

She furtively and slightly guiltily picked the tissue back up and pocketed it. Saiorse then came around to where I stood still holding the driver's side door handle and hugged me tightly. She hadn't done that for a while!

"You're right, of course. I'm going to try not to think too much about it until I see the consultant. Thanks for coming with me, and being the one to be honest and tell me that I'm out of order. I know it must have taken courage to do it, particularly whilst I'm acting so off the wall. I'll speak to you soon and I give you my word that I'll let you know when my appointment for the hospital comes through. By the way, since we're being so honest with each other... I don't know how to tell you this, so I'll just come straight out with it... Knickerless was in the Slug the other night. He tried to have a conversation with me but I just looked straight through him like he wasn't there. It was all I could do not to glass him, to be fair. Dunno about you but I'll never forgive him for what he did to you. My mind might be slipping but my loyalty is still intact," she smiled sadly.

"Thanks for that, Sas. I can always rely on you for that much, I know. I did know that Knickerless was back in town, as it goes, but I'm hoping that it won't be for long, so don't worry about me. I feel more sorry for his victims than I do for myself. Imagine bumping into him after what he did to them and their underwear! Anyway, don't get me started on that. Keep me informed about your appointment and I'll keep a space in my diary," I promised.

"You're such a decent person! I admire you for caring about the others, but you know, sometimes you've got to think of yourself. If you need me I'll be around. See you, sis," she replied.

"See you," I whispered as I watched with a little sadness while she made her way briskly (considering the height of her boots) out of the car park and towards the town centre. Her blonde hair shone like a halo in the wintry sunlight, and I found myself hoping that she would not let either herself or me down again. She seemed fairly genuine in her gratitude towards me, and relieved that she now knew that there might be cause for some of her more unusual conduct. Time would

139

tell!

And it was time I was getting over to Sal's!

It was twelve thirty pm by this time, so I couldn't be sure whether Sal would be at home or at already at her mother's. I tried to get hold of her on her mobile but for some reason she wasn't answering so I left a message for her to call me and set off toward her house. Twenty minutes later I pulled up in front of it and noticed with some relief that Peter's car was not there. I could do without the confrontation, as despite my bravado, I was feeling still pretty winded by news of yet another sighting of Knickerless. With luck this would mean Peter was out!

I knocked hurriedly on the door and was quickly answered by a furtive and slightly dishevelled-looking Sal. Shoving back her hair with one hand she was brandishing a large case with difficulty, and there were two black bin bags full of stuff at her feet, along with two further cases out in the hall behind her. I threw open the boot of my little Fiesta, dropped the back seats with a thud and swiftly began to load everything dubiously into the small space I had created.

In no time at all the back of my car was so full I was unable to see in my rear view mirror or out of the back window at all! Good job we didn't have far to go then, really! Still, at least we got everything in!

Whilst Sal went to have a last check round the house and lock up I sat silently contemplating the events of my morning and waiting for what would come next.

I had the beginnings of an unpleasant and heavy headache, which I could well do without! Last thing I wanted was to spend my precious time off nursing a poorly head; I had way too much to cram in to the rest of the day. I rummaged around my glove box, finding the remains of a packet of paracetamol and quickly cramming two into my mouth. They were difficult for me to swallow without water, but swallow them I must, so I threw back my head and rubbed at my throat in order to coax them down. They tasted harsh, foul and dry, so the harder I tried, the less able to swallow them I seemed to be.

Sal emerged from the house, the trace of a smile playing on her face, and I knew then that she would be ok. I hadn't seen her look so contented in ages, which was absolutely at odds with the situation we were now involved in. I knew that Peter wouldn't make things easy, but I was positive that with Sal's new found contentment the days in which he could make things complicated were now well and truly numbered!

Sal hopped lightly into the seat beside me and noticed that I was having a problem immediately. My head was now back in the tilted position, and to add to this I had white powdery residue around the edges of my mouth.

She stared at me concernedly. "Zoe, are you ok? Are you... foaming at the mouth?" she asked incredulously.

"Noo, hmm, cnn't swllooo thzzz," I mumbled.

"Sorry?" she pressed.

"Nnnnnmmm nmmmmwww" I told her incoherently. She watched with open, blatant curiosity whilst I frantically rubbed at my throat, pulling pained and revolted faces until the last of the vile-tasting tablets disappeared into my system. "Eugggghhhh!" I said finally and with feeling. "Sorry about that, I took a couple of tablets for a headache, thinking that I'd be able to swallow them without a drink. As you can see, I couldn't easily. I really, really need a drink now!" I explained.

"Let's go in the house and I'll get you one," Sal volunteered, determinedly unbuckling her seat belt.

I hurriedly stopped her. "No! Let's get to your mums and I'll get one there. I want to get going before Piggy gets back! I won't have you going back in there now just in case he turns up and starts chucking his enormous girth around. We're doing this the way you want it doing, and that means leaving now!" I said resolutely, pulling out onto the road.

As I rounded the corner out of the street I saw something that made me gasp.

Peter's rotund, lardy lady friend was turning into the street where Sal and Peter lived and into the eye of the storm. "Oh my God! That's her! That's the mucky tart I've seen him parading up and down with outside my

141

shop! It looks like she's heading towards your house, Sal. Do you want me to turn around so you can see for yourself?" I wanted to know.

As I said this I noticed Sal half-heartedly waving at 'Rotunda', and 'Rotunda' returning the wave with a jolly, cheery smile in Sal's direction. "Do you know her then?" I questioned in disbelief.

"Who, Penny? Yes that's Piggy's friend Robin's wife. She does Piggy's books for him before he takes them to the accountant. It keeps the costs down," she replied coolly.

"If she only does his books, why have they been meeting outside my shop and snogging the face off each other? Doesn't she need a desk to work at, instead of a pavement?" I asked.

"You're seriously telling me that's the woman he's been seeing? Ha! Oh that's priceless! She'll never leave Robin because he's a workaholic and he earns a fortune. She just does books for pin money as and when she can be bothered. Her house is a shit pit and her two dangerous dogs are riddled with fleas. I should have realised when you said he was with a mucky, round tart! They deserve one another. They're a pair! Both lazy, filthy, greedy and selfish! They'll destroy each other in no time flat! I honestly didn't think that today could get any better, but you – my best mate – have just put the glace cherry dead centre of the cake!" she laughed.

"Glad to be of service!" I replied, somewhat nonplussed.

Chapter 13

It took us a further twelve minutes (I was probably doing more than the regulation 30 mph, a fact of which I'm not proud) to reach Sal's mum's house. On our way over, we had discussed Louise's reaction to the new situation of moving out and into her nan's, and her mother having a new man in her life who was also Lou's old teacher. Sal had told me that Lou's reaction to the whole thing was "Cool", and therefore a bit of a surprise to Sal, who was ready for more of a fight. Turned out Lou was more fed up of her father's attitude to life and his daughter than Sal had realised!

I was so relieved to have made it to Sal's new abode without fighting the Piggy or choking on the vile remains of paracetamol stuck in my throat that I openly sighed with relief on arrival. I hurriedly helped Sal with her myriad cases and bags into the house, said 'how you doing' to her parents, drank a fresh-from-the-kettle hot cup of tea (third degree burns to the mouth!), said a swift 'hello' to Johnathan who had given up yet another lunch break to be with and help Sal (seemed kind, warm, personable and quite attractive on first impressions); then made a quick exit into town to dispose of the watch and sort out a treat for my own parents.

Town was packed-to-bursting and madly hectic. It was more than that; it was countdown-to-Christmas hectic, which would be easier to understand if we were more than just halfway through November. People darted swiftly hither and thither like shoals of confused, cold, washed-out fish trying to beat each other to the Christmassy, glittery plankton. I strode through them decisively into Quilly's Jewellers, because they had a tinsel-strewn window full of sparkly Rolex watches both new and 'vintage' (that's 'used' to you and me!) so I had a feeling that my luck might be in there. I was right, too!

It took white-haired old Mr Quilly (looking rather like a lean, short, drawn, Santa) himself less than half an hour to come through from the back of the shop, and with adroit fingers and sharp eyes admire, authenticate and value the watch. Not bad, considering he was pretty 'vintage' himself! I came away with one thousand eight hundred crisp, new pounds in my pocket, and I just couldn't wait to treat my parents to a decent break with some of it, so next stop would be Kendall's Travel via the odd clothing and shoe shop just for good measure. (Window-shopping only, of course!)

I glanced hurriedly at my watch. With some panic I realised that it was approaching two thirty. I wanted to look in on Alli before she locked up the shop, just to make sure that everything had been ok and that there was nothing I needed to be aware of for the following day, so the window-shopping might have to wait for Saturday, as would any Christmas shopping I'd been hoping to squeeze in. Kendal's would have to be next then we'd see what was left afterwards.

On the way through town I thought I'd seen Knickerless on the other side of the street. It turned out to be someone else, but somehow the incident still made me feel a bit sick and uneasy. Was I going to imagine that I'd seen him everywhere now?

Once I arrived there, Kendal's was pretty busy as people were piling in to try booking quick getaways for Christmas and I had to agree that it sounded like a great idea to me. I mused for a moment that I could join in the exodus myself if I left on Christmas Eve and then returned on New Year's Day because the shop was always quiet after Christmas. Funerals notwithstanding, because there were always plenty of those! I found my somewhat free-range attention being drawn to an offer on their 'last minute getaway' board for that particular week to Morzine.

I had always enjoyed skiing in my youth and I couldn't help thinking on some subconscious level that I was due a bit of a treat...

"Can I help you?" The pretty, dark-haired assistant caught me off guard, and before I knew where I was, I was booking the skiing week in Morzine in five-star luxury, all-inclusive. This was uncharacteristic of me for three reasons. 1) I had just agreed to do Christmas lunch at my house with Sas, and I hated letting people down; 2) I had spent a long time building up my savings so that I could afford an around-the-world airline ticket (something I'd been dreaming of for a while); and 3) I knew I would spend hours justifying the luxury of it to myself and be unable to. The guilt would stop me enjoying the experience! What was I thinking? It was too late to un-think it now as I had already handed over my bank card for the deposit!

Oh well, I needed a rest and this would do me good.

Some time later I emerged from Kendal's with a weekend in Rome at Easter for my parents, a skiing break for myself, a conscience full of remorse and nearly empty pockets! But my break did sound like it would be fun! Then it hit me that I was going to have to spend another chunk of money on skiwear and equipment. Oh dear, this was going to hurt (but hopefully only financially!). This would be another thing for me to add to my list of things to do at the weekend. Still, there at the top of this mythical list, though, was seeing Will.

I made my way back to my car and over to the shop. It was just after four o'clock when I arrived and Ralph was just on his way home. I told him that the shop would be closed for the week between Christmas and New Year, and he seemed a bit put out by the news. Considering he'd be on pay I found this a little odd, but was sure I'd get to the bottom of it sooner or later.

I found Alli with her head in the cold room checking off the orders for the following day. She was always very thorough.

"Hi Alli, thought I'd better check that nothing outrageous has happened in my absence," I called.

"Oh, you startled me. I didn't hear the doorbell go," she told me.

"Sorry. How has today been?" I asked.

"Just fine... except, you're a dark horse, aren't you? How long have you been seeing that gorgeous bloke of yours?" she teased. I looked at her in confusion.

"I don't have a bloke at the moment!" I told her.

"Oh!" It was her turn to be confused. "Well a man called Will came in this afternoon and asked me to remind you that you are meeting him at one on

Saturday…"

"Oh, I see. He's not my bloke, he's just a friend," I replied, possibly a bit too firmly.

"Shame!" she replied, somewhat deflated, then continued, "He also asked me to give you these." In her hand she held a beautiful bunch of pink and white roses with fern and gypsophila.

"Ooooh, they're lovely! You've excelled yourself, and he's put far too much money into my till with his extravagant 'coals to Newcastle' gesture," I exclaimed, a little ungratefully. I would have to have a word with him, because I knew only too well that he didn't have two ha'pennies to spare. Let alone what this would have cost him!

After ascertaining that Alli didn't need me I thought I would make the best of the rest of my day off by picking up a take-away on my way home and then maybe – if I could pluck up the courage – I might call my sister later and let her know that I wouldn't be around for Christmas after all. I had no doubt that she'd pass on the 'good news' to my parents and save me the unpleasant task. In fact, I'd no doubts at all that she wouldn't be able to tell them that I was letting them down quickly enough…

I called Dannie and informed her of my plans for the evening, asking her if she would like anything picking up from the Chinese Takeaway for dinner whilst I was on to her. She had (and this was by now no surprise) made other plans with Karin. They were going for a walk and then to meet some of Karin's colleagues at the pub. She very kindly asked if I'd like to be included in their plans and – as much as I liked them both – I really didn't feel like playing 'gooseberry' this evening. I was quite happy with the plans I had already set out for myself. In fact after my plans of the previous evening had gone so terrifically awry, I was positively looking forward to my quiet evening in front of the telly!

I paid a visit to the China Garden on my way home and picked up some Singapore noodles and chips. The smell in the car taunted me all the way home, so much so that I was ravenous by the time I got through my door and plated it up. So was Flo, but Singapore noodles are far too hot for small furred ones! They made my Chilli Chocolate ice cream look like porridge!

After a peaceful dinner and a lime and soda I made myself comfortable for an evening slobbing out on the sofa. I grabbed my throw from the back of the chair, some chocolate from the kitchen, and the remote control from the table, and made myself thoroughly comfortable. There's nothing quite like a good, old-fashioned wallow on a cold winter's evening!

Halfway through a comedy program the doorbell went! "Go away," I told whoever was at the door, from my warm and cosy position. I sighed dramatically and eventually heaved myself up from my comfortable position on the sofa.

I was feeling somewhat aggrieved because I had been looking forward to lounging the night away, on my own. Alone. Nowhere in my plans had I bothered – or wanted – to factor in space for anyone else! And anyway, I really wasn't fit to be seen at the moment. My hair was a veritable rat's nest and my makeup was a bit smudged. I tried to make a vague attempt at straightening both up in the hall mirror before answering the door.

Saiorse had decided to 'just pop by' to see if I'd had any joy selling the watch! Wonderful! I made her a drink and fetched my purse into the room. We discussed the break for our parents and she saw the itinerary and the bill for herself. I explained that I had spoken to mum, and although Saiorse actually owed her five hundred and forty pounds, she would round it down to five hundred. Then I told her that I'd accept six hundred pounds as her half of the hotel bill she'd run up with Tomm. She tried to argue this one, the contrition she had shown this morning all completely absent!

I was having none of it. I explained that I thought it was time she grew up and realised that actions had consequences. Some of which were costly. Between that, her half of the break to Rome and the money I was giving to mum on her behalf (I didn't trust her to do this herself), she had four hundred pounds left for herself from the sale of the watch. Predictably, an argument ensued. Unpredictably, I was grateful for it, because halfway through I shouted, "Right! That's it! I'm not doing Christmas with you! I'm not going to do Christmas at all! It'll only end in a fight! Do it yourself! At mum's! Leave me out of it!" As you can tell, I'm pretty sick of all our conversations ending in a fight! Also, I was now very neatly out of the festivities with my family, and had somehow managed to make it Saiorse's fault...

Anyway, I can't begin to tell you how relieved I felt! Nor how guilty I felt for the dishonesty of it. I seemed to be a bit 'out of character' lately and I was going to have to get a grip! Also, I was going to have to prepare for the backlash that would surely follow from my parents, and steel myself against their pleas that would surely follow shortly.

Saiorse stormed from my house, stopping only to count the four hundred pounds I had carefully placed on my coffee table in front of her. She spoke not one further word, and neither did I. There simply was no more to say.

I slunk back to my couch – Flo hot on my heels – and sunk down into my smug wallowing. Smug with just the slightest tinge of guilty! I was suddenly very tired and so decided that I wouldn't think about the consequences of my actions until tomorrow.

Chapter 14

At six twenty. I awoke with a start as the whistling milkman clattered his many and various bottles cheerily onto the neighbourhood doorsteps through the thick frost and slick and slimy leaves on the dicey streets. My neck was painfully cricked from the awkward position I had slept in, giving me a harsh headache as though someone were knocking seven inch nails in with a pile driver, and I realised with more than a little shame that I had fallen asleep mid-slob. I never allowed myself to do that! It just seemed so slovenly somehow.

Dragging myself up from under a still-snoring Flo, I shuffled slowly and agonisingly up the stairs to the bathroom to climb into a luxuriously soapy, red-hot bath, guaranteed to ease my aches and pains.

An hour later, I heaved myself out and got myself ready for what I was sure would be a very long day at work. I was starting to feel as though I was at the bottom of a deep, dark well, swimming in a mixture of tiredness, fuzziness, and couldn't-give-a-stuff laziness. This would be fine for dealing with the abuse I was sure to receive from my family, as in this state anything they gave out would just roll off me; but it didn't bode well when dealing with my clients! Inwardly I bitch-slapped myself mentally to snap out of it. Outwardly I looked like hell and couldn't wait for this evening when I could go back to bed and feel sorry for myself in peace!

I fed and watered Flo whilst she pottered affably at my feet; then, telling her to guard the castle, I left for the interminable day ahead. As I locked my front door the sharp, frosty air crept up unbidden to molest me through my clothes. It penetrated my warm, black wool coat from every angle, tweaking sharply at my fingers through my red woollen gloves, then wriggled through my other things to chill through my skin and into my bones. This was cold, but Morzine would be colder still … and the wrath of my family, it struck me, would be positively Arctic!

All the way to work I tried to shake myself awake

and prepare myself for the fight that surely would be the fruit of my rash actions of the previous evening! At the same time in a tiny corner of my head I couldn't help but wonder why my mother hadn't been on the phone already, to find out why I would chose to spend Christmas with a bunch of total strangers rather than my own flesh and blood. Not that they knew I was going skiing yet... it was simple. I was learning to be a little bit selfish!

Well, it worked for Saiorse!

Thankfully, most of the day passed in a fog of fuzziness. The shop wasn't too busy because most folk were by now saving their pennies for Christmas. Things were relatively peaceful and quiet luckily for me. This was, however, not good for my bank account, considering it would now need replenishing from my impulsive spending! And then Will called...

Up to that point, I hadn't really noticed in my semi-comatose state that it was finally Friday. Tomorrow would be Saturday. He wanted to check that we were still on for lunch. Same time, same place as last time. Oh, *yes please!* Something to brighten up my weekend! Inside I was glowing, even though I knew that I shouldn't!

I readily agreed, and after a bit of polite small talk, along with thanking him for the beautiful bouquet he had sent me via Alli, we said goodbye. Well, now I was tickled pink, wide awake, and grinning from ear to ear!

After seeing to the last of the orders then putting a delivery list together for a curious Ralph I awarded myself with a cuppa and a short sit down. As I sat I formulated a quick list of what I would need to do in town tomorrow, and what I'd need to get for my little break. Though the list wasn't long I knew it would be expensive. Skiwear did not come cheap!

When I next looked at the clock it was almost three thirty pm, and with relief I realised that I'd be able to lock up within the hour... yet another reason to smile! Today hadn't been anywhere near as bad, or anywhere near as long, as I'd expected! I stood and began to tidy the stalk-strewn shop and put away the buckets of impeccable, peacock-proud, multi-coloured blooms from the shelves and window into the cold room. I'd soon need to buy Christmas trees and poinsettias for the window. That would look cheery! I loved poinsettias! Such animated colour! Such intense, open passion!

Ralph was soon back from his travels, so between us, we locked up and made the place thoroughly secure before going our separate ways with a chirpy "goodnight". (Well, mine was chirpy-ish, his was a little wilted. What can I say? It had been a long week!) Apart from the usual sirens and car horns I drove home in the relative calm and silence, savouring the quiet time in my own little metal bubble...

Good job I did, because little did I know then that there would be small chance of calm and silence waiting for me in my little sanctuary of a home...

As I pulled into my street, I noticed two things. Firstly the people at number twenty-one had parked a fuchsia leather sofa in their front yard (why?), and secondly my parents' car was parked on my drive.

My heart sank! I thought it was too much to hope that I had got away with it! My mother wasn't known for taking things that irked her (like me doing a runner at Christmas) lying down. If I wasn't very much mistaken, she had the metaphorical garden shears on her person and was about to embark on a brief spate of clipping my wings to stop my festive flight!

I sighed weightily, hauling my tired bones from the car. They had obviously used my dad's key to let themselves in. I could see him remonstrating with her in the living room, since the curtains were open and the lights were all on, and imagine him pleading with her not to make things any worse. No prizes for guessing where Saiorse got her temper and wilful ways... and it wasn't my dad!

I sighed resignedly. Well the way I was feeling 'good luck' to mum, coz she was going to need it!

Wearily I slunk into the house, patting a happy and excited Flo as I went. On entry into the living room, the Kraken was unleashed!

My mother flew into a rage before I could even get fully through the door. "So, now when *exactly* were you going to tell *us* you were going away for

Christmas?" she ranted.

"It wasn't *exactly* a solid plan until Saiorse started on me last night!" I countered.

"Well, then, there's no reason why you can't abandon it and spend Christmas with us like you usually do," she snapped.

"Actually, there is an excellent reason. I rang a travel agent today and booked myself on a skiing holiday for the festive season. I've paid for it, so I'm going," I replied wearily.

"What!" she screamed.

"I said... " I began.

"I *heard* it, I just don't *believe* it! As quickly as that? Spur of the moment, was it?" she questioned.

"As a matter of fact, I don't think it was. I'm sick of Saiorse behaving like a spoilt ten year old and getting away with it! I couldn't bear the thought of another Christmas with us all tiptoeing round her like Santa's elves (nearly said 'dwerves' there. Thanks Mr Sidebottom!) She can have you all to herself and sit in the spotlight for the entire festivities now. I'm sure she'll be thrilled! Though I can understand why you wouldn't be. She is rather draining... " I finished.

"Well! Let me tell you, *madam*, you can both be rather draining! You are doing a pretty good impersonation of a spoilt ten-year-old yourself right now! What on earth were you thinking? Spending Christmas away from your family! Who are you going with, I'd like to know?" my mother was raving. Only trouble is, (and I'm not sure why this happened) I wasn't actually hearing her. Instead, I found myself counting her words as they poured from her mouth.

Curiouser and curiouser! What was going on?

"Well, *say something!*" I heard her say.

"Fifty two," I replied without thinking.

"What! What kind of an answer is that?" she retorted heatedly.

"I don't know, but it's the only one I have, so it'll have to do you!" I smirked.

"Are you laughing at me?" she barked. Then, turning to my father, she commanded, "Don't just stand there! Say something!"

He looked from one to the other of us for a long moment, and finally, wearily, he spoke. "There's nothing to be said. I think Zoe is doing the right thing, putting some space between Saiorse and herself. Though I don't necessarily think that the space is best placed at Christmas!" And then, looking directly at me, "Zoe, love, I think what your mother is trying to say is that although we'll miss you, we hope you'll have a lovely time. All being well, you'll come home safe and sound, and calm enough to sort things out in a reasonable way with your sister. We really did think that the two of you had put your warring behind you after the trip to the doctor's, but there you go. It would be lovely for your mother and I if you could be the bigger person, let whatever passed between you both last night go, and just get on as if nothing had happened, but we'll try to understand why you can't. You've not been yourself recently, though. You've been a bit stressed so maybe the break will help?"

"One hundred and sixty," I responded.

He and my mother exchanged puzzled looks. "Is that all you have to say?" he asked, slightly confused.

"I think so. Seven, yes," I said thoughtfully.

"*Fine!*" my mother spat. "Time to leave!" she told my father pointedly, heading for the door. I followed them, removing my coat and shoes whilst simultaneously rummaging for my slippers in the shoe cupboard. My mother was already settling herself in the passenger seat of their car when my father turned to me at the door and told me, "For what it's worth, I think the change will do you good. You look tired and you've been edgy since we heard that Nick was back in town. I'm worried about you. If you need anything, you only have to ask. Will you be ok?"

"Forty five," I sighed in answer.

He slight frown crossed his features, but he took both my hands and reiterated, "Anything at all."

With that he was disappeared into the night, leaving me to a peaceful evening alone with my dog.

I collapsed into bed at a little after eight o'clock, where I slept fitfully due to a strange, technicolour, vivid dream I was having. I dreamt I was being chased, in a rainbow coloured mankini, across a silvery, cowpat-strewn field full of alpacas by an enormous number one with rabbit ears and a squirrel's tail. I ran rapidly and without looking back until I fell into a large, milky puddle full of mousse and drowned. As the creamy fluid filled my lungs it tasted sweet – like chocolate – suffocating me gently with its sugary perfection. Death by drowning wasn't half as unpleasant as it might have been...

What on earth could it mean?

Chapter 15

I awoke late and had to rush to get ready for work and my lunch meeting with Will. (I'm loath to call it a date because it just wasn't – unfortunately!) I had been hoping to take my time and make an effort, but instead, after jumping in the shower, I had to chuck on my jeans and a cream polo neck – which I was sure to get covered in green slime before the morning was out – and then I could chuck a petrol blue leather jacket and scarf on over the top of it all, making it look halfway ok. If I was right and I did slime myself, I'd just have to eat lunch in my jacket to cover the dirt ...

I daubed a bit of makeup onto my pallid-looking face – possibly being a little too heavy with the rouge – squirted a bit of Coco Mademoiselle on my tired, little person, and piled my hair somewhat haphazardly onto the top of my head.

I was definitely no Kate Moss, but I would just have to do!

Flo barely looked up from her happy slumber as I ran here and there, sorting myself out. She merely opened one eye, wagged her tail a little, then rolled indolently onto her back. These dark mornings were taking their toll on us both in the 'difficulty waking up' department. We needed to move to somewhere warmer with a slower pace of life, and fast!

I did manage to rouse her long enough to get her to go outside for a stretch, though she wasn't pleased. And she just managed to stay awake long enough to eat her breakfast but I knew she'd be curled up and fast asleep before I had chance to make it out of the street. Lucky dog!

By the time I'd made it through the traffic to work, it was nine seventeen by the clock in my car. Already an orderly queue was forming outside the shop door (ok, there were two people waiting), so I hurriedly opened up – apologising profusely as I did so – and served them as quickly and efficiently as I possibly could. This was no mean feat when some people like to come and swap gossip for half an hour before placing an order, I can tell you.

Mr Bartlett breezed in and bought his customary bunch of multi-coloured carnations for Mrs Bartlett. He remarked on the festive feel that was now gathering in sparkly, tinkly little pools around the shop. Also, he was wondering when we'd be stocking Christmas trees. He loved to surprise Mrs Bartlett around this time of year with a beautiful, majestic, pine-scented spruce tree, instead of the usual carnations. Always had to be tied with a big, pink bow and delivered by Ralph, and she was always as surprised as if it was the first time Mr Bartlett had done it!

Wasn't romance wonderful?

The phone was busy for a while. Several orders were placed for Mrs Griffiths, who had sadly passed away on Thursday night from a heart condition she didn't know she suffered from. It was a great shame for all of us, because Mrs Griffiths had the biggest heart (as well as the biggest smile) for miles around and was always doing something for charity. She was a lovely lady, so I'd be sure to take extra care in making anything for her. Her funeral would be a chance to give special thanks and make an even bigger effort than usual. Not just for me, but for many of the folk around here. She would be greatly missed!

By eleven thirty, Ralph had taken out all the orders, the floral tributes for early Monday were sitting on a shelf in the cold room with a delivery list, and the shop was gleaming like a new pin. After paying him from the till, I told Ralph to go home and enjoy the rest of his weekend. He muttered something about a houseful of women driving him out to the pub as he left, but to be truthful I wasn't really hearing him. All I knew was that he'd said whatever it was in thirty-four words.

This was a bit worrying, and I probably should have paid it more attention. Did everyone else count words, I briefly wondered?

I locked up and made my way quickly into town so that I could get as much of my own shopping sorted before meeting Will in Brown's at one thirty for lunch. The town centre was predictably packed with people on a mission! Time, tide and Christmas shopping would wait for no man. To prove it, there were quite a few with their partners buzzing hurriedly from shop to shop, hoping to bag several bargains and keep credit card bills down to a miniscule minimum!

'Good luck with that!' I thought.

It didn't take me long to get kitted up for my skiing trip. I found a sports shop with a bit of a sale on some of the previous season's gear, and managed to get some bright pink salopettes and a pale pink ski jacket for just under £290 for both, and a selection of socks, thermals and fleeces for another £180, or thereabouts. This last was all in shades of pink and white, so I'd look like a giant, skiing marshmallow flying down the mountain. Maybe I should have gone for all white, so that no one would see me coming until it was too late!

By now it was one twenty-five, so it was time to head towards Brown's where Will would, with any luck, be waiting for me. I bustled my way through the thickening crowd down the high street and towards the bistro, not stopping to browse in the shop windows as I normally would because I didn't want to be late. Also I was finding the crowds rather claustrophobic, almost to the point where I couldn't breathe. The damp air played havoc with my hair, turning it instantly to 'brillo pad', the stiff breeze teasing it out from the pile on the top of my head. I would look just 'delightful' by the time I arrived ... like a bag lady with a penchant for skiwear!

As I approached Brown's I spotted Will sitting at exactly the same table as the previous week, in the window. He was chatting to the pretty, blonde, young waitress, who seemed to be quite openly basking in his attention. Was he a bit of a flirt, I wondered? Jury was out on this; I'd have to watch him! Except that I wouldn't, because whatever he was or wasn't, he definitely wasn't mine to watch ... yet! Secretly I lived in hope ...

I pushed my way in to the crammed Bistro with my widest, brightest smile plastered to my face, trilling a cheery "Hello!" as I simultaneously parked my many bags next to our table (in such a packed place it was a health and safety nightmare!) and removed my jacket (see, no slime!) and scarf. By now the pretty, blonde, young waitress was looking slightly less interested in the job at hand as she manoeuvred herself carefully out of the way of my load.

Will smiled back at me and asked, "Been getting to grips with your Christmas shopping?"

"Sorry?" I asked abstractedly.

"The bags. Been getting to grips with your Christmas shopping?" he repeated, fixing his eyes on the load of bags I had set down on the floor by our table and a little too close to the waitress's feet.

"Oh, I see! No," I told him. By now the waitress was beginning to show her impatience by frowning at her order pad and then scowling at me.

"That's an awful lot of shopping you've done there, then!" he declared in surprise.

"Yes, I suppose there is quite a bit there, isn't there?" I stated nonchalantly.

"Been treating yourself?" he persisted conversationally as I sat down and began to peruse the menu.

"Umm, yes. Long overdue and much needed winter wear," I mumbled into the menu. I wasn't ready to discuss my little break yet.

The by now surly waitress rattled her order pad, looked pointedly at her watch then asked loudly "So, can I get you both anything, or would you like more time to decide?"

Will's eyes went back to making his selection from the menu and a bowl of chilli, some nachos and a large Americano coffee was what he decided on. 'Chilli kisses! Good job I liked chilli!' I found myself thinking. Then I made the mistake of making eye contact with the waitress and telling her "Fifteen." Because that was the number of words she had spoken in her last sentence. No harm was done, because luckily for me, fifteen on the menu was 'a chicken and pesto Panini', which I would happily eat. After the waitress had told me this I said "five" which turned out to be a medium hazelnut latte.

I was by now eyeing up the desserts whilst hoping she wouldn't speak to me again because I couldn't stop counting her words for some unearthly reason, and I was worried that I might end up with a rice pudding that I loathed. My eyes alighted on a stodgy, gooey, chocolate fudge pudding that I really would quite like to have today, since I'd skipped breakfast and used up all my energy rushing around. I wanted to have at least one thing I had deliberately chosen though, rather than anything to do with the waitress's last sentence! This problem with counting words was becoming a nuisance!

I looked up to find that by now the waitress was already sloping off to another table, so we were able to talk without being overheard, frowned at, or – worse still – spoken to again!

What a relief!

Will was watching me with interest as I absent-mindedly put the menu back into its slightly worn wooden holder and moved the salt and pepper for no apparent reason into the middle of the table. "Are you ok? You seem a little distracted," he eventually enquired.

"Eight... Sorry, got a bit on my mind," I responded automatically.

"Eight what?" he laughed.

"Two... eh? Oh, eight nothing, ignore me. I'm miles away, lost in one of my many to-do lists," I smiled, feeling somewhat foolish. Mentally, by now I was booting myself to kick out whatever it was that had a grip on me. 'Concentrate!' my mind yelled at itself.

"I see. Would it be easier if we made lunch a quick affair, so that you can get on with whatever it is that has you so concerned and preoccupied?" he tested in a measured fashion.

"Nope! It's fine, really! I'm all yours!" I returned, perhaps a bit quicker than I ought to have.

"Oh, well, in *that case...* " he replied with a wicked grin, "I'm going to make the most out of it! Are you sure you can only do lunch?"

I stared at him, seeing the glint in his eye and wondering if I could get away with grabbing his thigh under the table from where I was sitting. Not one of my better ideas, because due to my distracted state of mind I had no sooner thought it than I found myself actually doing it.

Somehow, half of the pristine, white tablecloth glued itself to the jumper I was wearing so the cloth ended up being pulled off the table as my arm shot out to grab at him under it, sending the salt and pepper cellars and menus flying in both directions, narrowly missing two other diners. Talk about embarrassing!

I laughed uncontrollably whilst trying to apologise (not a very convincing stab at an apology, in all fairness), the tears of mirth running helplessly down my face as I did so. If I said Will looked surprised, I'd be understating the situation by a country mile!

However, in seconds he recovered and he too began to laugh like there was no tomorrow. In the end he was able to ask me, "What was that all about?"

"I think I was trying to pat your leg in a sort of an attempt at scolding you for your naughtiness, but it went a bit wrong," I said in between guffaws. I could hardly tell him that in a moment of wild abandon I had spontaneously moved in for a grope, now could I?

Both waitresses were now scrabbling about the cosy, bustling, little, bistro retrieving the salt and pepper pots from nearby tables and then recovering our now bare, oak table with the cloth. Neither looked overly impressed with my display, it had to be said, and no one else was laughing.

We chatted about the happenings of the week now behind us, and plans we had for the week ahead whilst waiting for our food. As the drinks, arrived Will remarked that it was a good job the drinks hadn't been on the table when the cloth had been thrown off it, as a bit of scalding would then definitely have occurred! This started us both off again giggling like schoolgirls for a time.

The waitresses brought out the food and rolled their eyes at each other as they set down the plates in front of us. A couple of other people were regarding us over their meals and either smiling at our silliness or tutting at our childish sniggering. We didn't really care, though; we were locked in our own weekend world where something could 'twang' at any time, and one of us could lead the other astray. What an exhilarating feeling!

What a worry!

While, we ate we people-watched as we had done the week previously. It was more of a task this time, because the early Christmas shopping crowd rushed past the window like a high river in the flood season. Singling people out for special attention was a bit of an achievement. We made up our own meaningless stories about members of the public and their lives. Some funny, some bizarre, and some just plain, old-fashioned ridiculous! Each of us was trying hard to outdo each other in the 'comedian' stakes. By the time we had finished lunch I discovered that I had no room for a dessert after all. I was full up on laughter and a creeping desire to eat Will with a teaspoon...

When I next looked at the oversized, union jack clock on the bistro wall, I was amazed to find that it was by now three thirty, and the grey, milky daylight (such as it was) was now hastily beating a retreat as the darkness of the evening chased it from its throne in the winter sky.

"Gosh, where did the afternoon go?" I asked Will, a little sadly.

"Mmm, soon be Christmas," he replied with the faint trace of a smile.

"Amen to that! I'm ready for a break from work!" I informed him.

"Yes, me too. Although being stuck in the house with Wendy won't exactly be my idea of festive fun!" he grimaced.

"Then don't!" I declared boldly, and ventured, "Come to France with me. I'm going skiing!" I have to say, this wasn't how I'd intended to tell him I was going away.

He appeared taken aback for a second, then exclaimed, "Wow! You kept that quiet! Who else is going?"

"No idea, just me and a whole bunch of people I don't know and have never met!" I grinned.

He gazed at me for a moment in wonder and then told me, "Ms Parsons, you really are full of surprises! Aren't you worried about going it alone?"

I thought for a second and then replied, "You know what? I don't think I am, no! I'm looking forward to the anonymity of it, somehow. I wouldn't have even considered doing something like this six months ago, but lately ... well, let's just say life's too short!"

"Well, good for you! And much as I'd really love to come with you, I'm afraid I can't afford it. But thank you for asking me along. Maybe next year?" he ventured.

I smiled. "Yes, I'd like that! Here's to next year!" I pronounced decisively.

I stood to put on my jacket and collect my bags, and as I did so Will helped me. He insisted on carrying my bags whilst seeing me through the chilly, rapidly emptying town centre to my car, as it was by now fully dark. Every colour of merry fairy lights twinkled in the trees by the church, and the frost on the ground glittered like a festive rainbow as it reflected the shards of light. I could no longer feel the cold, because from deep inside of me there emanated a warm, fuzzy feeling. Almost like I'd been at the mulled wine!

As we approached the car, I opened the doors and popped the boot so that Will could put the bags into it as he had ordered. I thanked him and began to turn to open my door but before I could, somehow I was up against the car and we were lip-locked. Lip-locked, and holding each other like we were the last two people on the planet. Like no one else existed in that glacial, November evening... corny but true!

Several minutes later, we were not just lip-locked by grappling through our cold, gloved, hands with each other's clothing. I became loosely aware that from across the street a couple of older men were laughing and demanding that we 'get a room'. Will drew slightly away breathing heavily "Shall we?" he tested.

"Get in the car, we're not far from my place," I commanded. Before we could say anything else he was in the car and we were speeding (yes, really) along the wintry streets towards my welcoming, cheery, cottage home.

I said cottage, not cottaging!

Oh dear, there I go again, off at a tangent! You can

tell where my mind was going, and it was roughly in the same direction as my by now red, hot, buzzing, little body. I could feel the pure, white, heat burning its way through my jumper.

Or maybe it wasn't so pure… we'd soon find out!

Chapter 16

We hardly made it through my front door before we were at each other again. Hands were in all places as we struggled to undress each other at great speed in the middle of the hall (who said many hands make light work? Not true; there seemed to be many hands yet it seemed to be an impossible task!) Flo was now circling our legs like a shark waiting to choose its dinner. As she nudged my leg for the umpteenth time I realised that she'd probably be desperate to go out, so I instructed Will to go to the bedroom (pointing the way because I didn't want him to get lost in amongst the many clothes in my dressing room or end up in the spare room before we'd even begun) while I fetched a couple of glasses, a decent bottle of red wine, a corkscrew and let out what was by now my frantic dog.

That done, I made my way as rapidly as I could up the stairs, kicking my boots under the hall table, picking up the jackets we'd carelessly thrown onto the floor, and locking the front door as I went (a bit of OCD there). As I approached my bedroom with more than a little anticipation, I could hear Will moving about the room, so I gently nudged the door open (didn't want to find that he was behind the door and knock him cold!) sliding inside almost timidly.

Will smiled warmly as he caught sight of me and moved to take the bottle from my hands with the corkscrew, and began to carefully remove the cork. That done, I took the bottle from him and poured two generous measures of wine for us into the oversized glasses from my kitchen. I had hardly set down the bottle when he was beside me, pulling playfully at my jumper so I impatiently helped him to remove it. Then, so as not to be outdone, I pushed him into a sitting position on the bed and removed his thick, grey, woollen jumper and the t-shirt beneath it.

He had quite a fit-looking six-pack going on. He obviously liked to keep himself in shape beneath those suits. I have to say I was quietly impressed! I was also relieved that I'd put on some decent, matching, underwear, even though he was in the act of removing it and would probably not even notice my pretty, cream lace bra.

It was a very long time since my naked body had been seen by a member of the public at large, so I was somewhat worried by what reaction it might solicit. Luckily, he didn't flee screaming from the house crying 'freak!' as he went, so I was confident that I could go ahead and fumble with his trousers ...

A couple of seconds later and we were both completely naked, rolling around like marbles in a bag on the bed. The first time it was blindingly fast and furious. I think we must have both been bottled up for far too long! I had no reason to doubt from this display that his relationship with his girlfriend wasn't particularly active...

The second time was slower but much noisier than it ought to have been. Mrs Mack did not approve and went to great pains with a saucepan to show it. Flo added to the fray by barking loudly, darting hither and yon around the room whilst panting loudly.

But then, so did I!

The third time, though, was our ill-fated undoing. Somewhere into the proceedings, I slipped off the bed and ran playfully around it. Will ran after me, and as I jumped back onto the bed to escape his clutches (yeah, right!) he slipped his head between the bars of my beautiful, antique, wrought iron bedstead, yelling "Little pig, let me feel your entrails!" I know you're thinking that it's not the best line you've ever heard. Me neither, but it did make me laugh. What made me laugh even more – at least to begin with – was that he couldn't get his head out from the bars afterwards.

When I eventually stopped laughing I went to his aid. But he was well and truly stuck. I flailed around the bedroom and bathroom looking for something to free him with, eventually settling on the out of date 'tingle' lubrication gel from my underused 'special' drawer. If only I had bought some more Vaseline after I used up the last on my hands! I rubbed the 'Tingle Gel' liberally around his head, neck, and ears, but it made no difference unless you counted that now they were red hot and prickling like he'd been rolling in nettles. My hands were certainly tingling, anyway! Next I fetched the lard from the fridge but apart from the terrible mess it made of his hair it offered no real help or relief at all.

By now we weren't laughing so much (a few nervous giggles maybe), plus he was complaining that his head was on fire, so I decided to drag the mattress from the bed and pour cold water over him. Who knew, it might even shrink things enough to get his head out of its iron trap? I popped a bowl underneath his chin, fetched some iced water and began to slowly pour it over the afflicted area. This made him shriek in shock and gave Mrs Mack another reason to attack her wall furiously with her pan. I swear she spends her entire time listening through my wall!

After five excruciatingly long minutes of this we were still getting nowhere. The water was bouncing like little drops of mercury straight off him due to all the lard and assorted other gunk on there, so I gave in and tugged the mattress back into place. Next I tried pushing his head from the front. Whilst he alleged that he enjoyed the view immensely, to the point that it was almost worth the pain, it actually had no effect on alleviation of our unfortunate predicament!

Three quarters of an hour later, we were both completely exhausted from the effort of trying to release Will's head. This was not the head of Will I wanted to be messing with at this time and I was becoming frustrated. Ok, frustrated is the wrong word, I mean more ... exasperated!

Then I had a bit of a brainwave. Some of my dad's tools were down in my garage; perhaps there'd be something there I could use? Telling Will to wait there (as if he wouldn't) I pulled on my dressing gown again and dashed to the garage. Raking frantically through my dad's stash of hardware I found some bolt croppers, a bottle jack and a blowtorch. I'd hurriedly decided that I'd try heating up the bars and moving them slightly first off, the jack secondly and the bolt croppers as a last resort. Either way it would ruin my lovely bedstead, but what the hell!

As I mounted the stairs with the blowtorch, jack and

bolt croppers (took some doing because they were quite cumbersome) in hand, I was startled to hear a key turning in the front door lock. I froze, turning to find myself confronted by Dannie and Karin. "Hello, Zoe. We thought we'd pop over and collect some of my things for a day at Mam Tor tomorrow. Do you fancy a bit of a walk with us? You could bring Flo along too?" Dannie began to say. Then, upon seeing me all tooled up enquired "What on earth have you done? Have you had some kind of problem? Is there something we can do to help?"

I looked nervously upstairs and after a few seconds carefully replied, "No, it's ok. It's nothing I can't handle, I don't think. Kind of you to offer, though."

"Are you sure? Karin is quite handy around the house!" she sniggered as Karin giggled shyly.

"No, really... " I began.

"Let me take a quick look for you. I don't mind. It looks like a very odd mix of tools you have there. Are you certain that a blowtorch, bottle jack and bolt croppers will help? Is it your central heating system?" Karin tried as she came to join me on the stairs.

"Problems with your waterworks, eh?" Dannie guffawed throwing Karin a sideways glance "You definitely need a nurse for that!"

"No! Honestly! It isn't and yes, I think these tools should do the job for me." I told her a little louder than I meant to.

Karin looked a little affronted as she reacted "Well, if you're sure you know what you're doing ... " and she moved down to stand beside Dannie again. Dannie now moved towards the stairs asking me, "Well I need to get my walking boots from your spare room if that's ok?"

Once again I eyed the landing nervously "Where are they? Shall I fetch them for you?"

"Whatever for? Is the problem in the spare room? Is my stuff damaged?" she wondered.

I laughed, a little worriedly. "Oh no. It's in my room."

"Well then, if it's alright, I'll get my things myself," she said emphatically. She and Karin exchanged quizzical looks and I led the way up the stairs. "Shall we stay and keep you company for the evening? You seem a bit fraught. You're worrying me," Dannie tried.

"No I'm fine. Really. You two go and enjoy yourselves," I informed her, adding, "I'd better set to otherwise I'll be here all night!"

"Well, let us know if you want to come out tomorrow. I think the fresh air and exercise will do you the world of good! Are you quite sure we can't help?" she advised, whilst taking a step towards my door.

"No! Don't go in there!" I almost shouted. "I ... Well, I've got someone in there!"

Dannie turned toward me with horror upon her face "Zoe! What sort of perversion requires a blowtorch, bottle jack *and bolt croppers?* Be careful, Zoe, it looks... *dangerous!*" she finished.

"I can't say! I'll tell you maybe tomorrow," I whispered. "Now go! And have a pleasant evening!" I directed. And with that I rushed back into my room, bolting the door behind me.

Immediately I set to, wrapping the now protesting Will's head in a damp towel and lighting the blowtorch. This only had the effect of making Will squeal, due to the heat of the bars on his neck and ears. I could see it was starting to leave a couple of angry-looking red marks where the bars and the lard were frying him and so I stopped and poured water onto the towel to cool things down.

Next, I scalded my fingers ramming the bottle jack in between the hot bars just below Will's rapidly purpling-red head. He now laughed at my resourcefulness and told me that I was quite handy, 'for a girl', and that he was grateful that I hadn't invited my friends in and forgotten about him. He was nearly left to spend the night there for the sexist part of that remark, I can tell you! It amused me to think of him hanging in there for the night, head between the railings like some sort of attractive, crimson gargoyle at the foot of the bed whilst I entertained my friends downstairs. It didn't amuse him very much though!

As I beavered away at the job in hand I heard Dannie and Karin shouting their goodbyes, whilst laughing really quite loudly and raucously from the foot of the stairs (heaven only knows what they were thinking by now), so I reciprocated (without the laughter). Then the front door clicked to and the key turned in the lock. They were gone. I saw that as one worry less.

Anyway, within ten energetic minutes, he was free whilst my prized, shiny, well-loved item of furniture was – I thought – irretrievably mangled. He did offer to try and fix it, but I declined politely. I thought I might get my dad to look at it if I could think up a plausible story for how it came to be so bent. There was no way I could ever tell anyone the truth!

No one would believe me for a start!

Except for possibly Dannie and Karin. But they now thought I was some sort of maniacal pervert with a thing for heavy tools, and my intuition told me that they would probably prefer to see it that way than know the unvarnished truth. It was a lot less interesting than the version they had in all likelihood concocted from the evidence they had.

Will and I sat companionably on the bed for a while, giggling like teenagers over our antics, knocking back the wine, him asking if he'd ever be forgiven and me telling him, "Oh no! You're *barred* from here in future."

"That's no good!" he replied, "*barring* unforeseen circumstances, I've been hoping to make this a regular feature of our weeks!"

By the time the wine had gone and all 'bar' jokes had been spent, we were so fatigued that both of us fell fast asleep. Curled up tightly together with Flo at our feet, I had the best night's sleep I'd had in I couldn't remember how long. It beat my usual nightly ritual by far. I just hoped I wouldn't wake up feeling guilty! There was a part of me that would be happy to never wake up.

I'd be happy to lay here forever!

Chapter 17

And I might have at least had the pleasure of one lovely whole night lying there if only his phone hadn't started to ring piercingly loud from it's position in Will's discarded trousers at three in the morning!

The shock threw us both into instant turmoil as we'd both been sleeping quite heavily. I was somewhat surprised that the ringtone blasting out was 'What a catch' by Fallout Boy, I must admit...

He bounded up bewilderedly from where he'd been previously snuggled and scrabbled about the floor to retrieve it from the now vibrating item of clothing. Squinting through the darkness at the display, he stated flatly, "It's her!"

I said nothing, just nodded grimly from my position on the bed and turned on the lamp. We both blinked rapidly in the sudden, harsh luminescence of the room and Will began to speak in a very bored monotone, devoid of any kind of feeling, to the accursed Wendy. I couldn't bear to listen to their conversation whilst I was still basking in the afterglow of our antics so, feeling punctured, I slipped on my dressing gown and trailed down to the kitchen, Flo in my wake.

The full implication of what we had done was just beginning to hit home as I turned on the kitchen light. I was his 'bit on the side', his 'other woman'. How had I let myself come to this? It was so uncharacteristic of me to allow myself to break so easily and give in to such a thoughtless act of self-centredness. I had taken something that belonged to someone else. Shameless little me! That was usually Saiorse's speciality, not mine! Although at least I now understood why she walked around with that big smile plastered on her face for so much of the time. It had been a lot of fun... I smiled wickedly then to myself.

Gosh! That had been a very brief attack of guilt for me. My guilt was legendary and could usually last for weeks.

Will strode purposefully into the kitchen just as I was putting the kettle on "Not for me, I have to go I'm afraid," he stated sadly, pointing at the kettle. He was already dressed in his now heavily crumpled clothing. His hair was plastered in every direction with its 'just dipped in an oil slick' form and there were angry red lines down both sides of his head where the heated bars had done their worst, giving Will the overall appearance of someone who had been sleeping in the gutter. And in some ways you could argue that he had, I suppose... I allowed myself a smug smirk at that thought.

"That's a shame," I answered him warmly with a small smile. "I was looking forward to our next misadventure. I thought we could maybe try a bit of scarfing?" I twirled my blue, towelling, dressing gown belt mock-provocatively in his direction.

He stared in mock horror, replying, "Are there really no lengths you won't go to for thrills, Ms Parsons? They do say the quiet ones are the worst, and now I know that's true! I imagine your friends will probably be scarred for life at the vision of you all tooled up for action! They won't forget that – or let you forget it – for some time I shouldn't think. Heaven only knows what they will think of me!" He stepped toward me, opened his arms and hugged me tightly. "I never thought or dared hope we'd end up here like this. Not after what you told me last Saturday. What changed your mind?" he wondered.

"The devil took me, I think. I'm not normally this kind of girl, but just lately my ideals have changed a bit without me realising. This is 'the new me', I think. And does that mean you care what my friends think? Will you be around long enough to meet them?" I answered.

"Mm, well, there was nothing wrong with the old you, but the new you is certainly 'livelier'. Yes, I want to be around for a long time. Can I see the new you again, do you think?" he quizzed.

"Why not? When can you get away?" I asked as I stepped away to look at him. All the better to see what he was really thinking ...

"Tomorrow evening. I'll make up some excuse and come round here, shall I?" he stated eagerly.

"If you like," I began, then as an afterthought, "Can

171

I just ask you why, if she has someone else, she's still checking up on you? I'd have thought she'd have better things to do with her time, if you get my drift?"

"The alarm went off, and as she's home alone it spooked her. If 'loverboy' had still been there she wouldn't have cared less but because he isn't, she needs someone to protect her," he detailed matter-of-factly.

"I see. So you still have your uses?" I queried.

"Only utilitarian ones. Nothing that makes my heart sing, as you can probably tell. She ceased to do that long ago. Thing is, if we have been broken into, she has nothing worth taking. All the decent, saleable stuff is mine!" he replied sadly.

"In that case, you'd better get going! You wouldn't want to lose what she hasn't already taken from you, would you?" I pointed out, adding, "shall I call you a taxi?"

"That's ok, there's one on its way," he told me.

He must be in a tearing hurry to protect his things! Nice to know where I am in the pecking order from the outset, I suppose...

"How resourceful of you. Did you call as you were getting dressed?" I asked, trying (but failing miserably) not to sound bitter.

"Yes, from my mobile. I knew I'd have to get straight back and I can hardly expect you to drive me at this hour. And we've been drinking anyway," he answered with a slightly hard edge to his voice.

No, he couldn't expect me to and I had no intention of offering! I wasn't sure how I liked being fourth in line behind his house, his possessions and her!

"Hmmm, well you'd better get your jacket and your shoes on then and wait in the hall. I'll wait to hear from you tomorrow, shall I?" I reacted as nonchalantly as I could.

He nodded and went into the hall to recover the remainder of his things. Then as he was doing up his shoes he stopped saying, "I *will* be back tomorrow. I honestly don't intend on making this a one-off if you don't."

I knelt down, hugged him tightly and told him,

"Well I should hope not! I've told you I'm not a one-night-stand kinda girl. That *hasn't* and *won't* be changing. I'll expect you here around seven, shall I? I'll make us some supper."

With that, his taxi arrived and after a brief interlude for a brief bit more lip-locking he was gone.

Feeling a bit lost now, I went back to the kitchen and made myself a soothing cup of tea, located a stray packet of Nice biscuits from my cupboard, let Flo out again, and then the two of us made our way back upstairs to my still-warm bed. It smelled of Will. And me. And sex. I knew I'd find it difficult to sleep, so I turned on my TV to watch a bit of mind-numbing, pointless, early-morning programmes. I thought that at least ought to help. Flo hopped around fluffing up the duvet, quickly settling herself as close to me as she could. Meanwhile I opened the biscuits, giving one to Flo, who crunched it gratefully, and eating several myself; scattering crumbs as I went. It didn't matter; there was only me here and I didn't care!

As I lay there in the mass of crumbs and stains and lard-covered pillows, several things occurred to me. Firstly, I would need fresh bedding in the morning. Secondly, being a bit reckless was infinitely more attractive than always being responsible. Thirdly, that I loved Will's company. Fourth, I didn't care now who knew it. Fifth, I ought to get the family's presents wrapped and delivered as soon as possible, so that I could get on with the enjoyment of the festive season without the pain of having to deal with the people who were determined to wreck it for me. Sixth, I might need to go food shopping in the morning if I was going to feed Will in the evening. Seventh, I would have enjoyed a bit of a walk along Mam Tor, but I couldn't do with either playing twenty questions with Dannie and Karin; nor did I particularly relish playing gooseberry. To that end I would text Dannie and let her know that I wouldn't be coming. I didn't want them hanging on in the morning to hear from me – or, worse still, coming here to get me – so I picked up my mobile phone from the bedside table and began immediately.

Hi D, thanks for your kind offer of a walk, but as

I'm walking like John Wayne I think I would only hold you up. It's been a long night thanks to the visit to A and E, so I'm going to have a bit of a lay-in... if I can find a position that's comfortable enough to sleep in ☺.
Zx

That ought to get their imaginations going!

Eighth, I didn't want to be alone here any more. I definitely wanted to be with Will. Ooooh! That sounded a bit bunny-boiler even to me! Now I was scaring myself! I needed to calm down and not get too attached too quickly. He was bound to have big faults, and one day – sooner or later – I would be bound to discover them. Although somehow I doubted he'd have faults as big as Knickerless!

Where did that come from? I shouldn't be thinking about him at all, and certainly not now!

By the time I got to the ninth thought, I was so shattered that I switched off the TV, the lamp, and my brain, ready for a good, long sleep. Flo huddled in more tightly still, relieved just to have her place in the bed back to herself, so I threw my arm around her and before too long we were snoring in perfect harmony.

Then, as I dosed I realised, I'd never be completely alone. I had Flo!

Chapter 18

I awoke to find the fragile winter sun picking its way –
with no thought for my still weak eyes – through my
curtains. Peering at the clock, I found that it was nearly
eleven. I stretched and yawned, rubbed my eyes, then
reached over to the lard-soiled pillow beside me just to
check that the previous evening hadn't all been some
kind of comical figment of my imagination or some
bizarre dream. The pillow was still there. The lard was
still on it. And, best of all, the bars at the foot of the bed
were still all bowed out of shape! I allowed myself a
minute of complacent fulfilment.

Flo was by now aware that I was back in the land of
the living, so came to the top of the bed to lick me
energetically and sit on my head as she always likes to
when we have a bit of a lay in. I allowed her to play
and we fought good-humouredly over Hedwig the
stuffed owl as I wasn't in any particular rush to move. I
was all too busy taking long looks at the gnarled
bedstead. Admiring our handiwork and remembering
the night before!

When I did finally find the energy to move, I
removed all the bedding, opened the bedroom windows
to allow the room to air, and then decided to hoover the
mattress before remaking the bed with some lovely
fresh linen. Then I tidied away all the tools, bowl and
jug and tingle gel tube from our efforts to remove Will
from the bedstead and put everything back to rights. All
except of course for the bedstead. I'd need to think
about that one!

That done I ran myself a bath and popped a bit of Jo
Malone bath oil in as a treat. It felt wonderful to sink
below the water and just wallow.

I had been revelling in it for about ten minutes when
my phone started to ring, so with considerable effort I
forced myself out of my little heaven to answer it. It
was Sal and she'd very obviously been talking to
Dannie.

"And just what were you doing last night that
required a man, blowtorch, a bottle jack and some bolt

175

croppers?" she laughed.

"Gosh, word has spread fast, hasn't it?" I returned, one eyebrow raised.

"Well, tell all!" She was having a bit of trouble getting her words out because she was laughing really quite hard.

"You won't believe me if I do!" I warned.

"Try me!" she stated.

And so it began. I had to recount that story several times during the course of the day – Dannie and Karin obviously took their phones for a walk with them – but it never ceased to make me smile. It never lost the power to make my friends laugh either. Also now they were very much looking forward to meeting Will. I would have to tell him that word of his sexual proclivities had spread, and he was now famous (or infamous) amongst my pals for them. Not too sure how he would feel about that …

I spent the rest of the time that day running here and there cleaning the house, shopping, walking the dog and making a delicious tartiflette with green salad and home-made sun dried tomato bread for supper. I was almost tempted to grab the butter when the bread came out of the oven, I was so hungry. I'd had a bit of porridge for a very late breakfast but no lunch as I'd sort of missed the boat for it. I noticed that it was almost six o'clock so, after uncorking another bottle of red so that it could breathe, decided to go upstairs and make myself presentable. This took me around half an hour. After a quick shower I found some matching black and green lace undies, dug out a peasant style top in black with green beading and embroidery on it and some black jeans. Pretty but relaxed. Then I threw on some makeup, some grey and green beads, ran a brush through my hair, and with a quick squirt of Chanel I was good to go.

On my way back downstairs I unearthed the family's presents and cards from the growing pile in the dressing room, selected some festive red and silver deer patterned wrapping paper and labels, located the selotape and scissors then – via the kitchen to put the tartiflette in the oven – went into the living room to act

176

on thought number five in the list of things I'd given headspace during the wee small hours. Once they were wrapped I'd take the chicken's way out and leave them for my dad to take with him when he came to let out the dog for me tomorrow. It'd save yet another argument that I could not be doing with. I was at last in a happy place and, in an uncharacteristically selfish burst, I wanted to stay there!

As I was wrapping the Kath Kidston handbag I'd bought for Saiorse the doorbell went, giving Flo an excuse to dash excitedly up and down the hall with a piece of wrapping paper in tow. Rather like a festive Andrex puppy, but older. I brushed the stray bits of paper offcuts from my person and into my hand, balling them up as I went towards the front door and stuffing them deep into my jeans pocket. I could see Will on the other side of the glass so as I opened the door I pulled him playfully in over the step fixing him with a lip lock as he fell inside. Immediately he responded and once again our hands were all over each other.

After a few moments I removed his coat whilst he took off his shoes, but instead of discarding them everywhere as we did the previous evening, we hung up the coat and put the shoes under the hallstand. I showed him into the living room that was so homely with candles burning here and there and the fire glowing away. 'The Scripts' were on the CD player so you could just hear it as background, the wine and glasses were already on the coffee table with some of the home made bread cut into chunks with garlic and basil oils and olives that were out as nibbles. "

I love your home, it's so welcoming. It's a good reflection of you," Will told me as we stepped in and sat side by side on the sofa.

"Aw, thanks. I like it here, it's not a palace but it's perfect for us girls, isn't it Flo?" I replied, looking to Flo for confirmation. She wagged her tail hard, making 'thump' noises on the varnished boards.

"Can she talk? Does she ever answer you?" Will laughed.

"She just did. With her tail," I pointed out with a smile.

"Me too!" he retorted, leaning in for another everlasting kiss.

We came up for air a good twenty minutes later and after untangling our limbs I took the opportunity to pour the drinks and check on the contents of the oven. The tartiflette was perfectly golden in its white porcelain bowl, so I piled it, some plates, cutlery, the bowl of salad and the rest of the bread onto a tray that I took into the living room and parked on the coffee table.

We ate slowly, talking all the time, laughing a lot, and just generally enjoying each other's company. Don't ask me what we talked about because I can't remember. I was far too busy watching how his eyes crinkled when he laughed and how he savoured every mouthful of food.

As we cleared the dishes from the room and stacked the dishwasher after supper I asked him if there'd been hell to pay when he got home the previous evening. Somehow Wendy hadn't noticed or had chosen not to remark on the lateness of the hour when he returned or even the state he returned in. She had only been concerned that she was protected and that – save for her – the house had been empty. She'd taken herself straight off to bed once she was satisfied that the house was secure and Will alleged he'd then fallen asleep on the sofa downstairs.

I hoped he was being honest because the truth always had a way of coming out in the end...

As far as Wendy was concerned, he was out with some old school friends the previous evening, and he was out with the same friends this evening too. She'd been told not to wait up, but Will suspected she would be waiting when he arrived home if only because she'd invited some 'friends' of her own around. Will was sure it was just the one 'friend', and if he had been bothered enough he could have gone home early and caught Wendi and her 'friend' Nick in the act...

Did he just say what I thought he said?

There were loads of Nicks in the world. It didn't have to be the same Nick, did it? I stopped midway through closing the dishwasher door and turned to look at Will.

"Did you say his name was Nick?" I asked as indifferently as I could manage.

"That's right. Nick Souter," he replied. I paled at the mention of Nick's name and hung onto the work surface to stop the world from sliding on its axis. Once again our paths crossed ... well, almost!

Will noticed immediately and reached out, pulling me to him. "My god, Zoe! You've gone white! You look like you've seen a ghost! Oh no! You weren't one of his victims were you?" he probed gently.

"Victims? You... you know what he *did*?" I questioned confusedly.

"I told you last week that I'd prosecuted her new friend for something a while back? Yes, I know what he did. Were you a victim? I thought I'd seen you somewhere before. Was it in court? How awful for you!" he tried again.

"Yes, it was in court. I was his biggest victim. I was the idiot he was engaged to at the time," I responded morosely. All the old feelings of revulsion, shame, inferiority and emptiness washed over me like a tidal wave of epic proportions. I was never going to be abled to wash that Nick right outta my hair...

Will pulled me close to him, telling me "I'm so sorry for what you must have gone through. All those pairs of other women's underwear he'd abused and hidden under your nose, so to speak. Wendy has no idea, of course; I want her to find out the hard way about his little 'fixation'. That way it'll hurt more. I'm not at all sure he isn't just seeing her to hit back at me, but of course it isn't me he's hurting. I couldn't care less about her. Although I do wish she hadn't let him into our house. It just feels like a violation. Still, as soon as the market picks up I'm going to sell the house anyway so I'm not going to lose too much sleep over it!"

"One hundred and twenty-three. They weren't under my nose, they were locked in his gun cabinet. Not that he had a gun! Though I thought he did," I informed him, without realising I'd been counting his words. "So at least he wasn't armed when he was stalking the women or stealing their knickers. He just stole them from the washing lines. But yes, it was a massive shock. Not *just* because he'd violated all those other women after stalking them without me even being aware of it, but also because I couldn't have been enough for him either. I thought I knew him! I will never forgive him for any of it! Maybe you have the pair of them all wrong though? Maybe they will run off into the sunset together and we'll never have to see either of them ever again? Nick always has to get what he wants. He can't bear being told 'no!'" I advised, a little tearfully.

"One hundred and twenty-three what? And no, she won't do that!" he grunted. "He's just a groundsman, there's no status in it for her. She likes being able to tell her friends that her boyfriend is a solicitor and that we live on Knob Hill. He's just another bit of fun for her! Another dirty, little secret! Mark my words, he may not like the word 'no' but he'll get used to it if he's seeing Wendy!" he reacted resentfully.

"Well, we can at least hope! Maybe fate will be on both our sides for once and move the pair of them on?" I said almost to myself, dwelling on the fact that I was now counting without noticing I was doing it. I have to admit I felt slightly alarmed at that. The little voice of my friend Moonbeam was in my head telling me to "Be careful what I wished for!"

"Yes. Let's hope. They can't take that away from us, can they?" he laughed softly.

"No. They can't take that away from us," I said quietly.

We spent several hours just talking, hugging, fondling and kissing each other. It was tender, heartfelt, sensitive and attentive. A world apart from the exploits of the previous evening. Two people crushed together by the weight of someone else's self-interested games. I had never wanted anyone more than I wanted Will then. And I had never hated anyone more than I hated Nick. I desperately wished he would get out of my life and stop popping up like an evil jack-in-a-box at unexpected moments to give me such terrible, unanticipated shocks. My whole relationship with him had been punctuated by this, and it was a continuing pattern regardless of whether I ignored his existence or not!

I could always try to find him and ask him to leave.

I could always get someone else to find him and threaten him. Make him leave.

There had to be a way to get rid of him. And hopefully if he went, Wendy might leave with him?

This required further, careful thought. But I'd wait until I was alone and just enjoy concentrating all my energies on Will for the time I had him here.

By now it was after midnight and we both had work in the morning. Neither of us wanted to break up our little party though, so somewhere along the line we decided to continue it upstairs. It was an inevitable conclusion. After locking up and letting Flo out I made us some coffee and we retired upstairs. Will guffawed at the bedstead whilst trying to look contrite, so I let him in on the fact that I had been forced to tell several of my friends due to the jungle drums in the form of Dannie and Karin and their mobile phones telling everyone half a story. He didn't seem to mind too much and laughed along with me as I recalled the conversations and shocked tones of my friends asking why I'd needed tools for a night in with him.

We managed to have fun without damaging any more of the house and fell asleep in a pile of mixed limbs sometime around one thirty. Will set his phone alarm to go off at six so that he could go home to change and get ready for work. It would be an early start for us both but we wanted it that way. The more time we could spend together the more contented we would both be.

For now.

Chapter 19

And so soon it was Monday again. The weekend had flown past like Concorde on a mission, but it had been lovely to spend so much of it with someone who made me feel so comfortable in my own skin. Will seemed to put no call on me, seemed to make no judgements and didn't mind that I was a bit ... well, wild at the moment. Having said that he didn't really know me of old to know that I was behaving so out of character. How would he react I wonder if the old Zoe came back and ousted the new, improved, dangerous Zoe? We'd deal with that when it happened!

Will awoke on the alarm and forced himself out of my warm, damaged bed. We squeezed into the shower together − sharing the soap in a random, getting-to-know-you session − and then while he dressed I pulled on my dressing gown and made some tea. Flo was desperate to go out but then torn because she was so enjoying having Will there to play up to. I could hear him spiritedly tackling her for her toy on the landing (squeaky floorboards) as she barked lightly and ran in small circles at his heels. They were soon done with their game though. Flo came belting into the kitchen with Hedwig clamped firmly between her jaws, and Will wasn't far behind her. He came and sat down in the kitchen as I was plating up some toast and setting it on the table.

We ate quietly − almost thoughtfully − all the time smiling at each other as if sharing a private joke. Finally, as he was taking his last bite, Will asked, "Are you around tonight, or are you busy?"

"Much to my disappointment I'm busy. I have tickets to go and see 'Calendar Girls' at the local theatre with a couple of friends," I replied, unsmiling now.

"Oh, that's a shame! Although not for you, obviously. I suppose I'll just have to find something else to occupy my time tonight then." He said with a mischievous glint in his eye.

"As long as its 'something' and not 'someone' I

shan't worry," I threw back.

"Are you kidding? You haven't left any room for 'someone' else! You're both addictive and insatiable!" he grinned.

"Well, it had been rather a long time since my last... encounter." I smiled wickedly. "Obviously it showed!"

"Someone else's loss was definitely my gain there!" he told me. "So how about Tuesday? Would it be ok to come over on Tuesday night? Unless you'd rather go out?"

"No, I don't think either of us has money to burn at the moment. And we need to be a bit careful about being seen, don't we? Come round here and we'll watch a film and have a curry. I'll make the curry, you fetch a film. Better make it about eight though because I have a lot of work for a local funeral to see to on Tuesday. Is that a fair arrangement?" I asked.

"Oooh, sounds perfect! I'll look forward to it," he replied, brushing away a couple of stray toast crumbs and standing up. He opened the dishwasher and loaded his breakfast pots into it along with my empty plate then turning to me he said "Much though I don't want to, I have to be going. I have a meeting at eight thirty and I can't be late."

I hugged him. "That's ok. It was lovely to have you here for the night. You'll need to move quickly if you are going home to change, or else you *will* be late!"

I saw him off then began to make myself ready for my own working day. Although I would very much have preferred to hang around the house in my pyjamas, watching daytime TV and eating junk food I forced myself back into the bathroom to continue my ablutions and make a bit of a silk purse out of this untidy, unruly sow's ear.

By eight thirty I had sorted myself out, taken Flo for a short walk, made my bed (in more ways than one) and was on the road on my way to work. The traffic wasn't too bad for a Monday so it didn't take too long to get there. I was quite grateful for this because my concentration was darting from one thing to another in my head and not leaving much for use on driving my little Fiesta. Still, luckily no one died!

On arrival at the shop I opened up and sorted out pretty quickly. The deliveries stood to attention on the counter top with their neat little list ready for Ralph to take away, the flowers were in their place on the shelves ready to be seen and bought, the till was set up and the phones were ready for a (hopefully) busy day ahead.

Ralph lumbered into the shop just as I had finished, asking "What happened to you? You look like the cat that got the cream?"

"Do I? Well I have no idea why. Maybe I've just had a good weekend?" I replied, reddening a little (I could feel my cheeks burning) and turning away.

"Come on then, spill! Why did you have a good weekend? What have you been up to?" he pushed.

"Nothing much. Booked to go away at Christmas. Bought myself some new skiwear for the trip. Got a new pet man," I grinned broadly.

"A new *what* now?" Ralph asked incredulously. "Did you just say 'pet man'?"

"That's right. My old Nan used to call all her boyfriends her 'pet men'. They were all quite flattered by it I think," I answered.

Ralph looked a little concerned. I wasn't sure if it was because I had a boyfriend or because I had referred to him as a 'pet man', but it was amusing to watch. "Ralph, you seem worried by that news," I said finally.

He looked at me for a few seconds as if considering his reply, then told me, "Not worried exactly. I suppose I thought you were going to remain forever a spinster of this parish. You seemed to have a bit of an aversion to even the thought of having a boyfriend until now. I always got the impression someone had put you off for life – as if maybe you'd met with one of those men who rips the heads off cabbage patch dolls, and then burns the stuffing from inside it for laughs – so it's a bit of a surprise to find that you've suddenly hooked up with someone over the weekend. How well do you know him?" Ralph questioned. "Has he been a friend for a while? Is he decent? Hardworking? Trustworthy? Zoe-worthy, even?" he persisted.

"Wow, Ralph! You are more perceptive than I gave

you credit for! My previous boyfriend was a perpetrator of many a cabbage-patch massacre, so well done for spotting that! My new pet man is a friend – although it has to be said a relatively new one – and yes, he is hardworking, clean, kind to animals, decent unless the occasion calls for indecency, and I think he is absolutely Zoe-worthy. Though of course time might prove otherwise. But thank you for caring, Ralph," I informed him, patting his arm gently for effect. Then as an afterthought I added, "He's been in the shop before. If he comes in again I'll introduce you."

Ralph turned to the job in hand and began to pick up the orders from the counter. "Huh! Well I hope you're right! I hope he does know how to treat you properly! I wouldn't want to have to go and break his legs before Christmas because he's done something to upset you. It's not a very seasonal thing to do to someone, is it? Break their legs. Is he going with you to wherever you are going at Christmas? Will he be needing his legs for it?" he chuntered, only half to himself.

"Oh Ralph! Will is a solicitor so best you don't break his legs! He'll sue you! And I'm going skiing to France on my own. It was booked before we got together," I told him.

"Isn't he bothered that you're off on your own? That's a bit brave, isn't it? Aren't you meant to do it with others? Safety in numbers and all that?" He sounded worried now.

"I will be. It's a kind of a singles tour, so there'll be plenty of people to buddy up with. I'm quite looking forward to it. Although I'd be looking forward to it a whole lot more if Will was coming with me," I replied wistfully.

"Hmmm, well, I'm not sure if you were my girlfriend that I'd be ok with you wandering hither and yon on your own. What if some nutcase takes a shine to you? I'd be moving heaven and earth to be with you if I were him!" And with that he turned to take the deliveries out to the van.

It was quite touching, really. Ralph was turning into my own personal bodyguard, and whilst I supposed I should be cautious I was finding it rather... reassuring!

The rest of my day was pretty uneventful until one thirty. I'd just had a jacket potato from the local takeaway. It came with chicken and chilli sauce so it warmed the insides nicely. As I was clearing the container and plastic cutlery into the bin, I heard the over-the-door ping a warning, so I turned to greet the customer as they came through the door. As I did so, I stopped dead in my tracks.

It was Knickerless.

"What do you want? You've got a nerve coming into my shop! Go on, get out!" I shouted.

"Now, Zoe! Don't be hasty! I just wanted to buy some of those red roses from you. Are you so minted that you can turn down custom?" he asked, grinning like an idiot.

"My financial situation is no business of yours! Leaving roses as a calling card these days are you, you filthy pervert?" I yelled, loud enough to wake Mrs Griffiths from her eternal slumber.

"Don't be silly Zoe!" he replied, no longer grinning "Of course not! I don't do those things any more! I've paid the price, can't we just forget about that now?" he said more quietly.

"Never! You put me through hell, demean me – and several dozen other women to boot – shake the very foundations of my beliefs and my life, then stroll back in here like you've been away on a short holiday and I should arrange a celebration and kill the proverbial fatted calf! I know what I'd like to kill, I'm looking at it right now! Get out, and don't come back!" I spat.

"So you won't sell me some roses then? Zoe, I don't want any trouble, I just wanted to let you know that I'm back in town but I don't want any trouble. I'm seeing someone and I'm working, so my life's pretty settled. I was hoping that after all this time there'd be no hard feelings," he tried.

"No hard feelings?" I shouted, incredulous at his audacity. "Who do you think you are? Your life was settled with me once! You promised me that you'd stay away from this town when you got let back into society. Your promises are still as empty as your trousers, I see! Of course there are hard feelings! Not just mine, either! I don't imagine that any of your victims will be overjoyed to see you back round here! You really are one shameless piece of work, aren't you? And how on earth have you managed to find someone dim enough to date you? Is she for real, or does she just not know the truth about you? Give me her address and I'll happily send her some roses for free! With a beautiful card explaining what a sick, sad, little person she is seeing!" I finished with venom.

"Of course she knows about my past! There'd be no point trying to keep that quiet in a small place like this! Someone would be bound to tell her if I hadn't," he defended.

"Then she's as bad as you and deserves all she gets! Just as you do! Now get lost and don't come back! Stay away from me or else!" I threatened.

He stared at me for a long moment and opened his mouth as he had found something left to say but then closed it, turned quickly then slammed out of the shop.

I sat down heavily on the stool in the back of the shop to get my breath back. He was turning into my worst nightmare. We'd only been talking about him the previous evening and here he was back on my doorstep, stirring up all the old feelings of disgust and ire! I'd have to think about an injunction if this continued. Luckily I was sleeping with a solicitor.

Maybe I could get Will to sort out an injunction for payment in kind? That could be enjoyable.

Slowly I went into the back of the shop to make myself a drink and compose what was left of me. Before I had chance to even climb off the stool, the shop door again swung open, and this time a wiry, unkempt man ducked almost furtively into the shop. Looking like a poor man's Clouseau in a heavily crumpled raincoat, he looked deliberately around the walls, the floor and the counter tops before selecting a cute Christmas arrangement with a deer in it. Holding it out with a ten pound note, he asked, "Did I just see Knickerless Nick in here?"

Shocked I replied confusedly "Yes, you did. Do you know him?"

The man grimaced a little. "I know of him, yes. I

was hoping I'd never come face to face with the filthy pervert though!"

I stared at the dishevelled gent wondering, "Were you one of the newspaper reporters at the trial? I'm sure I know you from somewhere?"

Taking the change and the wrapped arrangement I was now proffering, he told me, "Something like that, yes. Thanks for this." And with that, he was gone.

So, Nick was being watched by a reporter? Made me wonder what they knew that the rest of us didn't. Perhaps Nick was up to his old tricks, and the man I'd just met was following hi in the hopes of catching him in the act? Nothing would surprise me; after all, leopards don't change their spots, do they?

It took me a large mug of green tea and five minutes to catch up with myself after Nick and his stalker left, but in my mind I quickly resolved to try and put the episode behind me. Just pretend he didn't exist. With luck he and Wendy would disappear sooner or later and do us all a favour. I couldn't wait to tell Will all about it, though, and make him an offer on an injunction. It registered at the back of my mind, though, that Nick must mean business in the relationship stakes if he was buying Wendy roses...

By the time Ralph came back from the afternoon deliveries the shop was clean, tidy and ready for closing. I'd channelled some of the anger Nick's visit had stimulated into cleaning and organising the shop and the shelves, speaking to Len to order some festive bits and bobs for resale, and all the many flowers for Mrs Griffiths' funeral from the locals and her family.

Ralph took one look at me and knew that the Zoe he now saw before him was not the same chirpy, happy Zoe from this morning. He clucked and fussed around me like a large, round, mother hen around a sick chick, trying to pry out of me what had sent my previous good humour on a trip never to return, but I couldn't bring myself to tell him. I could barely even concentrate on his questions. All I could do was count the words he uttered in each sentence.

After all this time – much though I hated to admit it – my life with Nick was still too raw and embarrassing to deal with, and provoked me into 'shut down' mode however hard I tried to fight it.

I made my way home in a single-minded mood. It didn't take me long to get back in the house and the kitchen where I could pour all my ill will into some 'revenge' bakery. I took a couple of tins of a particular dog food from the cupboard, added herbs, garlic and extra thick gravy, then put the mixture into the rich, buttery, herby short-crust pastry I'd whipped up with my own fair hand and extra added wrath. Flo was driven to distraction by the smells, so when the pies came out of the oven I set one aside as a treat for her. After letting her out and helping myself to some quiche, salad, and new potatoes from my fridge, I got myself ready for a night at the theatre.

I was now all the more resolute that tonight would be a good one. Something had to make up for the disappointment of today!

And it had started out so well, too!

Chapter 20

Despite my best efforts, those of my friends, and the Thumpington and Clagdale Strollers, the evening passed slowly with little to recommend it. I watched but did not see the local theatrical production of Calendar Girls. The audience laughed uproariously, they were clearly enjoying what was a very spirited performance but - protected by my fuzzy blanket of disbelief and despondency – I missed most of the jokes because somehow I only heard words in terms of numbers.

My friends were all so kind, they understood (not about the counting thing, I couldn't tell anyone about that! They'd think I'd lost the plot!). They were all so thoughtful and considerate and – once they heard the whole story of what had happened with Nick – fully empathised with how I felt. Loose comical scenarios were bandied around for 'payback' and revenge on him but nothing really penetrated the impenetrable Plexiglas barrier I was beginning to build in my head. The only things that made me smile all evening momentarily were the raunchy the texts I received from Will.

I couldn't wait to see him again and fill him in on the encounter with Nick in the shop. I wondered briefly what he would make of it all and how he would feel about another man (and I use the term very loosely) sending Wendy roses. Would it bother him, or would he feel nothing at all? How would she hide the fact that they'd come from Knickerless? Would she be brazen enough to keep them, or be devious enough to realise that she'd need to throw them away?

Anyway, it was a relief at the end of the night to make it home to the refuge of my little, old cottage with its welcoming atmosphere and my waggy, licky, fluffy, dog. I knew I'd feel safe here protected by these solid, brick walls. Safe from the hard knocks and bangs of the outside world. Even when others come into my life wielding large, rubber mallets and dangerous jackhammers that mean to crush and smash holes in the hearts of the innocent and unaware, my own impenetrable front door would keep me sheltered and protected. It's much more than just a little, old cottage to me. It's my fortress too!

The following day I had such a lot to do. There were fourteen different sprays, wreaths and large floral tributes for Mrs Griffiths from various neighbours, friends and family of the deceased. We local shop owners wanted to send her a tribute from all of us too. Ralph and I conferred with them and between us we'd decided to give her an 'angels' wings' wreath of double white chrysanthemums complete with a halo of white roses and baby's breath. She was always around inspiring us all to do our bit by fundraising for the locality and other national charities. She had led local Guide troops, taken charge of playgroups, raised funds to build a new community centre, and – in her younger days – fostered many children along with gentle, kindly, old Mr Griffiths. He would miss her greatly now she had gone. I had a 'gates of heaven' to make from him, and a harp from several of the children they had fostered who were now all grown up and had clubbed together to get something 'substantial' for the very worthy lady who so loved them, us, life, the universe, and everything.

I arrived at seven thirty and started on the orders immediately. Len arrived at half past eight just as I was using up the last of the previous day's flowers with the order for everything I needed to fulfil all my obligations. Ali was coming at ten and between the two of us it would be a long day but I couldn't think of anyone I'd rather work so hard for. Mrs Griffiths was deserving of a funeral fit for a queen, and by the hands of everyone who loved her she would get one too.

By six that evening everything was ready for early delivery the next morning. The funeral was set for ten the next morning. The shop was now clean and tidy, the unused flowers were safely stored in buckets in the cold room, the delivery list was made out, and Ali had been paid from the till for all her hard labours. The shop smelled gorgeous, too. Like a bottle of freesia eau de cologne that had lost its stopper, the blooms mingled their scents and touched every millimetre of the usually musty air in the shop making it heavenly.

As Ralph emptied the bins and locked up the back door I said a silent prayer for Mrs Griffiths and thanked her for gracing us with her personality and her loving self. She was truly one in a million and we'd all miss her loads.

Quietly, respectfully – almost reverently – we turned out the lights on the shop and in hushed tones said our goodnights. It had been a tiring, busy day and I couldn't wait to get home, get clean and see Will again!

Once home, I sorted out Flo, set the curry on in my slow cooker, then took myself upstairs to get a quick shower and change into something clean and comfortable. It didn't take me too long, and by just after seven thirty I was more than ready for a sit down and a chill-out. I poked the curry with a wooden spoon, put some rice in a pan, and the Indian snacks were on a tray ready for the oven. Time to light my favourite candles and pour myself a glass of something crisp and white. By the time Will arrived (suitably early at ten to eight) I was almost down to the bottom of my first glass and – due to the fact that I hadn't eaten since breakfast time – feeling a little bit squiffy!

I dragged him through the door and sucked the face off him in a way that was definitely not ladylike, and possibly rather slutty to anyone watching. It didn't seem to put him off though. Quite the contrary, he came on as strongly as a glass of water after a Fisherman's Friend! Took my breath clean away!

After a few minutes of this, we removed his outdoor things and grappled our way into the living room where we toppled onto the sofa and landed in a somewhat frenzied, haphazard heap. Clothes were shredded then hurled hither and yon about the room as we tore into each other like vampires in a blood bank, enjoying a happy meal. I had never wanted to 'bite' anyone in the same way as I did him. I could just gobble him up with a spoon, and then gnaw noisily on the bones!

He remarked later that he had no idea that I had a secret life as 'Elvira, Mistress of the Dark'. His new Superdry leather jacket would never see the light of day again, and his ridiculously expensive jeans looked like

192

they'd been made by Vivienne Westwood at the height of her punk days by the time we'd finished. I'm still not sure where or how it happened. It was for a short time as if I was temporarily possessed by the spirit of a vampire! Everything was happening so hastily and in such a blur! This didn't detract from the fun though! Flo took herself to hide behind the sofa, out of harm's way.

By eight fifteen we were panting like marathon runners after a particularly difficult, uphill course. Both of us were covered in angry, juvenile love bites, and naked, sweating and grinning from ear to ear! I poured us both a drink from the well-chilled bottle of chardonnay and as he quaffed his gratefully I proceeded to empty a little of mine onto his torso then feverishly lick it off. He moaned loudly as if I'd stuck him from behind with a baseball bat and we were on for round two.

Eventually, and with tremendous effort we were through and lying together on the floor (the sofa was just not enough) in a tight clinch. "Are you hungry?" I enquired.

"Ravenous!" he smiled.

"Shall we eat?" I tested.

"Thought you'd never ask!" he replied.

I pulled one of the throws on in a loose sari fashion and went with an effort into the kitchen. Five minutes later Will followed me, wearing his slightly torn shirt and what was left of his boxers. I hooted at the sight, so in retaliation Will grabbed at my sari and made to loosen it from my aching, bruised and bitten frame. I smiled wickedly, warning him, "Do you really want to start something you won't be able to finish?"

"Hah!" He began "Who won't be able to finish it? Shall we just see about that?"

And so we christened the kitchen table in a way that no kitchen table ought to be christened. I'd need a new saltcellar in the morning!

Eventually we did get around to eating. It was all the more delicious for both of us being voraciously hungry too. There weren't too many scraps for Flo to hoover away! We didn't get to watch the film he'd brought though, because we spent several hours afterwards just talking and getting to know more about each other. We discussed our day, the trip I'd had to the theatre the previous evening, our families, our childhood, the state of the world and how the perpetrators of crime seem to have more rights these days than the victims. This led me to Nick and his visit to the shop the previous day. Will had almost managed to make me forget all about it. Almost, but not quite. He really must try harder next time!

I recounted the story to Will of how Nick had called in to the shop, explaining how enraged and upset I'd become just at the very sight of him. I communicated my angst at Nick's stubbornness, selfishness and plain short-sightedness of what he had done and was still doing. How he was making me (and probably all his victims too) feel by remaining here in town after promising he wouldn't. I then filled Will in on Nick's admittance that he was seeing someone. And that he wanted to buy roses for her. Roses that were - in all likelihood - for Wendy. Roses that Will would have to have seen had I sold them to Nick...

Will was quiet for a time. He stared into his glass, took a good, long swig, looked away and then finally he said, "Well, he got roses for her from somewhere, because there was a vase in the hall last night when I got home full of them. What can I use to kill them off?" he wondered with a false smile and a glint of anger in his eyes.

"You mustn't do that! She'll know that you know where they came from then! It'll give the game away and it might be enough to make her dump him! Better to kill Wendy and Nick than take it out on some innocent flowers!" I told him, slightly shocked that he seemed upset, and for myself only half-joking about killing off Nick. Also I was anxious that he might thoughtlessly, needlessly give the game away if he got too upset.

Suddenly I needed to know, "Are you angry because you still want her, or angry because they are rubbing your nose in it?"

"Want her back? God, no! I'm angry because she's

rubbing my nose in it! And you're right of course, I can't let on that I know what she's up to. I'll just have to hope she falls so heavily for him that she'll agree to split up with me. Then we can be a proper couple," he spoke warmly.

I had no doubts in my mind that he was serious, so I tried "Do you honestly think that if she knew about us, or if you left her or chucked her out now, she'd do away with herself?"

"I think she would, yes. If only to spite me! Because she's a solipsistic, vindictive, gold-digging cow," he stated dangerously softly. "She hates me but loves what she thinks I can provide as I told you before."

"Well, the pair of them ruined my night last night so I don't intend to let them ruin tonight as well. Come upstairs with me and I'll make you forget all about it!" I promised, taking his hand and pulling him upstairs.

We didn't get much sleep, but we didn't accumulate any more bruises either!

Chapter 21

The next morning (after only a couple of hours sleep) I woke up to find that Will was already up, buzzing around the bedroom and dressed in his ripped, violated clothing. He looked like a victim of some kind of aggressive assault! There was a mug of steaming hot tea on my bedside table along with yoghurt, a banana and a small spoon. This made me smile. Bananas on a bedside table just seemed to cry out for batteries somehow!

Flo moved in for a tickle as I sat up and beamed now at Will. "Are you going home, or straight to work dressed like that?" I asked. "People will think you're the victim of some terrible attack."

"Are you kidding? I look like an extra from Michael Jackson's Thriller video! See?" he said, pulling at the neck of his torn shirt to reveal a couple of pretty annoyed-looking scratches and a love bite. "I'm this colour practically everywhere, Ms Parsons, and thanks to sleep deprivation I have eye bags down to my knees!" He sat on the edge of the bed now holding my hand. "You are one mad woman, and I spend every minute I'm not with you wishing that I was!"

"Me too. Even though you bring out the depraved side of me. Are you coming over tonight, or will it be difficult to get away, do you think?" I queried.

"I have a meeting at five, which should probably end around six thirty to seven, but I can come around then if that's ok? I can tell her that I'm working late. I don't care what she thinks. If she thinks at all it'll be a first!" he smiled. "I have to go now. Drink your tea before it gets cold. I've let out the dog and fed her already, so you only need to see to yourself. Oh, and the wreckage in the living room!"

"You are so sweet! Thank you for that. I'll spend all day looking forward to tonight. You'd better get going. Don't wear your best clothes to come over tonight, because I'd feel terrible if anything happened to them!" I smirked naughtily and he leaned in for a lip lock.

After he left I drank my tea and ate my yoghurt. I

couldn't somehow bring myself to munch on the banana yet. Next I took myself downstairs – Flo in my wake – to make good the damage in the living room so that my father wouldn't think the place had been ransacked when he came round to let the dog out. I threw away the leggings that I'd worn the previous evening but were now clung to the fireplace, because they were a little like me... beyond salvation! As was my beautiful, fuchsia, silk underwear, which now enhanced the television and the chair, respectively. This relationship was going to be costly in more ways than one, if this level of lust were to continue!

I made a mental note to myself to maybe let him get through the door without tearing up both the guy and his garments this evening. He'd be thinking I truly was insatiable at this rate!

Soon after, I stood under the harsh heat of the water in the shower watching the drops as they beat down abrasively on my naughty, gluttonous, little body. The soap sadly washed away the smell of Will but it did nothing to remove the bruises and bites I was covered in. I leaned back against the glass tiles on the wall, closed my eyes and let parts of our exploits play out like graphic technicolour in front of them. The memory of it was hotter by far than the water and would keep me amused all day. I dragged myself away, dressed, put on my best work persona and, telling Flo to guard the castle, made my way to work.

As I arrived at the shop, Ralph was loading the many tributes for Mrs Griffiths into the van. He'd already opened up, put the float into the till, turned the phones over so that they were no longer on answerphone, and put the flowers on display front of shop. I smiled to myself at his thoughtful diligence. He really was a gem!

He looked up from his work as I came in remarking, "Someone looks tired! Was yesterday a bit too much for you?"

"Something like that, yes," I replied, smirking.

He searched my face and then told me, "You look as though you've not slept. Have you had a rough night? You're a bit peaky. Are you ok?"

"Yes, I'm fine. *Better* than fine. Just a bit tired," I reassured him whilst thinking to myself that 'rough' was the word. 'Rough' conjured up all kinds of images from last night! "Do you need a hand to get this lot into the van?" I wondered.

"Nope, got it all covered! You just get that kettle on, have a sit down and I'll be back to help you before you know it!" he informed me with a wink.

Contrary to his promise, Ralph didn't return right away. In fact, the hearse conveying Mrs Griffiths' body to her final rest came past the shop before Ralph returned. Her husband had ordered a Victorian coach-type hearse with two magnificent white horses to take Mrs Griffiths to the peaceful, picturesque churchyard of St Barnaby's in Clagdale where she had spent so many hours worshipping.

As the Hearse passed, all of the local shop owners – myself included – came out to bid her a fond farewell. The ensemble paraded past dutifully at the traditional snails pace and all us onlookers stood forlornly and deferentially to attention with heads bowed.

Mrs Griffiths, in typical Mrs Griffiths style, had other ideas about how her last tour of the town she had so loved should go. She never did know when to quit, and she was not about to make today any different from any other. We all watched in a mixture of horror and incredulity as the hearse doors somehow pinged open of their own volition and Mrs Griffiths' coffin began to quietly, and almost surreptitiously slide out. Luckily she didn't get too far before it was spotted by one of the coachmen. They held up the entire procession while she was reverently slid back into place and the doors firmly shut once more.

It would seem that Mrs Griffiths had wanted to ride in the car with Mr Griffiths and the rest of her family. And what Mrs Griffiths wanted, she generally had a way of getting! That was how we'd come to have a brand new community centre, after all! Two minutes more and she'd have been wedged firmly in the front seat through the windscreen!

We would never forget the thoughtful, helpful, kindly old girl, for many, many reasons. This would be one more reason never to forget her!

When I'd stopped laughing (wrong on many levels, but you needed to be there to understand), I went back into the shop to answer the phone. It was ringing fit to bust, so I picked it up and began, "Scents of Humour, Zoe speaking. Can I help you?"

"Zoe, it's me. I'm sorry to call you at work but I wondered if you'd seen Duncan on your travels? He's been a little out-of-sorts recently and he seems to have vanished," gabbled a distraught Joy from the other end.

"Oh, dear! No, I'm afraid I haven't seen him for a while now, Joy. In fact the last time I saw him was at your house about a month ago when I came for tea. When did he disappear?" I questioned.

"This morning. It was around five o'clock-ish because I heard the door go and it woke me up." She was beginning to cry now. I could hear muffled sniffs coming down the line. Knowing Duncan it was likely that he'd suddenly taken it upon himself to take up fishing and had decided to go and catch some sticklebacks for their tea!

"Are you sure he's not just gone off for a walk or something?" I tried.

"At five in the morning? In the pitch black and the cold? It's unlikely but as I said, he's been a bit quiet and out of sorts so it's not impossible, I suppose," she responded.

"Well there you go then! He probably just wanted to clear his head a bit!" I reassured her.

"Hmm, maybe. Look, if you see him will you do something for me, will you let me know? I'll keep my mobile switched on. I'm going to go for a drive round, see if I can see him anywhere," she told me, sounding a little frantic now.

"Of course I will. In fact, I'll do better than that! If I see him, I'll bring him in for a cuppa, give him a good ticking off, and get him to ring you himself!" I promised.

Joy was always worried for Duncan, but now she seemed positively alarmed. "Thanks. Got to dash!" she finished, and with that the line went dead. I didn't expect to see Duncan around here. I expected she'd find him sat by some lake or river somewhere, makeshift rod in hand, bobble hat jammed hard to his head (rather like one of Mr Sideeebottoomme's dwerves!), trying his hand at fishing. Duncan was eccentric like that. If the notion took him to do something he would just follow it. Sometimes in the past I'd wished I could be more like him. Although lately, I mused, I had been!

Ralph returned a short while after this, bearing two large, plump, white ham, salad rolls and a couple of cholesterol-laden cream buns from the bakery over the road. I couldn't be bothered to ask what had taken him so long because it was so unlike him to be tardy with his timekeeping. With Ralph there was likely to have been a very good reason and he'd no doubt tell me himself when he was ready. I made us two large mugs of coffee and we sat in the back of the shop perched on stools at the workstation in amicable silence, munching on the goodies Ralph had brought.

After a while he let on that the traffic through our little town had been held up for quite some way by the cortege of Mrs Griffiths, hence the lateness returning to the shop. I filled him in on her attempted untimely escape from the Hearse and we laughed together at our dear old friend who never gave in!

Then he asked me why I hadn't slept. I thought about telling him but decided that in all fairness, it would just be way too much information. Instead I told him that a friend had been round for tea and we'd been carried away talking and forgotten the time. (Not quite the truth, but not quite a lie either.) This seemed to resonate with Ralph. Then he began asking about Will, as though he knew this was the friend who came to tea.

Ralph had become concerned that I might get hurt because he'd remembered that Will had been in recently buying revenge foods for his 'girlfriend'. Much though I didn't want to (believe me, I know how bad it sounds to others), I carefully, painstakingly explained Will's tricky living situation with the unfaithful Wendy to Ralph. I needed him to understand that I in no way felt afraid that I would be injured by the situation I was now in. I'm not sure why I needed him to understand. I just... did!

He asked if I didn't think that Will had fed me the old 'my missus doesn't understand me' routine, and whether I could stomach long term being 'the other woman'. I reassured him that I didn't mind and I could cope and – because I couldn't bring myself to divulge the entire situation to Ralph, including Nick's part in it – I don't think he believed me. In fact we ended up agreeing to disagree about the whole thing, which was a shame because I rather like Ralph; he's got good morals and a kind heart. But maybe that's his problem...

The old Zoe had those things too. The new one, not so much!

As we were starting to get a little heated in our 'agreeing to disagree-ment', a lady came in for a revenge pie along with a tub of chilli-chocolate ice cream. Ralph served her and I could hear the lady giving her story to him as he went about his work. She had been given a brooch – a family heirloom – by her mother, and her husband had sold it behind her back to pay off a gambling debt she was unaware he had run up. She was devastated at all his deviousness and lies and wanted to feel a little like she'd had some payback. She'd heard about our 'revenge foods' through a friend, so had decided to be a bit devious on her own account by feeding him firstly the pie, then burning his mouth out with the ice-cream as payback for lying. It seemed like a great plan to me! I doubted it would stop such a selfish man from ever lying again, but maybe if she fed him the chocolate and scotch bonnet chilli ice-cream *every time* he lied, it might purge him of his bad habits!

Whilst Ralph was in the middle of listening to this story we had another visitor.

Much to my surprise, Duncan came strolling, in bearing Joy's brown, pink gingham-covered wicker basket. It was loaded to its brim with creamy coloured, earth-covered mushrooms of all different types. Duncan was clearly thrilled with his morning's work and seemingly oblivious to Joy's distress. I peered down into the parcel he held out to me a little dubiously. I was certain that some of them weren't mushrooms at

201

all. In fact, I wouldn't want to play 'Russian roulette' with my life and try tasting them for him, not one bit! Nevertheless, I congratulated him on his finds and brought him into the back of the shop to warm up with a cuppa so that I could give him a ticking off for frightening Joy and hopefully, get him to phone her.

Whilst I made him a drink, he sat listening through the partition as the lady in the front of the shop spoke to Ralph. As I came to sit with him he remarked in a low, hushed tone so as not to be overheard, "You know, some of my funnier mushrooms would make an *interesting* revenge food."

I didn't quite follow him so confusedly I asked, "Come again, Duncan? I'm not sure I follow you."

Suddenly he lunged down to search through his basket on the floor. Just as suddenly he bobbed up, proudly clutching a small, brown pointy-looking 'shroom with a rather straggly stalk.

"This, for instance, would have a *magical* effect all of its own in one of your revenge pies." He winked conspiratorially for effect and I suddenly caught his meaning.

"Oh!" I cried. He waved his hand to his mouth manically in the 'hush' position so I dropped my tone. "Oh, wow! Yes, I see what you mean! Well, it's a thought!" I said pensively.

And it really was ... but not for the reasons either of us would have imagined.

I gave Duncan tea and a large slice of my mind for upsetting Joy that afternoon. He soon saw the error of his ways and very quickly called her to apologise. She came around some twenty minutes later in her little red Micra to pick him up because a low, damp, grey mist had settled in over us and she didn't want him to get wet walking home. I don't think it was ever really a worry dressed in his green wellies and a wax jacket as he was. Still I think he secretly enjoyed Joy fussing over him as much as she did, and so as long as they were happy so was I.

Despite Joy's relief at seeing him again, an argument ensued about the offerings of forage Duncan was now planning to cook up for their tea. Joy was adamant that she would have nothing to do with the suspicious items within her now rather grubby-looking basket. Duncan was not pleased! He's spent hours finding them, and he wanted to make something yummy as a treat for her. Joy was having none of it and in the end – as much to get them out of the shop because their argument was scaring the customers – I agreed that I'd use them up so that they wouldn't get wasted. (I could always make an excuse later for why I'd failed to use them up before they were past their best. Or even lie and pretend that I had used them up.)

This seemed to satisfy Duncan. He happily allowed Joy to take his hand and lead him from the shop much like a child is lead by its mother. Under her immense umbrella of earth-motherly love and kindness I watched them walk out into the dank, fallen November sky and into their own world of tenderness.

I spent a couple of hours then making up the orders for the following day, while Ralph continued to help me out by serving the steady stream of customers throughout the afternoon. I was grateful to him for his help and I made sure that he knew it. Nothing more was said with regard to my relationship with Will, and so things between us were very much as they always were. He held forth with his dry observations and I listened and laughed. It was an easy friendship.

Home time soon rolled around again. As we cleared away the flower debris, wiped down the workstation and cleaned out the buckets, I spotted the inoffensive basket of highly offensive mushrooms watching me from its place on the floor. Not wanting to take it home in case Flo tried to eat them I absent-mindedly kicked them under the counter and vowed to throw them out the following day.

Then I took down my coat from the hook and put it on, plucked the prettiest bouquet from the 'peaches and creams' bucket, rolled it up in tissue paper and handed it to Ralph, telling him, "Give it to your missus. It'll earn you big brownie points, I think."

He grinned. "Nice one. Won't do any harm to have a few points in the bank for the next time I need a favour, will it?" With that we locked up and left for home.

I managed to find the time to treat myself to a soak in the bath when I got home. It was such a tonic for my aching, battered body. I'd thrown in a 'Ceridwen's Cauldron' (that's a bath bomby thingy) as an extra special treat. It felt wonderful to sink into the foamy, oaty liquid and let my mind drift wherever it may.

After half an hour I was out, sorted and ready for action again. I decided to make something simple for tea, so made spaghetti and meatballs with a green salad and ciabatta bread from ingredients I had in my cupboards, fridge and freezer. If we were still hungry after that, there was a box of chocolates in my emergency stash of goodies we could share.

As I was digging the ciabatta bread from the farthest corner of my freezer, my doorbell rang. It was only six thirty so I figured that Will must have got away from his meeting earlier than he expected. I threw the errant loaf onto the work surface, wiped my damp hands on the towel, fixed what I hoped was a warm smile (but was possibly more like a grimace) on my face and went to let him in.

It was a surprise to find Sal on my doorstep. She looked frozen so I brought her in and sat her by the fire. We were soon drinking coffee and catching up on each other's news but I had the distinct impression that she hadn't come here on such a bone-numbingly chilly evening just to swap gossip. We could have done that over the phone, like we usually did. Soon enough, the purpose of her visit was revealed.

"Zoe, Knickerless was up at our school today. He was asking about you," she eventually divulged.

"Yes? He's been into the shop too. What was he doing up at your place?" I wanted to know.

"He was doing the school gardens. He said he'd seen you. Said he thought you were 'unhinged'. Pretended that he was worried about you. I told him straight that if he was *that* worried about you he should leave town and get out of your sight *altogether!*" she replied matter-of-factly. Then added, "*Are* you ok, Zoe?"

I laughed. "I'm fine. In fact I'm much better than

fine! I'm happier than I've ever been! And if he would disappear by some small miracle I'd be just ... ecstatic!"

"So you're still seeing this bloke with the thing for tools then?" she smiled.

"As much as I can, yes." I admitted. "How are things going with you and Johnathan? Still great?"

She gazed into the middle distance. "Better that that! They're terrific!" she confessed.

The doorbell went again and so I answered it. This time it was Will so I introduced him to Sal. I looked at them, my best friend and my lover. I loved them both, and they seemed to love me.

I was blessed!

Chapter 22

Sal stayed with us for about half an hour after Will arrived and then – discreet as ever – she made her way home. During the course of the conversation, we made loose arrangements for a night out, Sal and Johnathan, Will and I. We thought just a quiet meal at Ros's and a few drinks would be fun. It was relaxed enough at Ros's that we'd all be able to get to know one another better, but it was just far enough out of town that we wouldn't be accosted. As you would expect, none of us wanted to bump into either Peter or Wendy and Nick. That would be sure to put a terrible blight on the evening!

After Sal left we finished making tea together whilst swapping comical stories from the working day. Will told me that he'd told Wendy he'd been mugged by a vast troglodyte of a man and had then to spend some time at the police station making a statement, so shocked was she with his battered, ragged appearance when he arrived home that morning. I chortled long at that! Mr Solicitor telling lies to his girlfriend about a fictional crime in order to cover for his feral antics in bed with his 'other woman'! Wow! Would she be surprised to know the truth!

In return I recounted the incident with Mrs Griffiths and the hearse. Now it was his turn to laugh long and hard. He knew the resolute Mrs Griffiths from run-ins he had had with her. She'd been round to his offices on more than one occasion to bully and secure donations from all of Will's staff and colleagues. He could therefore imagine her ire at being made to travel alone when she'd wanted to be in with her husband and other assorted relatives.

After we'd eaten up all the meatballs and spaghetti and mopped up the sauce with the bread, we settled down to watch the TV and destroy the box of fancy special chocolates I had found in my private goody collection earlier on in the evening. Both of us were pretty weary, so a tranquil snuggle on the sofa with a lovely cup of cocoa was more the order of the night than another night of full-on, raunchy, garment-ripping, fervid sex. Besides which, we both needed to let the damage from the last session heal, and neither of us could afford to replace the clothes we had already ruined with our waywardness! How soon we were turning into Mr and Mrs Cocoa and Slippers!

As we watched the TV we fed each other with the chocolates whilst kissing and cuddling lovingly. It was the polar opposite of the previous night, but none the worse for that. Flo settled down happily beside us and later, as we undressed each other for bed, Will sighed, "I wish it could be like this forever. Just us, and Flo and this madness!"

I smiled. "Maybe we'll get lucky? Maybe they will shrivel up, disappear, and leave us to it?"

"Wendy never does the right thing, so it's unlikely," he replied, laughing. But it was a small, bitter laugh.

"Perhaps if we cover her with salt? You know, like you do with slugs? I reckon it'd work on Knickerless! A knickerless world!" I mused. "It'd work for me!"

Now he laughed a deep, lusty laugh as he said, "I just bet it would, you dirty bitch!" And with that we fell onto each other laughing.

Hours later, in the wee small hours, as I lay awake, enjoying being wrapped up in Will's arms and listening to him unobtrusively breathing, I thought again about how fortuitous it would be if Wendy and Nick were to disappear. It *could* happen. They could go cliff walking... and be caught in a landslide. Or one of them could fall into a frozen pond and the other could go in to rescue them, leading them both to drown... or both be killed horribly by a mass murderer on the rampage. Or, more romantically, have a Romeo and Juliet-style poisoning incident. Of course, we'd have to find a way to persuade them both to take the poison. I could help them out with the poison, though; I could give them some of Duncan's suspect mushrooms to speed things along!

Oh! I could *give* them some of Duncan's *suspect mushrooms* to speed things along!

'No!' I thought, 'I'm just tired.' And with that

207

thought I fell to sleep.

I dreamed fairly vividly after that. Mainly of pouring salt onto enormous Wendy and Nick slugs, then watching gleefully as they gradually, agonisingly, desiccated into piles of dried-up nothingness.

Paradoxically, I woke up more tired than I'd gone to bed in the first place. I'd set my alarm for six thirty, and it took a couple of times of hitting the snooze button before I managed to drag myself out of bed. I wanted to get up before Will and make breakfast for the two of us but when I did finally get up, it was to discover that Will had already left because – as he had mentioned during the course of the evening – he had an early meeting with clients. I was a little disappointed, but not fazed by this. I supposed that it went with the territory. I'd committed myself to this when I'd agreed to be his bit on the side!

Well, I was awake now so I might as well make good use of the time. It didn't take me long to sort myself out after which I ate a quick breakfast and then ran round the block with Flo. I had a little time left then just to make the bed, empty the dishwasher and fill the washer before setting out for work.

Len was waiting for me when I got there. Along with my usual flower order he also had my Christmas trees. Four seven-foot trees, eight six-foot trees, six five-foot trees, six four-foot trees, five three-foot trees and a couple of the cutest, tiniest baby trees I had ever seen. I would need to take one of those home with me, since there would be very little point in putting up my big tree as there was going to be no one there to see it! All of the trees were beautiful, silvery-green, healthy spruces and they smelled of Christmas! My favourite season was here in all its glory! Bring it on!

Ralph arrived just in time to help me move the trees into some semblance of order for display. Some of them were just trees, all netted for stacking and others were potted with their root balls still intact so that they could be used again if you were judicious in handling and taking care of them. From them I chose a beautiful five-foot potted one to stand in the window.

Between the two of us, Ralph and I popped it into its

new home, taking pride of place in the middle of the window. It looked magnificent in its metallic, shiny, silver pot. Once we had finished arranging the other trees I would be able to find the Christmas decorations and 'Christmas' it all up with a vengeance!

It didn't take long, between us, to get everything ship (or even shop) shape, ready for the day's business and once Ralph had disappeared with the deliveries it was quiet enough for me to be able to get on with decorating the tree and finishing the Christmas window.

After a bit of fishing in the storeroom I came across the boxes of decorations. They came in all shapes and sizes but were either shades of blue, white or silver. There was also some white and silver angel's hair in a box along with a string of blue and white Christmas lights that I knew I'd have to test before I put onto the tree. There was no sense in wasting time on a string of dead lights, after all. I carried everything through to the shop front then realised that Aurelie – our pretty, little, indigo angel for the top – was missing from the box of decorations, so I went back to foraging through the store room in search of the all-important feature for the finish.

When I unearthed her, she had the appearance of someone who had partied rather too hard the previous Christmas. Her face was smudged with earth from some nearby plants, and her dress was a little dusty. She was desperately in need of a little TLC and an urgent appointment with a bubble bath. It didn't take long before she was restored to her former splendour and happily drying out on top of the radiator.

The rest of the morning was spent serving customers, making up a couple of bouquets for the afternoon delivery, and generally turning the shop into Santa's grotto. Ralph was suitably impressed with the effect when he returned.

As well as the blue, white, and silver tree, there were blue, silver, and white balloons, a small circular table bedecked with a midnight blue cloth, two tall white candlesticks, and a couple of silver flowery candle rings. I'd strewn a few white rose petals on the table just for added effect and piled the floor with fake Christmas presents. Lots of different sized boxes covered in different types of blue, white and silver paper and ribbons. White and silver tinsel adorned the walls and here and there were small snowmen wearing velvet scarves and holding sparkly, silver roses. On the counter where there once stood a jar of Haribo sweets that we gave to children (with parental consent) now stood a large blue, glass bowl full of silver foil covered chocolate baubles (again, supposedly for kids, but they'd have to fight Ralph and I for them I felt.) and gold foil covered chocolate coins. Very festive, if I did say so myself!

Ralph put on the kettle as I stood back behind the counter admiring my handiwork. As I was doing so, the shop door opened tentatively pinging loudly as it did, and in walked Knickerless ... again! He was nothing if not persistent! And thick skinned! Or just plain thick, maybe; I hadn't quite decided.

I leapt out from behind the counter frenziedly, like a hungry tigress that had spotted a big, fat gazelle, and immediately began yelling, "Oh. My. God! Do you never learn? Get out of my shop, you sick pervert! Leave me alone!"

His jaw was practically on the floor. I don't think he'd ever seen me so angry before. After his arrest, I only ever saw him again in court, because I made him go and live with his mother until he was thrown in jail. I couldn't bear even to see him, so there was no way I could live with him. During the rest of the time we were together, I rarely lost my temper. Certainly not to this extent.

After he'd recovered his composure, he began, "Now Zoe, I know you're angry with me and I can understand why. But the thing is, this is my home. It's where all my family and friends are, and now I've got a girl here too, I don't want to have to leave. I've come to ask you again to forgive me and put the past behind you. I don't expect you want to be friends, but can't we just agree to ignore each other? It's such a small town, and everyone will always harp on about what I did if the few who were victims can't find it in their hearts to let it go."

I was incredulous! "Let it go? Let it go? Are you for real? How dare you come in here and try to make me feel like I'm doing something wrong by not putting the past behind me? Have you any idea how seeing your evil, sick, twisted face around here makes any of us – me, or any of those poor women you victimised – feel? I doubt it, because if you had even an ounce of empathy in your pathetic, selfish, hollow, worthless soul you wouldn't have come back here! Now, for the final time, will you get lost!" I told him with some force.

He looked as if he was about to continue but by now Ralph was by my side. "You heard the lady. I've no desire to knock you into next year, but I will if you don't leave right now," he stated firmly in a tone that let Nick know it was pointless to argue. Nick stared from one to the other of us – a stony-faced, impenetrable, human wall – and knew that he was beaten. He turned and left without uttering a further word.

As soon as he left I began to shake violently, so great was my anger. Ralph turned me to him and enfolded me in a mammoth bear hug until it subsided. Much like a father with a small child. I could feel him stroking my hair and patting my back lightly as he told me, "There, there. It's all going to be alright. He's gone now, and he won't come back while I'm here." At that moment I was grateful for his kindness and his presence in the shop. I was grateful for the hug, and I was grateful that there had been no other customers around to witness me losing my temper so spectacularly.

Ralph sent me into the back of the shop to drink the tea he'd made me while he took over front-of-house. As I sat sipping my tea, I noticed through the trellis that the thin, unkempt looking reporter was there again. His raincoat was still badly creased while his jeans looked like they could do with a good wash. His wispy salt-and-pepper hair was in need of shampoo, and he looked so tired.

This time he was fiddling with the Christmas trees on show outside the shop window. He appeared to be hiding – not very well – in amongst them. He didn't bother to buy one, and this time he didn't come into the shop to ask questions either. I surveyed him with interest as he shiftily held one after another of the larger trees in front of himself peering with narrowed eyes at someone I took to be Nick in the distance. I couldn't help but wonder what he was doing, what he had found.

Ralph hadn't noticed him and continued all the while to calmly, cheerfully serve the handful of customers. Mostly they did come in to buy trees, as the festive spirit caught on like a winter flu virus. One man had to wrestle a six-foot netted tree out of the hands of the reporter in order to buy it. Still Ralph didn't notice the commotion going on outside, and I couldn't be bothered to move to stop it.

My attention now turned to Ralph, I could hear him asking after the old folk and offering those customers with children something from the blue bowl. He even offered those customers he knew lived on his route home free delivery as an added extra drop of kindness. Kerry was a very lucky woman! Ralph was a wonderfully warm person who had a marshmallow heart as big as himself. That was pretty-damned big!

I decided to text Will and let him know what had just happened with Nick and maybe warn him about the reporter. I didn't suppose Will would be very happy if he was to find his face all over the newspaper because of his association to Nick's latest squeeze! This set me thinking that maybe if this reporter knew something I didn't, Nick would be leaving in a black Mariah soon enough anyway... we lived in hope!

Personally, I would've considered taking out an injunction on Nick; but then, if I forced him to leave town he might have to stop seeing Wendy. I definitely didn't want that! I wanted them to run off into the sunset together, and the sooner, the better!

When I had calmed down and had a reply from Will, I went out into the front of the shop to join Ralph. He asked, "Are you sure you're ok? We can always phone Alli, see if she can come in for a couple of hours?"

Smiling, I told him, "I'm ok now, thanks to you. In case you hadn't guessed, that was Knickerless. Do you remember me telling you the story of the pervert I lived with?"

"Yes, I guessed as much. What on earth is he doing back here? I thought he'd agreed to move away when they let him out?" he questioned.

"He did. That's why I'm so angry. I'm not surprised, though; he never did know how to keep his promises," I answered gloomily. In reply, Ralph tutted loudly, uttering under his breath about yellow, cowardly sickos, and how they had no place in society.

After about ten minutes he asked if I'd be ok while he took out the afternoon deliveries. I thought for a moment and then told him I'd be fine. I also told him that once he'd finished the afternoon deliveries he should go home. He'd earned his money this week, and it was only Thursday!

Ralph looked at me doubtfully. He wasn't at all sure that he should be leaving me but I insisted. Eventually he agreed to take out the deliveries, pop back to pick up the trees he could deliver on his way home whilst checking on me, then go home early.

In my head, I'd pretty much decided that I was going to do something similar myself. I would finish tomorrow's orders, make up the delivery list and then go home early, armed with all my receipts, to do the last months books. There was also a pile of washing and ironing that I needed to attack if I had any energy left afterwards. Will wouldn't be round this evening; he had some fundraiser that he had to attend with Wendy. Part of the art of not being caught out was being seen to be carrying on as normal, so these things were part of the act. Therefore I resolved to use the time wisely in order not to fall behind with my chores.

The rest of the day passed fairly mundanely. I was glad to eventually get home. Even if it was to a pile of chores I hate! Flo was pleased to see me. She danced doggy attendance on me as I lit the fire and put on the TV. Then I put out her tea and grabbed myself a plate for the fish and chips I had treated myself to on the way home.

After I'd eaten my fill and removed the pots to the dishwasher, I pulled up the coffee table, set up camp and began to do the books for the shop. It was my least favourite job of all of them. I was a 'creative', not a mathematician, so it was with mammoth effort that I saw the job through to the end. Some two and a half hours later it was done. Everything was recorded and neatly filed in its rightful place. The sense of relief was overwhelming! Now to tackle the ironing then I could reward myself with a lovely soak in the bath! Great!

By the time I'd finished all my chores it was nearing eight. The hectic pace of the last few evenings was beginning to tell on me, I was bone-weary. Because of this, I decided to have a soak, wash and condition my hair, have a delightful chocolate face pack, then grab an early night. Heaven!

Taking a large mug of Earl Grey with me, I ran a bath – a lovely, bubbly, deep one – covered my face with face pack, grabbed a magazine, and then jumped into the water for a long session. Delectable! My phone began to ring soon after but I ignored it. Whoever it was would just have to wait! As I lay in the tub enjoying the peace I found myself unable to settle. Flo popped her head over the side and began to lick firstly at the face pack and then at the honey and oatmeal soap bar on the side. I playfully covered her nose in bubbles, which she joyfully licked off with her overly long tongue.

As pleasant as it all was I still couldn't settle somehow. I washed my face and then grabbed the jug and began to wash and condition my hair. While I was doing this, my phone began to ring again. Still I ignored it. I was indisposed. They would have to wait. I continued until the job was finished. I was squeaky clean, warm and smelled like a cookie. That would do nicely!

Once dressed in my turquoise cotton pyjamas with my hair towel dried I picked up my phone to see who had been trying to get through to me. I didn't recognise the number, so I wasn't too worried about missing the caller. If it was so important I was sure that they would try again.

Going downstairs, I let Flo out for her last 'business appointment' of the evening, and when she came in I locked up, checked the windows, shut off the lights, and the two of us made our way up to bed.

We had barely made it into the bedroom when, right on cue, the phone began to ring once more. This time I answered it.

It was Knickerless the Persistent. How had he got hold of my number?

It turned out that my lovely sister had given it to him. So much for 'never forgiving him for what he'd done to me', and loyalty to her sister, then! She thought it would be helpful if he and I talked. I would *never* be talking to her *again* after this. She had really taken the bourbon this time!

As soon as I'd found out where he'd got my number I clicked the phone closed and cut him off. I so wished I could do that to *him*. Press one little button then... no more Knickerless! Life could be a dream!

I turned off my phone then, and plugged it in to recharge for the night. Having set my alarm I turned off the lamp and settled down to sleep. Except now that I was so wound up, I couldn't seem to drop off. Tossing and turning, I began to think of all the reasons I had for eradicating my pain-in-the-neck ex and possibly also his girlfriend. Why should she have all the fun? She was out there somewhere with Will – whom she only wanted for what he could provide – having a lovely evening thank you very much. Then, for dessert, she had Nick – to whom she was welcome. Hell, I'd even gift- wrap him for her – so what kind of karma allowed for that level of avarice?

All the while I was becoming more and more angry, more and more vengeful and less and less able to sleep. This was not good! I'd be a wreck tomorrow at this rate!

Time to get up and make some cocoa then. All this served to do was remind me of the last time I'd sat on the sofa drinking cocoa with Will. The drink was sweet, but my bile was bitter. Maybe a little more TV would help distract me. I tried a weak comedy but it didn't hold my attention, so then I flittered from channel to channel until I alighted upon the cookery channel. It was some chef or other on a Tuscan hillside, and he was chucking porcini mushrooms into a large pan of creamy-looking risotto. The risotto looked very appetising, it had to be said. I hadn't made risotto for a while. Maybe next time Will was over I'd make it for our supper.

While I remembered I checked the kitchen cupboards for Porcini mushrooms because I was certain that I'd seen some dried ones in a packet in there somewhere. It was either that or use Duncan's gift but that would make one very dodgy offering! Laughing to myself at the thought, I put the Porcini mushrooms to the front of the shelf and went back to my place on the sofa. Making a mental note of the recipe for the risotto, I watched as the chef threw in some shitake mushrooms and a little pecorino cheese to finish. Nope, you definitely wouldn't want to use Duncan's mushrooms, it would doubtless ruin the delicate flavour! And quite possibly ruin your life as well! Though there were plenty of people I would like to ruin the lives of... it would make a terrific revenge food, would it not?

I tuned out of my head and back into the chef just as he was telling us, "And unlike other risottos, this one is much better if served chilled. It's a terrific summer dish!" with a big, cheesy, televisual grin.

Idly, I wondered if Nick and Wendy liked a bit of risotto. I could whip up a batch especially for them if I could figure out how to get them to eat it... couldn't I?

Suddenly I was feeling ready for bed again. Switching off the TV I yawned. Life was so much simpler when you had a plan. There was something to be said for rational organisation and so tomorrow I would work out the finer points of my idea, think it through properly.

For now, I needed to sleep!

Chapter 23

Friday was here once more, and this time I was eager to face the day. My last thoughts of the previous night were still running chaotically round my head, causing mayhem with my 'inner saint' and conscience. The devil inside was rapidly gaining ground, and his flag was permanently pitched now at the top of the highest mountain of my righteousness...

Hard times lay ahead for my guardian angles (Damn you Mr Sidebottom for sneaking under my skin and transforming my grasp on the English language!), I felt.

Within an hour of arriving at work, I'd filled the three orders I had for funeral work, and was on with a bridal bouquet and a couple of bridesmaid posies for a registry office wedding that afternoon. As I did them, I wove in a little myrtle for good luck whilst saying a quiet prayer for the couple wishing them both well on their foray into marital bliss. I didn't know that many couples who had lasted the distance any more, so my belief in it as an institution was waning massively.

I looked up at the wreaths on the shelf above me. Death; now there was a whole other thing. There was something you couldn't *not* believe in! There was something that would come to us all whether we liked it or not. Question was, should it come to some quicker than others? Did some people deserve to be dispatched sooner rather than later? I stared at Joy's basket, still nestling innocently under my counter, then back to the wreaths.

Dare I?

The recipe for mushroom risotto was still turning circles in my head, so I made a loose plan to look on my laptop later and google 'field mushrooms'.

Well, it couldn't hurt to know *exactly* what was in the basket, now could it?

Just after lunchtime, when the last of the days' orders had gone – including the wedding flowers – I grabbed myself a cuppa and perched at the workstation with my laptop. The mushroom basket stood next to it on the worktop, and google was busy running a search for me. I smiled wickedly at the thought of what I was doing. Somehow the fact that murder was highly immoral and totally illegal was just… passing me by!

Google was brilliant. I popped on some latex gloves (wasn't going to risk handling the mushrooms bareback!), and within minutes I was able to identify several of the species from the basket. Some of them were indeed edible. There were Amethyst Deceivers (so pretty I could always use them in my arrangements), attractive yellow Chanterelles, blue-green Aniseed Funnels, Fairy Ring Champignons, a few 'shrooms, a Hen of the Woods, several dozen Wood Blewits, a couple of large, not-at-their-best Fly Agarics (these were *not* for consumption) and last but not least, a small quantity of Amanita Phalloides. It was this last category I was most interested in. They were big, fat, white, juicy death caps!

I had a perfect mix for my 'revenge risotto'. This would be fun!

I closed my laptop down and took off my gloves. Just as I was clicking the kettle on, Will popped in to see me. He purposefully swept in, pulled me towards him across the counter, and kissed me full and hard on the lips.

"God, I needed that!" he smiled when we finally came up for air. "How are you? I missed you last night. Wendy was a complete cow. She made a holy show of the pair of us with her flirtatious, drunken antics. My work colleagues think she's such a laugh, but they wouldn't if they were stuck with her!" he rattled as he came through to the back of the shop with me.

"I'm fine thanks, I think," I smiled. "Sorry you had a lousy evening. I had a very productive one. I managed to do my books, and all my chores. Then I thought I'd look for some new directions for my revenge foods," I told him.

"Ooh, any good ideas?" he asked.

"Well…" I started, "as a matter of fact, yes. My friend gave me these mushrooms the other day. He'd been foraging in the fields nearby and landed up here with them. His partner wouldn't use them because she wasn't sure how safe they were, but he knows I like to cook so he thought he'd leave them with me. Anyway, I've just been checking with google to see if they're all edible and, well, yes they are. But some of them will make you a bit ... poorly," I finished, not quite truthfully.

Will peered dubiously at the contents of the basket, then at me "When you say 'poorly', how 'poorly' do you mean?"

"Just a bit sick and stomach-ache-y," I reassured him deceitfully.

"So, Ms Parsons, what are you going to use them to make?" he asked sounding impressed.

"I thought a delicious wild mushroom risotto, with a sprinkling of pecorino cheese," I said.

"Sounds great. Can I try the first batch out on Wendy?" he requested spontaneously.

I smirked. "Better yet, why don't you suggest she invites a 'friend' round for tea while you're out, and be sure to leave enough in the fridge for the two of them? Nick loves mushrooms. He's a vegetarian. Though he will eat fish," I remembered for no apparent reason.

Will looked thoughtful for a moment. "Sounds like a plan," he readily agreed, adding, "when did you hatch this?"

Now I was totally honest. "Last night, watching a cookery programme. The chef was making this wild mushroom risotto in the middle of a field on a camping stove, from mushrooms he'd just picked himself. He did caution viewers to 'pick carefully', and that was when I realised what I could do with my gift here. I could always just make one that'll send them on a bit of a trip, if you'd prefer. See these? They're 'shrooms!" I smiled as I pointed at the bizarre, gangly, little mushrooms.

"Well! You had a busy – and as you say – productive time then." He laughed. "Save your 'shrooms, you can sell them to teenagers instead!" he joked.

We made arrangements to meet at my house later on that evening and then he was gone. I served a couple more customers, tidied up the shop, phoned an order in to Len for the next day's flowers, turned the sign to closed, the lights off, and made my way home.

When I arrived, I found Dannie's car on the front and the lights on inside. "Hello?" I shouted as I went through the door. Dannie was sitting in the living room with her feet up reading a magazine.

"Hi, hope you don't mind, but I'm home for the night. Kerin is on a course for the next couple of days, and I didn't much fancy hanging round her place on my own. Is that ok with you?"

I thought of my plans for another mad evening, christening various parts of the house with Will, then replied in a falsely cheery tone, "Of course I don't mind. I would say make yourself at home, but it'd be a waste of words!" Then I added, "What's that lovely smell?"

Dannie had already made a start on cooking for us. I wandered into the kitchen, Flo hot on my heels, to take a look at what was cooking. There was a casserole bubbling away in the oven and a pan of potatoes bubbling away furiously on the stove. Luckily there would be more than enough to feed the three of us – and a hungry Flo – so I wouldn't need to set to and make more. Great!

I made Dannie and I a coffee then went to sit with her in the room so that I could listen to all of her news. When she had relayed it all I explained that Will would be joining us later, and that there was a strong possibility he might be staying the night. She was looking forward to meeting him, at long last, she said. Then I added that there was also a strong possibility he would have to leave quite early in the morning. This lead to me having to offer an explanation as to why he'd need to leave quite early.

Dannie was not generally judgemental, but just like Ralph she was concerned for me as a friend. She hadn't been aware that Will was still in a relationship and she was worried that I'd be the one who'd end up getting hurt if it all went wrong. I was grateful for her concern, so I said as much. Then I explained that I wouldn't be getting hurt because I wouldn't be getting in over my head. After Nick, I was just in it for fun. And sex. And free legal advice (not that I told her this, because if I did I'd have to explain that I was planning to do away with Nick and Wendy. I knew that Dannie would be more than concerned for me if she knew I was even thinking of it!)

Dannie, whilst not exactly happy with the situation, could see that I wouldn't be moved by her plea for caution. She took herself into the kitchen to see to the dinner while I took myself off to get a shower and change out of my work clothes. When I returned to the kitchen Dannie had neatly set the table, opened a bottle of Merlot to allow it to breathe, and was in the middle of whipping up a lemon sponge pudding and custard for desert. "Wow! You're a quick worker!" I told her, "It all smells lovely."

"Least I can do. Have a seat and I'll pour you a glass of wine," she declared, fussing around me like a mother hen. I must admit I let her, simply because it was so nice to have someone looking after me. It had been such a long time since anyone had.

Will turned up at seven and was a little surprised to find Dannie there. Once the introductions were over, and they had laughed at Will's misfortunes with my bedstead, it was time to eat. We sat together around the table, enjoying Dannie's yummy beef casserole with colcannon mash and huge chunks of buttered French loaf. The conversation flowed, as they swapped life stories and anecdotes. The sweet, citrusy lemon sponge and custard rounded things off well.

Soon we had moved into the living room with a jug of coffee and some wafer thin mints. The brandy came out because somehow the evening just demanded a proper, warming nightcap. By now the anecdotes were getting a little more raucous. Dannie was telling us all about her sexual exploits with Georgie, and how she hadn't realised Georgie's secret, when Will decided to tell us what Wendy had been up to the night before at the charity fundraiser they had been to. As he was launching into how Wendy had polished the bald head of Will's boss with her napkin, before planting perfect, deep, red kisses all over it in front of the guy's wife, Dannie stopped him.

"How can you stay with her, when she rubs your nose in it like that?" she asked.

"I can't afford not to at the moment," he replied shrugging. "If we sell up I'll lose a fortune, if I chuck her out I can't afford to live. If I had any other option I'd take it, believe me. I'm not with her by choice."

"Well, why don't you sling her out and move Zoe here in?" she said with a wink in my direction.

Will was at a loss. He looked to me for something to say. I smiled at Dannie and – even though I wanted to yell at her, "What are you trying to do?" – I told her, "We've barely known each other five minutes. Don't move us in with each other just yet, it's far too soon!" Then, out of curiosity, I asked her, "Would you move in with Karin if you were asked to? Even though you've only been seeing each other for a couple of weeks?"

Dannie thought for a moment and then answered "I think I would, yes. You have to understand that there are far less girls seeking girls out there, so when you find one that keeps your interest you hang on from the start. I think that's probably why gay relationships move so much faster than hetero ones."

We mulled that one over for a while and then Dannie spoke again. "You know what, I think I might go on up to bed now. I'm all in!"

"Of course, well, thanks for a lovely dinner," Will told her.

"Yes, thanks, Dannie. You've made it a really lovely evening for both of us. It was great not having to cook," I followed.

Will looked hurt for a moment, and turning to me said, "You don't have to cook, you know. We could always go out, or maybe get a takeaway if you prefer?"

"Terrific!" Dannie shot, "We'll hold you to that tomorrow night if you're not busy?"

Will brightened now. "Well if that's ok with Zoe, I'd love to!"

I looked from one to the other "Of course it's alright with me. I'd like that very much. Also, I don't mind cooking generally, but it was lovely to be spoilt for once."

On her way up the stairs, as a parting shot Dannie told us, "I've left the garage door unlocked and an assortment of power tools on the workbench for you there. Keep the noise down." I reddened a little, then we all laughed a lot at her cheek!

Shortly after Dannie went to bed we took Flo for a short, chilly run around the block, then settled down in bed ourselves for the night. Without power tools, I hasten to add. It was cosy there, all snuggled up in Will's arms. I enjoyed it whilst I could. All too soon, he'd have to make his way home. But hopefully not for very much longer.

Not if I got my way!

Chapter 24

The weekend passed quickly and was all too soon over. I'd enjoyed having Dannie around; she clucked around me in a way that reminded me of my grandmother, remarking that I was looking far too thin (well that was a first!) and peaky. It was good to have her company and her opinion on whether I should redecorate the lounge, cut my hair short or think about extending the house in the new year. Of course, I'd have to build my savings back up first.

After Dannie left on Sunday afternoon to stay with Karin, I was able to pay some thought to the mushroom risotto idea I'd had at the end of the last week. Will was over at my place on Sunday evening; in fact he'd been with us for most of the weekend, we spent a lovely evening together. Both of us cuddled up in front of the fire on a duvet with chocolate and a jug of coffee. If this relationship were to continue I'd have to widen my doorframes, or eat less chocolate and more fruit. Despite Dannie's remonstrations that I was getting too thin. But that was a whole other story.

We talked and talked, kissed and cuddled while Flo lay languidly at our feet with her owl. While I had his attention and we were alone, I asked him whether he thought it would genuinely be possible to 'kill two birds with one stone', as it were. Feed the offensive Risotto to both Wendy and Nick at the same time.

Inside I was laughing myself stupid at the thought of doing this. I wasn't just doing this for me any more, I wasn't just doing it for Will; I was also doing it for all those other women Nick had damaged with his perversion. I can honestly say that I really felt, at some level, that I was doing it for the good of mankind. Or womankind, even.

And in my mind, Wendy wasn't exactly blameless, with the inferior way she had treated Will. And for a pervert like Nick, too! She deserved what was coming to her.

Will decided that he'd set it up so Wendy would bring home her 'friend' on Tuesday evening. He would tell her he had to work late and that, rather than waste it, she should eat up the risotto he had prepared for their tea and placed in the fridge. She'd be bound to take the opportunity to have Nick in, and since she was a useless cook herself she'd probably try to impress him by passing off the risotto as her own. Obviously, she'd retract the lie when they both became ill, but by then it would be too late. He'd know she was a liar and no domestic goddess. He also added with glee that he knew if Wendy had to have any more time off sick, she'd be on a warning from work. Just a step away from losing her job completely! She'd been 'chucking sickies' quite a lot in order to meet Nick on his day off, when she should have been tending to her caseload at work, and her boss was growing tired of it.

I pointed out that the whole thing might result in a 'make or break' situation for Wendy and Nick. He might not be impressed with her dishonesty, having been so honest with her about his own life – that's if he had; I had my doubts about it – or the fact that she'd made him ill with her cooking. Will felt that he'd be happy to take his chances with that.

Little did he know, but there would *be* no chances for this hapless pair. Once the risotto was gone, so were they!

Will stayed with me until two in the morning, but then he had to leave because he had an early meeting the next morning again. Mrs Mack's venetian blinds hadn't seen so much action in years! They twitched every time Will arrived and every time he left, no matter what the hour. I wasn't too bothered; I sort of felt sorry for the old girl. I wasn't too bothered about Will leaving, either. It was quite nice to have a bit of bed space for myself after such a busy weekend.

Monday turned out to be a ridiculously busy day in the shop. The extreme cold snap that had arrived over the weekend took several infirm and elderly local people with it. We were sadly inundated with funeral work; so much so that I would need to bring Alli in at the back end of the week to help me out.

I also had a couple of small winter weddings and

225

thirty-one Christmas table decorations for a local hotel. These would grace their banqueting tables for the Christmas party season, so they had to be perfect. I got to work on the orders for the following day first, and once these were all done I was able to make a start on the hotel order. In between serving the many customers who came in for trees and arrangements, it took most of the day to complete the table decorations. By the time they were done, I was so tired of seeing deep pink roses, white lisianthus and gold-sprayed ruscus leaves, that I never wanted to see them again. Not to mention the glitter. It was everywhere!

Ralph showed up at three forty-five and helped me to tidy up, after which we loaded the arrangements for the hotel into the van. Ralph had decided that he'd take them on his way home, rather than leave them until the following day. This suited me; I was more than sick of the things by this point. He could have taken them to the local tip and I wouldn't have cared.

On my way out of the door I picked up the mushroom basket from the cold room. I had moved it from under the counter the previous Friday when I'd decided to use them instead of throwing them away. I wanted to retain as much of their freshness as I could. They looked ok. Not daisy-fresh, but they'd still be useable.

On seeing me with the basket Ralph looked worried "You're not actually going to eat those, are you?"

"Yes, as a matter of fact I am," I told him. "I've checked up on google, and all but a couple of them are edible. I thought I'd make a nice risotto for Will and I for dinner."

"Bloody hell, Zoe! Have you gone off this Will, then?" he exclaimed.

"No," I calmly reassured him, "I know what I'm doing or I would hardly be eating them myself."

Ralph saw me out to my car and waved me off. All I had to do was grab a piece of pecorino cheese from the supermarket on my way home, and I'd have everything I needed.

Pretty soon I was home and in front of my cooker, stirring away at my 'cauldron'. I had given Flo a pig's ear to chew while I got on with the job in hand. She happily crunched away from her favourite spot on the rug in the hall. Before too long, the kitchen was full of delicious, herby, mushroomy, scents. The multi-coloured fungi were a beautiful and appetising sight in the pan. They brightened up the bland Arborio rice a treat. I scoured my kitchen cupboards for a plastic, takeaway container and lid to package it in, then labelled the front carefully with a sharpie marker. The wording proudly announced that the contents were 'Mama's Memorable Mushroom Risotto. Best served Chilled. Enjoy!'

I guaranteed they wouldn't remember a thing!

The trouble was, due to the lovely mushroom risotto smells in my kitchen, I was now desperate for some edible risotto for my own. I allowed it to cool and the scent to disperse while I took a bath.

An hour later I was clean, tidy, and downstairs loading the washer when Will turned up. He was very obviously somewhat flustered and slightly aggrieved. I brought him into the kitchen, sat him down at my table, and quickly located one of the bottles of lager from the back of the fridge. Opening it, I emptied the contents into a glass, handed it to him, and he downed the contents without stopping to draw breath. So I gave him another. This time he did not down the contents in one but took a couple of short sips then began...

"When I got home this evening Wendy announced that she knew I'd been seeing someone. She said that now I should understand why she needed to have 'interests outside of our relationship', so she didn't see why we shouldn't have an 'open relationship' from now on. That would suit us both in our present situation. I was flabbergasted! I told her that I wasn't seeing someone else out of choice, but because I'd fallen hook, line and sinker for someone after falling firmly out of love with her after the second of her little 'dalliances'. And if she'd agreed to sell up and clear out when I asked her, then we'd both be free to see whomever we chose now with no problems. She said that it wasn't an option for her. She loved me, and our life together, and she'd rather die than not have me to take care of her. I told her that I didn't want to be her father, I'd wanted to be her husband, but now that was all gone. I wanted to be her ex. She threatened the usual 'I'll go to sleep and never wake up. I have my sleeping tablets' crap and I walked out. I couldn't even look at her. She as good as admitted to my face I'm not her man, I'm her surrogate father! I'm so angry!"

After a few minutes, I told him, "You already knew that. You told me she wasn't with you for you, she was with you for what you could provide. You were *always* her stability. Maybe she's just one of those people who will never settle to just one man? It's a genetic fact that some people can't settle with just one person. You shouldn't feel bad about yourself or anything you've done here. The problems are hers."

"I know that, but I just feel so... stupid! I've given her chance after chance, thinking we could get back to what we once were. The first few months were terrific, you know? There was nothing she wouldn't do for me... and all the time she knew that would never happen. She knew she just regarded me as her 'dad'. That's not just hurtful, it's sick!" he ranted.

"Huh! Maybe that's why she and Nick get on so well? They both have these strange, sick little perversions, so they fill a void in each other," I spat. By now I was more that a little bit annoyed. I really didn't need to hear that he and Wendy had been terrific together; as far as I was concerned that was just twisting a knife!

I think he realised then that he'd shared a little too much information. He deflated a little and said, "I'm sorry. You don't need to hear this. It's hard enough on you that I'm not a 'free man' without me laying the fights I'm having with her on your doorstep!"

I kissed his forehead and replied, "It's alright. But for what it's worth, in your shoes I'd be formulating a plan of attack. You need to find a way of escaping the bind you're in without doing too much more damage. To either of you."

He stared into my eyes. "You're a good person, you know? I think you may be right. It's time to get her out of my life." We held onto each other as if we were the last two people on the Titanic as it went down. It dawned on me then that he must have really loved her to have given her so much rope, so much of himself. It was going to take a while to heal those scars. Just as it was taking me a very long time to heal mine. Nick and Wendy had a great deal to answer for. Luckily I had the means to make them pay!

I peered over Will's shoulder and winked at the plastic, risotto-filled container on my kitchen counter. Vengeance would be mine! I only just stopped myself from once again emitting the standard 'mwahhh, hahhh, haaaah, haaah, ha!' evil laugh! I really must be more careful!

Then and there in the kitchen we had some pretty torrid, crackling, fiery sex. My countertops would all need treating with Dettol in the morning! And some of the shelves in the pantry. And I'm going to have a devil of a game removing the scratches from the fridge door... still, it was worth it! I think it was the safest way of getting all Will's fury out. 'Out with anger, in with love', as my lovely Wiccan friend Moonbeam would say.

When we both lay gasping for breath on the kitchen floor, covered in the residue from squirty cream, Cadbury's flake, marmite, and sun-dried tomatoes, Will offered to go upstairs and start the shower running. We took a long, hot, steamy shower together, carefully soaping each other's bruises and stains, then gently, with love and laughter running between us towelled each other dry. Afterwards, we sat huddled together in front of the fire with a large plate of croque-monsieur and mugs of tea, feeling like two children who'd been lost out in a storm, but had found their way home eventually. It was that warm, pink, fuzzy emotion you always get from feeling secure.

This was love.

I had been running from this. I had been trying to deny that I was in it for anything more than a bit of fun, but now I knew for sure. I wanted Will all for myself. I didn't want to share him, but I needed to be sure that he felt the same way. Only thing was, how would I find out without scaring him off? I didn't want him to think

I was coming on too strong. I didn't want him to think I was a 'bunny boiler'. So how to find out?

After a while, I asked, "Do you remember what Dannie was saying about gay relationships on Friday night?"

"Which bit specifically?" he replied cautiously.

"The bit about their relationships moving more quickly in order that the 'participants' won't lose each other to someone else?" I reminded him.

"I think so, yes. I remember thinking to myself at the time that us 'hetero's' should think about applying the same rules, simply because life is too short and too precious to waste love when you find it," he told me through a mouthful of croque-monsieur.

"I was thinking about it earlier today! That's exactly the conclusion I drew, too! How uncanny is that!" I exclaimed.

He smiled. "Well, if *you* think that, and *I* think that, then maybe we should stop messing around and just go for it!"

"Well ok. How are we going to do this?" I turned towards him now "Do you want to move in here, with me?" I asked.

"*What*? And leave her in my house? Not likely!" He countered. "I know, how about you move in with me. She said we could have an open relationship. That's very open, isn't it?" he smiled.

"*Get real!*" I laughed, "If I move in with you, she'll move Nick in! I've been there, done that, and I would never live with him again if you paid me! Besides which, what would your posh neighbours think? A local solicitor moves in his lover and his fiancée's lover. How will that look to the locals of Knob Hill? You are joking?"

He was laughing himself hoarse by now "Of course I'm joking! The look on your face was priceless, though! I'd love to move in here with you, it's a perfectly lovely home, but first I need to get her out of Knob Hill and make it saleable. I've already explained that if I sell it now – in it's present state – I'll lose money on it that I can ill afford to lose."

"But isn't that better than living as you are at the

moment? You might be poor but you'll be happy, Bob Cratchett!" I advised him.

"Hmm. Let me sleep on it," he replied contemplatively through another mouthful of Croque Monsieur.

It was difficult to know if he meant it or not.

A little later, as we were clearing away the supper things, he noticed the risotto sitting all innocently, minding its own business on the kitchen work surface. He asked if it was '*the* risotto', and I answered affirmatively. He asked if it would need heating up, and I answered that it was a strange recipe that apparently was best served like Gazpacho, cold.

Then I asked if he hadn't maybe blown the plan a bit by storming out of the house when she mentioned an open relationship, unless ultimately he wanted to end things with her. Didn't he ought to maybe go home, pretend to sort things out? Tell her she could have her 'friend' in while he was over seeing me? Sneak the risotto into the fridge and then wait. He wouldn't have to wait all that long, I assured him. Provided they ate it, the mushrooms were quite quick to take effect. They'd both be a bit poorly for a while. She'd be a bit quiet, get off his back and he could laugh at their misfortune whilst buying a bit of time to think. I didn't see the need at that point to tell him he'd have aeons to think. Or that both Wendy and Nick would become *very* quiet, *very* quickly. This was need-to-know only information.

He was best kept out of it.

When it all caught up with me, I had decided that I was going to feign ignorance. Say that I thought the mushrooms would only cause a bit of sickness. Say that Nick and Wendy were supposed to be a bit off-colour for a while and nothing more. Say that I was shocked and horrified at the result.

Say that it wasn't meant to happen!

Will took what I had said on board, and between us it was decided that he would leave there and then, taking the risotto with him. It was only ten o'clock so there was a good chance that Wendy would still be awake and he could have that conversation with her. It

231

wasn't the best solution, but it was the only one we had for now, and in Will's eyes it would at least buy him time to think. I warned him that if he got the risotto on his hands for any reason, he should wash it off because the slightest bit of it could cause illness; *that under no circumstances should he be tempted to taste it*! Unless he actively enjoyed staring at the bathroom walls! (Actually it would be more likely the morgue walls, but I wasn't giving that away either!)

I waved him off and wished him luck as he went. Then – after letting Flo out and locking the doors and battening down the hatches – I took myself off to bed. To sleep.

Where I – ironically – slept the sleep of the innocent.

Chapter 25

I awoke bright and early the next day, pulled on my thickest, warmest clothes, and took Flo out for a short, chilly walk. It had snowed a little during the night, so the orange light from the streets shone down out of the dark and turned the snow to sparkly peach. It was a silent, beautiful, winter world. We walked for a good half an hour before deciding that it was time to go home for a warming hot drink and some breakfast.

After eating, I had time to put my washing into the dryer and have a quick tidy round with a duster before getting ready for work. I could lock my front door that morning knowing that at some point in the day the world would change immeasurably. Feeling quite excited at the prospect of having Will all to myself, I slung my workbag over my shoulder and trotted off blithely into the chaos of the working day.

There was plenty to do there, so I got stuck in with gusto immediately. By lunchtime I had completed ten out of the seventeen orders for the following day and I knew I would have to get Alli in for Wednesday – and possibly Thursday and Friday too, if I was called in by the police for questioning! Realisation of the magnitude of what I was about to do began to set in, right there and then as I briskly snicked the stems mechanically from some double whites.

I began unexpectedly to think clearly. Well, now; the books were pretty much up-to-date so that was ok. Alli could take care of some of the work in the shop in the first instance. But what if – by some misfortune – I got held longer than a couple of days by the police? What if I went *down*?

What would happen to my dog? My house? My business? My life? It was an odd fact, but I hadn't once stopped to consider any of this in all the time I'd been plotting and scheming to finish Nick and Wendy off. All I could see was the end result... A Knickerless life! Wendy's end was just a happy coincidence.

Were they really worth it?

Did they honestly deserve for me to throw

everything I'd worked so hard for away? The simple, decent answer to that question was a resounding no! And the mess it would create wouldn't just be my problem. It would be Will's too. He was a solicitor! They would make him a, whaddyacall it, an accomplice! He had no idea what was about to happen, and I had implicated him.

What was I thinking? *Who* had I become? I used to be so *sensible*... oh yes, but sensible Zoe would never have got herself embroiled in this stupid situation. Sensible Zoe would have stuck to her no-nonsense guns from the outset and kept a safe distance from Will Gelder... Sensible Zoe would have ignored Knickerless's return and got on with her life! Sensible Zoe wouldn't have been dim enough to sabotage everything that was good for the sake of getting rid of a couple of things that were not.

But where had sensible Zoe gone? What had mad Zoe done with her?

Suddenly, sensible Zoe was back! She flew rapidly into action...

I banged my snips down onto the workstation and looked at the clock. It was one thirty. I was wondering if there was any point in going over to Will's house right there and then, but I was pretty sure that both Wendy and Will would be at work until around five. I could shut the shop around four, make my way over there and sit on the front in wait. Then, when one of them returned, I could ask for the risotto back. Be honest (ish), say I made a mistake and some of the mushrooms in the risotto were more than just a little dangerous. Or I could call Will and tell him. That was a good idea. I'd do that *right now*...

I picked up the phone and speed dialled his number. His secretary answered, he was still stuck in a meeting but she would gladly take a message. What was I going to tell her to pass on? "Tell him that the risotto I gave him to make his girlfriend ill would probably kill her, so he should just throw it away?" I didn't think it was wise, so I after a seconds thought I simply told her "Get him to call Zoe. It's *very, very* urgent!" That ought to do it! What would sensible Zoe do next? 'Keep calm

234

and carry on with her work' was probably the best plan.

When I hadn't heard from Will by three and all of the work for the following day was done I began to worry. A lot. Ralph returned from his deliveries he very kindly made me a drink. I snapped at him when he put it down too close to a white ribbon I had cut for a bouquet. He remarked that I was extremely tetchy today, then disappeared into the cold room to make out the delivery list for the work laid out in there. After this we set to and tidied up between us. I could barely speak to Ralph and was curt with the customers. All I could do was watch the clock and worry.

Ralph began to grow concerned for me. He grabbed me into one of his hugs as I was leaving. "Zoe, I'm worried about you. I don't think that seeing this 'Will' type is good for you. You're under a lot of stress with that pervert back in town, and your new man isn't in a position to protect you, what with him being tied to someone already. Go see your doctor, please. Then, if you need someone to protect you, I'm your man. Any time of the day or night. Alright?" he told me baldly.

I pulled away, sharply. "Ralph, I can't do this now, but thanks!" I replied, storming off.

Secretly, I was inclined to agree that I needed to see a doctor, but not for the reasons Ralph might have thought. I was starting to think I had the same problem as Saiorse. Ralph had unwittingly hit a raw nerve!

I didn't drive home from there; I went – quickly as possible – straight to number seven, Knob Hill, where I expected I'd have to sit and wait. On arrival at the house, I was surprised to see that there were several lights on upstairs, and some of the curtains were closed too... my heart sank into my old, black boots!

The scruffy reporter was hanging around by the wheelie bin at the side of the house, but after acknowledging me with a brief wave and a smile he disappeared off down the hill at a brisk pace. My eyes diverted from watching him in my side mirrors to the upper storey window of Will's house.

What if it had been Nick's day off and he and Wendy had spent the day together, as they'd secretly been doing for some time? What if they'd already eaten the dratted, dangerous, killer risotto? My heart was in my mouth as I approached the front door, lifted the knocker and knocked hard. Repeatedly. Like machine gunfire. They'd have to have been deaf not to hear that.

Or dead!

There was no reply. I knocked again but louder. Still nothing. Panic rose in my throat as the full tonne weight of what I had done hit me like a double-decker bus. I had never felt so completely sick in all my days. Hysteria took hold as – in my mind – I began to think of the scene inside the house. Nick and Wendy face down in plates of perfectly chilled, creamy, fungi-filled risotto. Nick and Wendy, spoons still in their rigor mortis-ridden hands, rich, cool, mushroomy risotto spilling from their open, lifeless mouths. Nick and Wendy naked on the kitchen floor with intensely flavour-packed, herby, risotto drying around their dead, open mouths and on the already greying, rapidly deteriorating, naked flesh of their stomachs. Nick and Wendy prostrate on the floor under the table covered in perfect, velvety, risotto, deep, claret-y red wine and black candle wax... the scenarios were endless.

But *nothing* could have prepared me for the actual scene within the house...

As I stood shivering at that big, Georgian, scarlet front door with its sizeable, brass, lionhead knocker, Will arrived home from work. I didn't even see him roll up as the hysteria had by now overtaken sensible Zoe and she was numb from the inside. Will tapped me gently on the shoulder, causing me to jump out of my skin.

"Zoe, what are you doing here?" he asked, his voice sounding somewhere between shocked and worried.

"Six! Oh, Will. Thank God you're here. Those mushrooms I put in the risotto, I didn't realise at the time but I think some of them might have been death caps!" I babbled.

"Meaning ... ? And six what?" he prodded.

"Four. Meaning, if it's already been consumed then Nick and Wendy will no longer be our biggest problem!" I exclaimed.

"Bloody hell!" He yelled hurriedly opening his door

and rushing upstairs.

Running hot on his heels, I followed him up the rather grand, balustraded staircase into a room to the left of the hall. As he entered the room, he stopped abruptly, causing me to slam into the back of him violently. He didn't move aside so that I could see whatever it was that he could see. He stood, blocking the door, stock-still and emitted a small, strangled moan.

Turning slowly, he looked at me and said, "Zoe, we can't go in there. It's a crime scene. I'm going to phone the police, and you are going to go outside and wait in your car until they arrive. Do not try to run; it will only look worse. I will help you all I can, together we can get through this. Do you understand?"

I nodded my understanding. "Fifty seven," I managed to mumble. I was too late! I couldn't believe it! They had already eaten it and were now lying cold, dead, locked in each other's arms forever. This really was their was their unwitting Romeo and Juliet moment, and I had caused it. Who was I that I thought I could play God like that? I must have been insane!

I made my way to my car and mechanically opened the door. I plonked myself down heavily and sat while waves of complete horror washed over me.

Suddenly there were blue lights and ambulances everywhere. I sat, rigid, numb, a hollow, empty shell there in the driver's seat of my little, purple car. Unmoving. Waiting. Afraid. I watched in horrified mortification as Will was lead away to a police car. I could see him; he sat, ashen faced, robotically his mouth moved, not his usual, uninhibited, animated self, explaining to the officer what had happened. I could see officers – both uniformed and not – everywhere, and other curious residents were coming out of their houses to rubberneck at the scene. As I watched, the snow began to fall silently, peacefully. So entirely at odds with the tableau unfolding around number seven, Knob Hill. I was totally unaware of the time passing as I sat there observing the bodies being stretchered dutifully out on gurneys. The 'Scene of Crime' team were busily scurrying hither and yon with bags of evidence, and a coroner came and then went in his flash car.

Then from deep within, something about it registered. They wouldn't have 'bags' of evidence if I had killed them with my cruel, culinary offering. They would have had 'bag' maybe, but no more than that! So, if I hadn't done it, who on earth had?

I sat there and waited for a couple of hours for Will, as he had instructed. A kindly young officer escorted him into the house and they reappeared twenty minutes later with Will carrying a large green duffel bag and his battered old laptop bag. He approached my car with leaden steps, so I opened the doors and let him in. He was pallid, gaunt and looked ten years older than he had just a couple of hours ago. He leaned in to me and I hugged him with all my strength.

"What's happened?" I inquired.

"Someone has broken in through the back hall window. They've found Wendy in bed with Nick, there's been no obvious signs of a struggle – so chances are whoever broke in had a weapon to threaten them with – and the pair of them have been strangled with a matching pair of black, lace thongs. The one used to strangle Wendy had been 'used' by Nick, they think, and there was a note attached. It read 'I enjoyed this very much. Nick Souter'. The police think that he may have been forced to masturbate into the thong by whoever killed them, before it was used to strangle Wendy. The police say they will have to seal my house off for a while; just until they've taken everything they need from it, so can I stay with you?" he related in a flat tone, staring almost detached at the scene outside.

"Well, of course you can. It goes without saying!" I said, relieved. Then wondered, "So they didn't die of mushroom ingestion?"

He smiled a weak, wan little smile, and pulling a plastic carton from his laptop bag, told me, "I checked the fridge while I was waiting for the police to arrive. No, they didn't die of mushroom poisoning. See? The risotto hadn't been touched."

Chapter 26

Nick and Wendy's killer was never brought to book. The police believed him to be the husband of one of Nick's victims, one Mr Ronald Matthews. His wife, Josephine, had been driven to distraction by Nick's sudden reappearance about the town. She had been the only unfortunate victim to not only have had her underwear violated, but to have been assaulted by a particularly frenzied Nick after he found her hanging white cotton 'big panties' on her line. The Matthews moved to Samoa on the evening of the killings, and of course as the UK have no extradition treaty with Samoa, they cannot be brought to justice. I was shown pictures of Mr Matthews by the police when they asked me to make a statement; although I was never a suspect they knew I was one of the first on the scene. My suppositions were all wrong, and that reporter was not a reporter after all. He was just an angry, affronted man looking to protect his fragile, haunted wife.

Nick and Wendy were cremated at the local crematorium and scattered about the local parks and gardens by their families. Will was very tempted to send a 'revenge wreath' to each of them, but for decorum's sake he sent the full hearts-and-flowers coffin top spray to Wendy instead. The card he sent bore a special message to her. The message read simply 'Hope you've retired to that warm place we always dreamed of from your happy partner, Will.'

The house on Knob Hill was sold in the New Year to a heavy metal bassist named Crack from a band called Snaggle Tooth for a very good price. He just had to have it, due to its notoriety as the Clagdale Amittyville. Will was not left out of pocket, and was abled to easily clear his debts from the proceeds.

Saiorse is now settled in a beautiful house with a wealthy, healthy, attractive, good-humoured quantity surveyor and is, for the moment medicated and happy. We occasionally go out together as a foursome. He recently bought her a beautiful, shiny, gold Rolex watch for her birthday. This time, hopefully, she will be able to keep it!

Dannie and Karin are still living together, blissfully contented and all loved up under a perfect sky, out in Florida. We visit occasionally, and are looking forward to an invite to our first gay wedding in the very near future. I believe it's being held in Disneyland on the teacups.

Sal and Johnathan are married already. Lou was chief bridesmaid and, everyone agreed, queen for the day in her soft lilac prom dress and satin shoes. All three of them smile out from the photographs and those smiles tell a tale all of their own. They are radiantly happy together. It's not before time and well deserved.

Joy and Duncan are still hanging on in there. Joy swears like a docker now, though, and Duncan has taken up origami. There are paper animals everywhere around their house. It's a regular 'paper zoo'. Joy is looking to get out of anger management and into bereavement counselling. Am I worried? Not much ...

Ros still has the mill, and it's doing very well. I provide her with arrangements for the entrance and the lounge area every second Tuesday. She provides us with a meal and a lock-in at the mill once a month. Great deal! There's nothing like a bit of good old fashioned barter!

Moonbeam is still... well, Moonbeam. She recently returned from living in Ibiza with a druid called Scrogger, and is living in a Yurt with a wizard named Marasimus. I see her every now and then bashing policemen with her placard at demonstrations, and I sometimes join her when she goes dancing like no one can see her, in flashmobs in the square.

Ralph got over his embarrassment at his declaration of a need to 'protect' me, we both agreed to forget that it had ever happened. He is now happily settled with his Kerry, spending less time at the rugby and down the pub with his friends now, though, as he has to decorate the spare room in readiness for their baby. He's due in May and they are both ecstatic at the prospect.

And me? Sensible Zoe? It took a little time for both Will and I to get over what we had seen in his house that day. Although we couldn't have wished for a better solution to our problems, it wasn't a solution that either of us should have wished for or wanted. This has been difficult to live with for both of us. Added to this, I don't think I'll ever fully escape the guilt from trying to take another life (or two) myself. I'm seeing Saiorse's counsellor for help with the 'trauma'. Everyone believes it's due to the scene in Will's house that I need the counsellor's help. Only Will and I know the truth. Then Will still thinks that the mushrooms in the risotto were accidental. I couldn't possibly tell him that I deliberately put death caps into it. I'm having a hard enough time coming to terms with that, I can tell you! Although in truth, I still have quiet moments when I say a private thanks to Mr Matthews for doing what I couldn't bring myself to...

On a more positive note, I'm now happily engaged to a local solicitor. No prizes for guessing which one! Will came skiing with me at Christmas; he loaded it onto his credit card, having been driven to it by mad Zoe. He proposed at the top of a stunning blue run in the Porte de Soleil, using a ring that belonged to his mother. A fabulous white diamond solitaire which, when caught by the sun, sent a vast rainbow of colour dancing out across the snowy plains. The run he proposed on, I found out later, is known as 'Cheltenham ladies' due to it being wide and easy. I can laugh about that now! At the time, he was in danger of coming home to a plateful of my special risotto, though.

Just kidding...

My business is going well, my dog is as waggy as ever, and my family love Will almost as much as I do. Will and I are making plans to be married next October. It's taking place in a fairy ring in the middle of a mushroom field. Moonbeam's friend Marasimus is presiding, and my whole family think that I've gone and lost the plot! They have no idea!

Sensible Zoe is still in charge for most of the time, but now occasionally she'll move over and give mad Zoe an airing. It's ok being sensible some of the time, but being a bit, well, zany...

It's inspired!